# All That Jazz

By E.M. McDaniel

# *Chapter One: Drama*

Why do people attend weddings? To get ideas for your wedding? To witness true love? To see if your ex is really going to marry this second becoming of you? I only attend weddings because I am in them. That's the only reason I'm here today. I was the maid of honour for my best friend Reign. I was able to stand there and witness her finally become one in matrimony with the love of her life. The whole wedding was beautiful from start to finish, while they were here. Now that they have left to go on their honeymoon, the drama begins. I assume this is the real reason why people also attend weddings. They want to see some type of drama and gossip about it later. They want to know if the side piece is going to show and stop the wedding? Will the mother stand up and object because she never likes the soon to be bride or groom? Will the bride or groom catch cold feet and say I can't marry you, because I'm in love with your father. Nowadays that can work either way, it can be the bride or groom making that last second confession. They don't care what kind of drama it is, they just want to see it. They have their phones ready to upload, hoping to be  the next viral video. If you're black or brown you send it to the shade room, white and others will send it to TMZ. If you really want to get paid you will upload it to YouTube and watch the views kick in. Hoping to get yourself a bag and fifteen minutes of fame. How do I know this for a fact? I'm watching  a few people who are doing it now, as I speak to you. They have me starring in the shit? I couldn't believe it myself and when Montez and Reign see it, that's my ass! I'm praying that  they are on their way to Peru and have cut off all communication until they are back from their honeymoon. Lord knows I don't want them to know that I am responsible for this ratchet bullshit at their reception. How did I get myself into this situation? Hell if I know. I mean I did have a weak moment. That was almost a year ago. I slept with the father of my children and now his ass is on one knee proposing to me. Some of you probably like what's the problem with that? Well it wouldn't have been a problem if I wasn't already engaged to Sean. In my defense at the time I slept with Marcus. Sean and I were just dating.Listen I know that's a lame excuse and cheating is cheating. All I'm saying is I had a weak moment and I fucked up. I know all you pretenders are going to say well girl you should have confessed before he proposed. First of all my name is Jasmine and not Usher ain't no damn confession when there's a huge ring in my face. Plus our black asses were in the mountains and who is really trying to go over a cliff for a mistake? Not this chick so I waited before I admitted my infidelities. I feel some of you judging me and that's fine. What the fuck you all wanted me to do. Say no baby I can't marry you because I was unfaithful. How many of you male or female would have done that? Exactly! Now bring your judgemental asses off you all throne with y'all lying asses. I hate when people try to play me like they don't do half the shit I do. Probably reading this while lying up with your D.O.T.S. or chick on the side now. I know I'm not the only one who has had a weak moment with the father of my children. Anyway I thought I made it clear to Marcus back when it happened that I wanted to be with Sean. Apparently his ass was thinking us co parenting equaled getting back together. I told him that there were some emotions still there but I had no business exploring it. We had been over for three years at that point. I can admit at the time I wanted to know if I could get him back. Yes I wanted to see if I still had it and I did. I also had built up frustrations that I needed release that day and I wanted to release them on him. That's what really was going on in my mind that day. I wanted to know if I still had it and if I wanted to put my family back together could I? Then when it was over guilt took over and I realized that Sean was the one I wanted and he was the man I wanted to spend the rest of my life with. It was working out fine but when guilt eats at your soul eventually it will make you confess. I did and he dumped my cheating ass with the quickness. It took a lot of hard-work and even time apart. At the end he finally came to his senses and put my ring back on my finger. Now that I have you all caught up. Let me get you to where I am at right now. I have a commotion going on in the back of me because people are holding back Sean for whipping Marcus ass. I turn around to try to calm him down. Although I shouldn't have done that because Marcus did do some mad disrespectful shit. He took Sean's engagement ring off my finger and placed it on the floor like it wasn't shit. That's no cheap ring nor is it something that I don't value. I love that ring and fought hard to keep that ring on my finger. To those who are new and don't know what the fuck is going on. Let me get you caught up real quick. I was dancing with my fiance Sean when the father of my kids pulled me from that situation. He removed my engagement ring and placed it on the floor and now he is on his one knee asking me to marry him. He's been there for awhile too because my dumb ass is really trying to go invisible right now. I'm thinking why invent this word when it's humanly impossible to do it. I was doing the mannequin challenge and failing at it. Something finally snaps in my brain and says "We are going to need you to make your mouth move before the shit gets too real and out of control." Now that I'm back to the current let me put this bullshit to an end.

"Marcus you had way too much to drink, please get up. You have embarrassed me and yourself enough."
"You don't want to marry me? Are you really going to stay with him and not come back to your family? You said we would be a family forever that you would be with me forever. Jazz do not do this, you know we belong together."
Jasmine reaches down and grabs her ring that Sean gave her and walks away. She takes Sean's hand and pulls him away from all the commotion. Sean looks at her to make sure she's okay. Once he had his confirmation that she was they walked out the reception. Marcus was left there holding his ring and watching the mother of his children walk off with another man.
"Can you bring our car around?" Sean asked as he hands the valet person his ticket. "What took you so long to answer him? Were you considering saying yes?"
"You know better?"
"Do I?"
"Sean I chose you when you asked me to marry you. As a matter of fact I chose you right after making the biggest mistake in our relationship. If I didn't want to be with you, I wouldn't have worked so hard trying to cover that mistake. I would have just broken up with you that day and went back to him."
"Then explain to me what took you so long to respond to him?"
"I was in shock and couldn't believe this man took off my damn engagement ring and put it on the floor. I was thinking about showing my ass. Then I thought about our daughters and how I

shouldn't do that to their father in public. I know what I'm about to say next sounds crazy but it's true. I was trying to make myself disappear. I was actually standing there trying to go invisible."
"You know damn well you couldn't do that. Jazz you ain't that damn drunk! Do you still want that man?"
"No. You know I don't baby. Please do not get on me right now. I swear it took me awhile because I was in shock."
"Don't get in your ass right now? You had me looking stupid and you want me to ignore that?"
"That's not what I'm saying. Come on Sean you know I love you and only want to be with you. Baby I'm sorry for making you think otherwise just now. That was not my intention."
"I'm really trying to calm myself down at this moment. While you are up here taking this shit lightly. I was actually trying to kill that muthafucker for being disrespectful. Just know Marcus has an ass whipping coming his way. The only reason he didn't get it just now was because people already had their cell phones out. I didn't want to be part of the Santos rage when they saw it."
"I wasn't taking it lightly, I'm pissed just like you! This shit already went viral, Reign is going to kill me. I am on twitter and I am trending. To make the situation worse they @ Damien Anderson to get more views and attention. "It really do be your own damn family trying to destroy you. I'm messaging all of them and cursing their asses out! How is this even happening? On their invitations it clearly says no cellphones at the wedding or reception."
"Jazz it's not like they stripped search them. Sneaking them in wouldn't be hard to do honestly."
"I'm messaging their trifling asses now. Anyone who has this video up I am suing. Montez and Reign said absolutely no phones at their wedding or reception.
"Don't do that! Then they will screenshot your message and also send that to the blogs. You are going to ride this one out, do not make this worse. I'm pretty sure they already sent the blogs a copy."
"Fuck!" she screams out. "I am so fucking screwed! I have turned a beautiful reception into some hood rich shit! I thought they had everyone keep their phones in that room. I didn't plan any of this but this is exactly why she sent those invitations out that way. People are so damn thirsty! You wait till I figure out who quenches their thirst first! Just wait!"
"We will figure it out tomorrow when we are sober up. It's out there now it's nothing we can do."
"Lies you tell!" Jasmine yells as she goes through her phone. She calls the one person she knows that handles stuff like this, "Mommy are you up?"
"Barely baby what's going on? Are you still at the reception?"
"No I left, but something made me leave early.
"I heard. I was just on the  phone with your dad. He told me bits and pieces about how Marcus embarrassed you at the reception? He also said Abs is on social media and you went viral because of Dame. What the hell does Reign's ex fiance have to do with this?"
"Marcus proposed to me and someone uploaded it. It went viral because the person tagged and hash tag Damien. Tag a celebrity and it makes it go viral. Assholes also made it seem like Dame was there, I swear I hate social media."

"Oh I get it because Reign was engaged to him and it was her wedding that made it spread. Well who did it? They were told specifically no cellphones were to be at the wedding or reception."

"I don't know, it's viral and has been reposted several times."

"Listen there's nothing I can do until the morning. I know you are mad, you have every right to be. I promise I will figure it out in the morning. Are you two headed here?"

"Yes we should be there in fifteen minutes."

"Okay, when your dad walks in I will tell him not to set the alarms. Make sure y'all do before going to bed. I love you."

"I love you too mom."

"You are beyond spoil."

"What?" she asks with an attitude. "Reign's wedding is viral and her best friend and cousin are the headliners. She is going to flip out, you know she hates being on social media when she's not controlling the narrative. To make things absolutely worse they used her ex fiance for click bait."

"Now that you said it out loud she is going to be pissed and that means Tez will be too. Let's hope it's old news when they surface back."

"Hopefully, I just have a bad feeling they sent it to her. Just like they did when Dame was caught cheating. They lit her mentions up and blew up her DM. I'm a dead friend walking at this point."

"She should be pissed more at Marcus than you. You ain't really do shit but hesitate for the fucking longest."

"I wasn't being hesitant or considering his damn proposal for the last time Sean. I was really wishing that shit was a dream or a bad joke on his part. I love you and only you. I want to grow old with you and give you beautiful babies and a beautiful life. I was not about to trade that in to be back with him."

"Next time say that shit to him! What you did tonight, you know what, forget it. Let's just go in here, take a shower, and get some kind of sleep."

"Baby I swear"

"I heard you Jazz! I listened and I heard you. Come on let's go.

# *Chapter Two: Decisions*

We went to bed late and he barely said anything to me. I kept trying to explain my actions last night but he fell asleep. He didn't say anything about forgiving me or believing me. I swear you cheat once and anything you do after that gets scrutinized to the fullest. At least he said hey beautiful this morning and gave me frustrated sex. Have you ever had that? Take it from me it's the best, its like straight fucking with some passion to it. He doesn't pull out and tongue you slowly as he releases in you. It's the absolute best if I do say so myself. He automatically had me in a deep sleep when we were finished. When I did finally wake up again, he was out of the bed and had me distraught because I was looking forward to round two. Since it's obvious I'm not getting that, I decided to get on my phone and try to see where the video came from. It didn't take long for me to get frustrated with playing detective by myself. I figured it was time to get up and shower and wash off my morning pleasure. When I was finished I headed downstairs and found my mom busy on her computer. I had the best person working on this. I am confident that she will nail whoever was responsible. My mom played no games when it came to her children or grandchildren. You want to see lilies grow thorns mess with Lillian's family and you would. While she was busy tapping away on her laptop; I noticed my dad, Sean, and Absalom outside throwing the football around. Damn my baby looked damn hot in those basketball shorts. He is sexy as hell and such a turn on when he is mad at me.I could tell he had some more frustration to release and throwing that football was not going to do it for him. I would tame him later and help him release some more tension. Right now I needed to join my mother and help her find the person who uploaded the video. We had some serious investigating to do.

"Are you ready for all this," Ab asked as he threw the ball to Sean.
"I'm all in, I know the drill, I have been here too many times that I better know it. You all are a tight knit family that has each other's backs and that's something I most definitely want to be part of."
"Last night it seemed from my observation you thought my daughter was going to choose him over you."
"You are right Mr. Butler, we both did. You asked me what you saw. I was just confirming and explaining why, that's all."
"I feel you Sean. Marcus was mad disrespectful last night. I personally didn't want to hold you back. I know Reigndrops is going to flip out when she hears about it. That girl hates social media with a passion. She's a female Prince Harry when it comes to it. She wants to control the narrative and not be anyone's story. She wasn't even there when this all went down and she went viral because it was her wedding. I saw on Twitter where someone said "Reign just standing there not even trying to stop it. She wants to be famous so bad." Of course that's my big sister that she was lying on so I @ her. I can't believe this woman was talking as if she knew Reign or Jazz. There were certain things I wanted to say but couldn't. That's when Sades saw it and she went in. Next thing we knew everyone was going in on that girl."

"People need to get a life she wasn't even there and Dame most definitely wasn't at her wedding or her reception." David said as he looked at his son with a smirk. "Um son you and Mersades have become quite close since you two met. Is there something you want to tell us?"
"We are just friends for the millionth time that girl has a boyfriend."
"Yeah and his name is Absalom Butler," Sean jokes as he throws him the ball.
"If she was don't you think we would claim one another? Man y'all are mad silly yo for real. Mersades is just a cool as female friend"
"That you wish didn't have a boyfriend. I get it son don't involve your true feelings until she becomes available, play the friend role. It worked for your dad and look I got your mama. I know the move. I have been there and done that."
"Alright let's get off Absalom and his "friend" Mersades. There's nothing to see here, right Abs?"
"Why did you do air quotations when you said friend? That's what we are nothing more, nothing less."
"I believe you."
"Man you two are trippin I'm going back in the house. You two have fun."
"Aw Abs man don't be like that. Come back dude we will change the subject," Sean said with a laugh.
As Abs walks back in the house he finds his sister on the phone pacing and trying not to curse out whoever was on the other end. His mother was still sitting at the table closing up her laptop and shaking her head. He wanted to ask so badly what was going on but thought twice about it. Instead he retrieves a bottle of water out the refrigerator and continues to observe in the background.
"You should have thought about our daughters before you uploaded the video. Don't you dare try to bring them up now that the damage has been done."
"You really going to have your mother sue their father? I told you multiple times I was drunk and pissed when I had him upload it. I fucking dose off and when I woke up the shit had already went viral. When I woke up I called him to take it down and we tried. It was too late it already went viral what the fuck you want me to do Jazz? I have been trying to get in contact with Reign or Montez but their phones are going straight to voicemail. Once I tell them what happened they will understand especially Reign. She will not go to the extremes like you and your mother are doing now. Damn! You have embarrassed me enough now you two are being fucking bullies!"
"Stop cursing Marcus before one of our daughters hears you!"
"How the fuck can they hear me unless your trifling ass have me on speaker!" Jazz looks at her brother and takes her hand and messes with his hair. As she walks by him, she takes the phone call outside in the front yard. She wanted to make sure Sean or her father couldn't hear them.
He couldn't believe what he heard, it was Marcus who uploaded the video. He had so many questions he wanted to ask. Who did Marcus hand his phone to? Why did he think that was time and place to do something like that? How did his mother and Jazz discover it was him? He decided only one person that could relate to him about this was Mersades. He grabs a plum from the fruit basket, rinses it off and heads to his room."

"Hey baby. I didn't see you come in. I was about to order breakfast from IHop did you want anything," she asked him just as he turned the corner.

He peeps his head back in the kitchen and says "IHop" in a high pitch.

"Yes sweetie. Do you want something or not?"

"Um yes of course I do! Can I get

"The usual" she says, cutting him off.

"Yes," he says, kissing her on the cheek and "extra grits please."

"No problem can you go out there and tell the guys to come in and give me their order."

"I got you mom." He walks to the door and yells "Sean! Dad! Mom wants you two in the kitchen!"

"Abs! I could have done that boy! Stop yelling in my house! Are you crazy?"

"No mom I'm not loco. I just thought it was best for me to do the yelling that way you keep your lovely voice," as he dodges her playful hits and takes off running to his room. He closes the door and jumps on the bed. He grabs his phone from his nightstand and sees that Sades already sent him a snapchat this morning. He retrieves her message and his face brightens up when he sees hers.

"Abs! I know you ain't still sleep boy! Hello Abs! Call me when you get this and make sure your face is washed. Abs really?! What are you doing? Hit me back!"

"You were blowing me up on snap beautiful. What's up? What makes you so anxious to see me?"

"Don't hey beautiful me. What were you doing? You haven't been on social media at all this morning. You sleep in today?"

"Not at all. I just came in from throwing the football with Sean and dad. I was about to hit the shower but saw your snaps so I'm staying funky just for you."

"Whatever Abs. So how's your sister doing this morning?"

"She's pissed. They found out who uploaded the video."

"Damn! That was quick? Well don't keep me in suspense, who was it?"

"Brace yourself, it was Marcus," he says slowly trying to be dramatic.

"Something is seriously wrong with you Abs," she said laughing. "Please don't quit your true talents of being a musician or cornerback. Because acting is nowhere near your future."

"I put a beautiful smile on your face so mission accomplished. How has your day been so far besides blowing me up on SC."

"Blowing you up? Stop it! You know I did all that to be nosy. I can't believe it was Marcus dang. He really hates my brother. Why would he do that? First of all his proposal was tacky and disrespectful. He just took Sean's ring off like he got it out of a bubble gum machine. Then he has someone record as if your sister was going to say yes."

"I honestly don't know what he was thinking."

"I don't know either. You should have let Sean get in his ass."

"Then your brother and Reign would have cut  them all off and me. Nah I did right by not letting it get to that. Plus I have nieces that I have to protect and they love their father."

"You're right. I'm just upset because they are really coming for Reign and none of this is her fault. My brother is going to be pissed when he sees it, this is about to be a mess when they come back from their honeymoon."

"Yeah especially since I heard Marcus say that my sister and mom are going to sue him."

"What? Really? Damn! Well can you blame her, it's bad on twitter. People keep asking how a bunch of nobodies are trending on Twitter. It's bad today, if you think last night was bad I suggest you stay off of it today. They already put me in time out."

"Now that I know who is responsible, I'm most definitely not going on today. My sister is handling it and I'm done with being a thug warrior on Twitter. What are you getting into today?"

"I'm going to the mall and movies later on tonight. I have no plans for today. I really probably go see MJ or take a nap."

"Date night tonight?"

"No, I'm hanging out with the girls. Dallas is gone with his brother for the weekend. He figured since I was going to be at my brother's wedding."

"Why didn't you invite him to the wedding?"

"I did. He bailed on me last minute and that's why I brought Neisha with me."

"Neisha seems cool. Is she single?"

"You want to hook up with my best friend?"

"No. I just asked if she was single."

"Uh huh."

"Why are you looking at me like that? I'm being for real, I was just asking."

"She is not in anything serious. Do you want her number?"

"If I wanted it I would have got it last night. You know I'm feeling you and only you. I wouldn't dare hook up with a best friend and ruin any possibilities."

"I can't be mad if you hook up with her or anyone else. I'm not going to lie I would be upset but I'm involved with Dallas. I don't expect you to wait on me. You are not doing that right?"

"What do you think?"

"If I knew I wouldn't have asked."

"I'm not waiting on you. I just haven't found anyone yet. I'm like your girl, I'm not into anything serious. Just having fun. What movie are you seeing tonight?"

"Come on you know we are hitting up Girls Trip."

"Oh."

"Hater."

"Whatever. You all have fun tonight."

"We always do. How about you?"

"No plans for now but we probably will go to the mall and grab something to eat."

"Alright. Well let me get off this phone and figure out what I'm doing for the rest of the day. I will talk to you later."

"One."

# *Chapter Three: Santos*

The bathroom was steaming as they bathed one another for the last time in Santa Catalina. They were so fortunate to have retired grandparents that wanted to give them their honeymoon getaways. Reign's wedding gift from her grandparents was Santa Catalina Island and Peru was paid for by his grandparents. They have been secluded from the world and in their own little bubble for two weeks. They had a brief interaction with their parents when they returned to the states for part two of their honeymoon in California. It was LAX when Reign received the news about what happened at their reception. Just like when Dame got caught with another female her DMs were filled with blogs wanting to get her side of things. Then of course the haters hit her up as well. She couldn't believe that her own cousin uploaded the video and then sold it to TMZ. Just to get back at her best friend for walking away from his proposal and choosing Sean. That was one revenge he was going to regret as Reign gave Lillian her permission to sue him. Montez took her phone after that and she was out of the loop again when they arrived in Catalina. As much as she tried to talk about what she saw and how mad she was at Jasmine for dodging her. He had no problems distracting her with romantic gestures until she no longer cared about the situation. Montez also had his parents facetime with MJ for another distraction. When she saw her son's adorable face, her anger and disappointment left. How could one chubby face pull that off? He kept his parents entertained by making cute little noises and faces that they had never seen before. He was so excited to hear their familiar voices that he smiled a lot and was trying to grab his grandparents phone. They knew their parents had him off his daily routines. All that hard work was all gone in two weeks and they knew putting him back on it was going to be a challenge. Before they ruin the rest of their honeymoon thinking about it. They decided to let their parents have fun with their grandson while they go back to enjoying their honeymoon. "What's the first thing you want to do when we go home tomorrow," Reign asked him as she was getting out of the tub.

"All I want to do is open up all our wedding gifts with you and my son. While eating some home cooked meal from my in-laws."

"I can't wait to see if people stuck to our gift registry or went on their own."

"You already know who stuck to that registry and they have grand in front of their name."

"Too funny. I think our uncles and aunties stuck to the list and maybe our parents."

"Yeah that's about it but I still can't wait to open them. Those tables were packed when we left the reception. You know how much I love free shit."

"I'm going to hold our son while you enjoy opening our gifts."

"I know you just want to get back to find out what went on at the reception when we left. I hope you at least wait a day and enjoy being back with our son. You already know Marcus is the reason, I don't know why you and Jazz can't just let it go. She chose Sean. I'm pretty sure the buzz on that will be dead when we get back. Help me understand why you of all people want to entertain it, Miss I Don't Like The Internet?"

"Social Media has this lie out there on me and I don't need a lie to taint my business. That's the only reason I want to address when I get back. I just want to understand what the hell Marcus was thinking that's all.

"Are you still going to sue him?"

"I gave Jazz permission to do that. If she still wants to that's on her."

"You can talk her out of it?"

"I could. I mean I will if his explanation is justifiable."

"Justifiable huh? I hear ya baby. Alright we have talked about that enough. Let me get out of this tub. You have me looking like an old man with these wrinkles forming on me."

"Trust me baby there's nothing old about you or your body."

"Are you flirting with your husband," he asked as he scooped her up and carried her to the bed. Determine to make their honeymoon memorable. He had convinced her to work on baby number two while they were in Peru. Something about making love to her husband made her more sensual and vulnerable. She had agreed to a lot that night being drunk in love. She couldn't explain it but it just meant a lot more to her now. Then it did when they were dating or engaged. The first night as newlyweds she cried while they were making love. That was the first time she ever did that, they made love plenty of times. He has always been passionate yet and still that first night as Mrs. Santos was very emotional. She now understood the religious part of waiting until you are married before having sex.

"I wish we would have brought MJ, I do not want to go back home right now. I want to make our honeymoon a family vacation now, he says to her as he plays in her hair."

"Now that it's the last day you want our son to be here so I will stay? Don't be using my son for your own agenda. You wouldn't let me talk about him at all while we were here or out of the country."

"What you mean I let you facetime him when we arrived here."

"You only did that because I wouldn't shut up about Jazz and Marcus."

"What? That wasn't why. I knew you were missing him. It had nothing about you going on and on about it," he said with a smirk. Besides, your son told me to keep you distracted before we left. Remember? I told you he asked me to work on a brother for him to play with."

"That worked in Peru that's not working in the states. You better hope your little friends accomplished their mission because if not. You and MJ will have to wait on his sister."

"It worked, not even worried about that. I just pray this pregnancy is easier on you, MJ had you going through it."

"Yes my lil stink butt took me through the wire and back in the beginning. Those first four months were scary after that though smooth sailing."

"I want a big family with you. If the next pregnancy goes like it did with MJ, we are two and done. I refuse to lose you to giving birth to our children. I know it's a woman's choice

"I'm glad you know that babe"she said, cutting him off.

"Your body but it's also my sperm. Therefore I can refuse to give it to you, even if that means a vasectomy."

"Wow! The Tennessee trip is still bothering you I see. We will be fine, Dr. Morales said so himself. He didn't find anything in my check up. I just had a rough trimester which is normal for most women who are pregnant for the first time. Besides I wouldn't put my life in danger now that our son is here and I'm your wife. I wouldn't risk that when we have other options. Again though Dr. Morales said I wouldn't have to entertain those options."

"He said for now, you nor Dr. Morales can't predict the future."

"We're good Tezzy, stop stressing."

"Just letting you know where I stand if the second pregnancy puts you at risk."

"I appreciate that but you don't have to have a vasectomy. I need your little friends if we decide to do the other options."

"I was being extra huh? Yeah I'm not doing that unless you force me too."

"Changing subjects because you are blowing my high. What are we doing on our last day in paradise?"

"I wanted to do this until we left."

"No sir, we are getting out of here our last day in Santa Catalina. Now get up hubby and feed your wife, I'm hungry.

# *Chapter Four: True Feelings Revealed*

       The newlyweds have been home for a week and decided to finally step out of the house. Reign's parents were throwing them a quick dinner with the Butler's to welcome them home. They had spent time with Montez's parents yesterday and now they were Charlotte bound this morning. When you own your own business you can take long vacations like this. No lie though I couldn't wait for her to return to the office on Monday. Reign's marketing team is great but my sis is a beast. I needed her for my new ventures that I'm about to buy. I know we have to first get past this reception that spiraled out of control when they left. We are in week three and I could no longer avoid the incident. When everyone had arrived the tension in the room was heavy, I was waiting for someone to address it. I was solo for the moment because Sean was stuck in traffic. My parents had the kids and they were still out shopping. Marcus had arrived before anyone, he was settled downstairs playing pool. When Reign and Montez finally did arrive, they headed to her old room to lay down MJ. When they came back downstairs she made eye contact with me then asked me to join her downstairs. It was time for us to discuss it once and for all. I guess she wanted it out the way before dinner started and everyone showed up. "You have dodge me long enough Jasmine. I'm ready to hear how my wedding went viral and how my ex was tied to it all. Who wants to start?"

"Can I just say I'm only involved in that damn video because of your cousin handing his phone to his people. I'm innocent in this whole thing. I didn't know he was going to pull that stunt and I damn sure didn't know it was being recorded."

"For the first time ever you finally told Reign the truth. It's all on me fam. I just thought what Jazz and I had was more than what her and Sean had. After seeing you and Tez finally getting married. For some odd reason it made me see that for us, Jazz. I had the ring for a while and with some alcohol encouraging me. I thought it was time to tell you how I really felt and how I wanted our family back. After spending time together again I thought you weren't really sure if Sean was the one."

"Why did you think that? I made it clear several times that I wanted him and only him. That where I was at, is where I wanted to be. I got caught up on what we had that day. How we shut down that closing sparked something in me for you that I haven't seen in awhile. I shouldn't had sex with you that day. I let that be known and told you we needed to just be co-parents. I thought you understood that's all we were doing. I didn't know you took that as me having doubts about Sean."

"I fucked up Reign and I am apologizing to you and Montez. I shouldn't have Rick upload the video and tagged Dame. Understand though I was drunk, pissed, and heartbroken that Jazz just dogged me out like that. She had you on her side since the break up and I just wanted payback. But damn you really about to sue me over it? That's fucked up!"

"You turn my wedding reception into some love and hip hop shit and you are coming at me for it! Are you serious? Then you tag Damien and for what? What was the purpose in doing that? Oh yeah, so you can sell a fake story to TMZ and have them go interview the basketball star. I'm off in Peru not knowing I'm being used for clicks and fifteen minutes of fame. Now you stand there and try to blame me for your actions. Are you fucking serious right now Marcus!"

"Hold on baby, calm down."

"Calm down? He's blaming me for this shit Tez and you are telling me to calm down?"

"We are trying to get this resolved. Someone needs to have a cooler head, that's all I'm saying baby."

"I'm sick of this. I'm not the reason for any of this shit Marcus! I'm not responsible for you and Jazz break up. I'm not responsible for her getting with Sean and I'm damn sure not responsible for the shit that went down at my reception! I was already fucking gone and we said on those invites no fucking cellphones. All this is on you, take responsibility for it and the consequences that comes with it!"

"You really think Jazz and I fail apart because of me?"

"Marcus"

"Nah don't Marcus me Jasmine. I will take full responsibilities on fucking up your reception and using it to make money and get a little fame. What I'm not going to do is continue holding on to Jasmine secrets."

"What the fuck are you talking about? Jazz what is he talking about? What secrets?"

"Tell her the truth Jazz or I will."

"More of an opinion then truth Marcus."

"It's our truth."

"Is it?"

"What codes are you two speaking? What am I missing?"

"The reason Jazz left me wasn't because I didn't want to marry her. She left me because of you! She put your needs and friendship above me, our kids, and our relationship. She said you needed us and that we should move to Greenville to help you. When I refused to do that she moved down there with our kids and left me. I thought the shit was going to be temporary and our relationship would survive because we were only miles apart. Then she started talking about Utah and moving to the midwest. I told her ass no and that she needed to come back home. That you and Montez were doing great and there was no point for her to continue staying with our kids."

"What?"

"She moved to Greenville because she felt you were suicidal after Dame's last infidelities. She didn't leave me because I wouldn't propose. She made that shit up and I like a fool went along with it. We were fine till she started talking crazy about moving to the midwest and taking my baby girls with her. Hell I thought you knew since you called me begging me to let your mom write out an agreement for me. I wasn't about to let Jazz mother's best friend rep me. I wasn't going to let my guard down because she is married to Uncle Rome. It felt like y'all were trying to take my rights from me and I wasn't having it anymore."

"Marcus I would never do that to Yas and Marcella. I know how much you mean to them and how much you love and adore them. I thought shared custody was the best way to settle this, that's all. I wasn't trying to take your rights or have my mother trick you into giving up those rights. Let's be real when you filed for full custody that was wrong and yes it pissed me off. That's when I let Reign talk to Charlene. I had no choice, you were being unreasonable."

"Wow Marcus! You really thought my mom was going to set you up to lose your daughters because her and Jazz's mom are best friends? You actually thought dad would have stood by and have them do that to his nephew? I know you are a great father just like Jazz is a great mother. I was just trying to help, I wasn't trying to destroy you."

"But you did Reign! Instead of convincing her to keep my girls close you backed her and her dreams!"

"Wait? Let me get this straight, because I supported my friend of being a badass entrepreneur I'm getting blamed for y'all chaos? I can't tell a grown person how to go for what they want. I can only support what they want. Maybe if you did that for Jazz, she would have stayed with you. How is that my fault?"

"Of course you don't want to fucking see it and that's why I didn't even bother telling you. You are always taking her side and she always takes yours. All I know is she gave up on me to make sure you were good. It didn't have shit to do with me not proposing. She lied to you about that. You were broken and she thought she was the only who could help you pick up the pieces. Once again Jazz put you and your life above her own."

"Wow. I never knew you felt this way Marcus. I mean you two hooked up and I told y'all from the jump how I felt about that. Then Jazz told me she was pregnant and I forgave you two. I never once got involved in you all relationship until that day. I am so confused right now. Where is this really coming from?"

"I just told you. I blame you that Jazz and I are no longer. If you would have left Dame instead of staying and let him continue to make a fool out of you. None of this would have happened but you don't give a fuck! You got your happy ending while destroying ours."

"Hold the fuck on man! This is where I draw the muthafucking line, don't ever come for my wife like that again. I will lay your bitch ass out! Be a man and take responsibility for you and Jazz not being together. If you really wanted that happy ending you would have brought your bitch ass to Greenville and made it happen there. You didn't do that and Sean did. You lost move the fuck on. But most importantly my guy stay the fuck out of Reign's face. I don't give a damn who you are, you will not approach her like that again." Reign gets between the two and pushes Montez back. Jazz steps in front of Marcus and helps her calm down the situation. They all stood in silence wondering who was going to be the first to break it.

# *Chapter Five: The Day of Reckoning*

Marcus opened up so many doors of secrecy that she knew nothing about. Jazz never told Reign the real reason for her split and Marcus was letting it all out. He blamed Reign for breaking up his family and ruining their lives. It got so bad that he was in her face yelling at her. Until Tez couldn't take it anymore and  lost it. He was trying to stay out of it because that's her cousin but he had his limits and Marcus reached it when he was in her face. Next thing they knew he had got between him and Reign, was ready to punch Marcus.Thank God, Reign stepped back in between the two and separated them. The loud commotion made Rome come down stairs, his presence alone helped maintain peace for the moment.  Now Reign was looking at Jazz wondering could she be the reason they ended. She had no idea that Jasmine walked away from her family because she thought she would do harm to herself. She really thought it was because Marcus didn't want to marry her. She had questions and  was trying to figure out how to ask. She felt like she needed to apologize to him but couldn't find the words. I mean they both lied to her and she was hurt that they did. If she knew at the time that Jazz put her relationship and family on hold because of her. She would've convinced her to go back to Charlotte. Finally Reign decided to pull Jasmine outside. She wanted answers and her best friend, her sister was going to give it to her once and for all.

"Is that true Jazz? I unknowingly ended your family and you lied to me about it?"

"You are not to blame for me and Marcus no longer being together. We had plenty of opportunities to make things right and get back together and we didn't. For him to blame you is ridiculous."

"Jazz did you leave him because you thought you needed to save me yes or no?"

"Reign its more to it then that"

"Yes or no Jazz," she yells getting frustrated.

"I can't answer that with a simple yes or no. Did it have something to do with it maybe, was it the main reason no. We were drifting apart before that and he knows this. I wasn't happy with him for awhile."

"When did you start being unhappy Jasmine? Because this is the first time I am hearing about this. You said nothing to me about being that way until now."

"When did we ever discuss my relationship? The focus was always on you and Dame. That I dealt with what was going on in my relationship on my own or tried to discuss it with him. You were allowing yourself to be consumed in Dame's life that you distanced yourself from real friends and your family."

"Let's not Jazz. Don't make it seem as if I didn't ask you about your relationship. Don't make me out to be selfish, needy, and all about me type of friend. When we both know that I wasn't. I asked you a lot about what was going on with you two. There were days I hated talking about my problems and wanted you to distract me. You would always say you and Marcus were doing great. Now you want to stand here and say that didn't happen?"

"I lied, it wasn't always peaches and cream. You were going through your own shit and I didn't want to add to it by dumping my problems on top of yours. After Marcella was born, I say around her first birthday. We had gotten comfortable and your cousin didn't see the point of getting married. He convinced me that we were fine the way we were. That all marriages were was a piece of paper to confirm everything. So no me moving to Greenville to be closer to you wasn't just because you were a wreck after Dame. Yes I told you it was because he didn't want to get married, that wasn't a complete lie. It just didn't happen at the time I moved here, and that's exactly why I can't give you a yes or no answer. It's just not that simple."

"Why didn't you just tell me this from the jump? Why is this now being told to me? I was stronger than you thought and yes that morning you found me at my worst. You act like I was suicidal and I wasn't. I just needed a fresh start where no one knew me and a location that wasn't too far from my family. I thought that's why you were coming, I had no idea it was because you felt like you had to save me from myself."

"At first yes I did. Once you and Montez were comfortable with one another. I went back several times to work it out with Marcus but he was still mad that I was back and forth in Greenville. The rest that I have told you about our situation was true."

"You do realize you had the whole family mad at him and it was a lie. I was pissed at him for not wanting to marry you and trying to take full custody of the girls. He was enemy number one and you let him be that. No wonder he didn't want my mother involved; he knew you were lying. Adding my mother to your team he knew he had no chance in hell of winning against them. Our mothers would have torn him apart. He was just as dumb though because no way I would have went along with your lies and since we are thick as thieves. Let me guess he assumes I knew this whole time?"

"He shouldn't be assuming that because I never told him that. I did put your situation as the main reason for me leaving."

Why are you two out here? I thought you wanted to have this conversation with all of us. Here you go again, taking her side and the hell with me!"

"What are you talking about Marcus? I haven't taken anyone's side, I'm trying to get to the truth. What the fuck is goin on with you? I love you cuz why you think I don't all of a sudden is crazy to me."

"I told you the truth. That's what really happened and now you are out here letting her still feed you lies!"

"That's not what's happening here. You really need to chill!"

"Hey what the fuck did I just tell you in there about being in her face! Are you taking me for a joke? Are you trying to call my bluff. Get the fuck out her face Marcus, my last time me telling your ass!"

"Fuck you Montez!" As soon as he said it he met Montez fist. He hit him dead in the mouth and before Reign or Jazz could get between them the two were fighting. Rome runs outside and tries to separate the two. He pushes Marcus towards the door and Reign grabs her husband. She wipes blood from his hands and tries her best to calm him down. Jazz stands there shocked and can't believe what just happened. What was going on with her baby daddy? Why was he wilding out? She had never seen him like that before his actions were alarming. Montez told him to stay out of her face why didn't he just listen. If he would have fought like this when they were together, they would have been still together. It's too late for this now and all he is doing is destroying his relationship with his cousin. She knows somehow he will blame this on her too, at this point she was hoping Sean would pull up. She was tired of being his punching bag and needed her fiance protection.

"Hey you alright," Montez asks as he checks her out.

"I'm fine babe I should be asking you that. What have I told you about being a thug? You don't always have to lay paws first lil Scrappy."

"What did I tell you? I'm going to protect you my way. Now Iyana, stop trying to fix my life. These dudes are going to learn one way or another not to get in my wife's face or personal space. Family or not."

"Where was that fucking energy when Dame was getting at her?" Marcus yells as he comes towards them again with Reign's father following close behind. "Huh Tez? You swing on me but not him. Where was that energy when he was kissing on her, hugging her, trying his damndest to get her back! I remember your ass did nothing, now all of a sudden you are Captain Save A Wife?"

"Marc man chill stop trying to push my buttons by bringing that lame up! I whipped his ass just like I did you and if you keep it up with the mouth. I'm going to lay hands again and this time you won't get up. Chill the fuck out man she has nothing to do with the demise of you and Jazz."

"How the fuck do you know? You came into the family late, you don't know them like I know them. Then your ass left her for three months and she hooks back up with Dame. But you can careless because you were in Brazil fucking Brazilian women. While me and uncle Rome took care of Dame for putting his fist to her face."

"Wait what?" Reign says as she looks at Montez. "You told me you didn't sleep with anyone while you were there. What is he talking about?"

"You believe him? He was in a country known for beautiful women and he was there for three months. You took him for his word that he didn't fuck not one of those women? Damn I thought you were smarter than that fam, being pregnant really had you stuck on stupid!"

"Watch your mouth Marcus," Rome says in a threatening tone.

"My bad Uncle Rome."

"He's lying Reign, you know he's lying. What are you doing? I know you are not believing this shit."

"I asked you straight up did you get with anyone while you were there and you told me no."

"Because I didn't, Reign you seriously can not be fallen for this. Baby you know I didn't you know me better than anyone. Don't start doubting me again on lies."

"You are right, I do know you. I ignored my intuition when deep inside I knew you slept with someone. You and I can't go two days without making love. I was a fool to believe you went three months without having it."

"I can't go without making love to you, that's our thing. I wasn't fucking randoms in Brazil and then turn around have unprotected sex with the mother of my child. Putting him and you at risk without being tested first. Come on Reign you know this."

"Do I? My best friend lied to me for three years and I didn't have a clue that she was doing that. Shit and I've known her my whole life," she says getting choked up. "So how hard is it for the love of my life to do the same," she says as she walks back towards the house.

"Reign. Reign!"

"Shit doesn't feel good when it's your family getting fucked with does it Tezzy?"

"Wow you are really doing a lot right now! Why the fuck did you do that Marcus, tapping on her insecurities like that? I lied to her, she knew nothing about this until now and you do this to your own flesh and blood? You know damn well we were having problems way before Montez entered her life. You ain't shit for this one!"

"Do what you always do Jazz, put her life before yours! Keep being her shadow while she shines. We couldn't completely be us or happy because you were too busy in her and Dame's world and when that shit blew up. You tagged along with her and Montez. Even hooked up with his best friend so you could stay in her life. You don't have a life unless she's in it somehow!"

"Fuck you Marcus!"

Montez was still standing there and his body was hot. He was staring at the door waiting for Reign to come back out and for her to say she believed him. He could hear Jazz and Marcus going back and forth but their argument sounded distance. Although they were right behind him. Then something inside of him just snapped and before Rome could grab him Montez had his hands on Marcus' throat trying to choke the life out of him. He rushed him so fast that the impact made Marcus hit his head on the garage door.

"If you ruined my marriage with your lies I swear to God that I'm going to kill you," as he ram his head into the garage door again.

"What the hell is going on out here! Montez let him go! Rome do something!"

"Woman don't you see me trying to pull him off! Jazz help me!

"Hell nah! Kill his ass Montez," she says as she walks towards the house.

"Jasmine Nicole Butler helped us separate these two."

"No mama Lene he deserves that and a whole lot more. I'm praying Sean pulls up and finishes him off."

"Jazz! Jazz!" She keeps going towards the door ignoring Charlene and walks in the house to look for Reign. She heads to her bedroom where she finds her breastfeeding MJ. She sits down next to her with no words being spoken. Only the sound of MJ eating fills the silence in the room. Jazz was trying to gather her words and Reign was focused on her son. "I believe Tez when he says he didn't fuck anyone while he was in Brazil. I don't think he would lie about that, especially since you were carrying his son at the time. No way he would risk harm to him."

"Mm."

"Okay. My thoughts on the situation you clearly don't want because I lied to you. I get that but you kept things from me as well. Things that I thought I should have had a heads up on and you left me in the dark. I forgave you for those moments. Why are you not doing the same right now?"

She looks at Jazz before cutting her eyes at her. She went back to focusing on her son eating.

"Remember me being upset with you for not giving me the heads up about Sean going to propose to me? We had it out and then I forgave you and we moved on."
She continues ignoring her and attends to her son.
"How long are you going to give me the silent treatment?"
"How long was it before you took my call when I heard about my reception?"
"I didn't pick up..... Ok heffa ha, ha, ha, so the silent treatment is over?"
"I wasn't giving you the silent treatment, I was just ignoring you. I wasn't expecting any of this when we returned from our honeymoon. I know Montez didn't sleep with anyone while he was in Brazil. I just wanted to make sure so I pressed him more on it."
"You do know by doing that he snapped and is trying to kill Marcus, right?"
"My parents won't let that happen. I'm listening to you now. Remember you told me let him be the man his parents raised him to be. What was it you said "let him take care of me and protect me. Oh and my favorite line from you. He's not Dame, and for me to stop treating him like he is him." That's all I'm doing, one thing I know about my husband, he hates being lied on. If Marcus was lying he was going to deal with him or if he was telling the truth he would have followed me and tried to convince me. Besides, Tez doesn't even speak to Marcus like that. How would he even know that, now if Sean was saying that I would have considered it."
"Glad you came back to your senses but did you have to let him whip your goddaughter's father like that?"
"Why didn't you stop him?"
"He ain't my man. Hell I stepped in when they were in the house. I did that while he was going in on my ass. My ass was done with that once he came outside and was still on that bullshit."
"Are you okay? He was saying some bullshit and hitting below the belt. Why do we go through this with our exes? We are close; they know this when they get with us. Shit doesn't change because they entered our life and damn sure will not change when they are gone."
"I have to be a low self esteem bitch to let that get to me. I have a life outside of you and you also have one besides me. If I am being all the way one hundred, it does sting, that's the way he sees me. I mean all I did was carry his two girls and are raising them as queens. You would think he would have a little more respect for the mother of his children. I just saw the fuck boy mentality from him. I'm praying that's just a one time thing. Speaking how I am stuck with him for eighteen years. Damn it! Sean just text and said he is on his way. Let me get out there and make sure Marcus is leaving. Are you coming with me?"
"No MJ is up so I'm going to take him down stairs and find a kid's movie on Netflix. Good luck with that."
"Only one that needs luck is Marcus. Are we still going to sue him for selling that to TMZ?"
"Sure am. I'm not letting him off for making a private matter of mine public just because he didn't get what he wanted. I'm not a celebrity. I left an athlete for those exact reasons. He's going to give me the money they paid him plus interest. No need for him to play the family card. Family wouldn't have done what he did."

"Well you know our mothers will make sure of it. Whatever I can do to help just let me know. I really need to get out here though Sean is coming and my parents are on their way with the kids. I'm pissed at him but I don't want our daughters seeing this."

"We have to protect our babies at all cost no matter what. Go ahead and do what you have to do." Jazz walks out the room and calls her mother. She explains to her what is going on and asks her to wait until she has Marcus gone before bringing the kids. Lillian let's her know she already spoke with Charlene. They were going to Target and let them pick out some clothes and toys before coming over. Once they had their plan together she hangs up the phone and just shakes her head. They were supposed to have a cookout and a small get together welcoming them home. Marcus was still on a mission to embarrass himself and the family because he didn't get what he wanted. The fifteen minutes of fame from TMZ has really gone to his head. That ego of his was doing more damage than good. He thought the family was pissed at him before he was about to find himself out after this. As she walks back outside she sees Marcus Rome and Abs talking. She walks over to them, takes Marcus by the hand, and pulls him to the side. They were going to act like adults and finally put this to rest.

"Are you done?"

"Just as much as you are."

"What does that even mean, Marcus?"

"It's clear where I stand with everyone so I'm fine with that. Just don't turn my girls against me like you did my family."

"I would never do that and you know that. How did we even get here? I thought we were fine until that foolishness at the wedding happened. After we slept together I made it clear Marcus, why all of a sudden are you saying I didn't."

"Maybe getting along and co-parenting put me back in my feelings. When the girls were finally getting along with Sean and his son, it started bothering me. I don't want no man taking my place in Yasmine and Marcella's life. I just wanted us back and I went by it all wrong."

"You think?"

"Jazz stops acting like you didn't play a role in it. It's just me and you."

"I'm not playing and that's your problem. You are treating this as a game and hurting us while doing it. I never once told you to hide anything about our break up. For you to stand there and say Reign is the real reason we ended is ridiculous. We ended because we changed. I wanted more and you wanted to remain the same. It hurts me that you keep saying I'm a shadow of Reign. I would never say anything like that to you."

"I wanted you to hurt. You walked away from us like it was nothing."

"That's not true Marcus and you know it. I wanted to be more than the mother of your children. I wanted our family to work and I fought for it. You wanted to fight once Sean became a factor. By then it was too late."

"Yet and still you were making love to me and opened the doors to us possibly getting back together. Then shut that door again because I wanted my family back home."

"I outgrew that life Marcus. I didn't want to work for someone else. I was happy working for myself and making my own money. You wanted me to go backwards, that was the problem.

Sean saw my vision, that we could be successful as entrepreneurs then someone's employee. He wasn't afraid to go after that dream with me."

"I guess there's nothing left to say. I'm going to leave. I will call you later to get the girls. Can you let them know that for me?"

"Of course. What about Reign?"

"I will work it out with her. We will always be family no matter what."

"I hope you two get back to how you were before us."

"With time I think we will." She watches him pull off and sits outside to wait for Sean to arrive. She felt bad about everything and wishes she could fix the past so the present wouldn't be this way. She loved Marcus and always will. He was more than the father of her children, more than an ex-lover she really lost her best friend. They were friends before they were anything else and now it felt like that was gone forever. Before she knew it tears were flowing from her eyes. She didn't want any of this to happen. Now she felt it was up to her to at least fix it between Reign and Marcus. Maybe she could convince Reign not to sue him and just handle it in the family. She would try to convince her later to do just that. As she was getting her plan together to present to her, Sean was pulling up in the driveway.

"Sorry I'm late, that traffic was a beast. I tried to beat the five o'clock traffic and still got trapped in that shit. Baby, what's going on? Have you been crying?"

"It's bad baby,  it's so bad!"

"What the fuck is going on? What's bad?"

"Reign didn't want to wait for you, so we already had it out. Marcus told her everything and that led to a heated argument between them. He was in her face one too many times and Montez lost it. They were fighting, Rome and Abs had the pleasure of pulling them apart not once but twice. I feel responsible for all of it and I just want to fix it.

"Jazz this is not all on you, these folks are grown. Take responsibility for your part and your part only! It's not your place to fix whatever is broken between Reign, Montez, and Marcus. That muthafucker didn't touch you or get in your face did he?"

"No, he didn't. He said some mess up shit to me but that's about it."

"What the fuck did he say!"

"I'm fine baby they're just words."

"Nah, you are far from fine. If they are just words then why are you out here crying?"

"Do not take what I'm about to say the wrong way. Before you and Montez entered our world we all were close. I couldn't stand Damien, but I was always cordial around him when we would hang out."

"You were being fake in other words."

"Basically but what wasn't fake was us; Reign, Marcus, and myself. We were the three amigos, now I don't know what we are."

"I get it baby I do. You want all of us to get along and be a strong family. I see it when you are around Dana, and I appreciate it. It's just going to take time to get us all on the same page. Right now, Marcus has to work on letting you go all over again and moving on. You gave him hope when you cheated on me with him. Then you take it back and he's angry and I get it.

That's why I am really trying to be patient with his ass but honestly my patience has run its course with him. He's lucky I wasn't here, Montez would have been the least of his problems."
"I know."
"I hope you do baby, come here. Everything will work itself out, you just have to let it. Okay?
"Okay."
"Damn I swear God really is looking out for this dude. I really don't like it that he has you out here crying. I know you are downplaying what happened, I'm not going to press you on it. For now anyway."
"Thank you. I really can't take another fight right now. I will give you all the info when we are home. Promise."
"Are you ready to go in?"
"I rather stay out here until my parents and the girls get here."
"Then we will sit here and do just that. I love you Jasmine."
"I love you too. Baby you just don't know how much I needed to hear those words. Today has been really rough."
"I got you. I will always have you.

# Chapter Six: The End

It was time to put the story to bed and give their side of the story. Rumors were getting way out of hand and Reign wanted the blogs to leave them alone. Jasmine had convinced Reign to drop the lawsuit on Marcus in exchange that they would act like they didn't when they went live. Technically the papers had already been filed. A court date hasn't been given yet, Reign was going to have Lillian file a motion to have it dismissed on Monday. She just wanted Marcus to sweat a little longer. I mean he is the reason they had to do this live in the first place. As Abs set the cameras up in the living room. They were doing last touches on their hair and make up. Once they were done they made their way to the sofa and Abs gave them the okay to get started.

"Hey everyone. How's everyone doing this evening? No one is headed to the clubs this beautiful Saturday night? Okay I see the dancing emojis coming in. Nope your girl is not headed to a club tonight. It's not girls night out yet for me. The honeymoon was awesome thanks to everyone who is asking. No worries I will flood your feed with pictures soon. I knew someone was going to ask and yes this is the reason for the live. It's truly unfortunate that I have to address this but here I am. It's a shame that my beautiful wedding and reception was turned into click bait. I also was lied on to, I was not at the reception when all of this happened. We were on our way to the airport when this incident took place. Also on my wedding invitations it was clear as day that guests were to leave their cellphones at home, in their vehicles, or if they had to bring them inside. They had to leave them in a room and they could retrieve them when they were leaving the facility. We said absolutely no cellphones period and this was the reason why. It hurts more because it was a family member who did it. Not just any family member, someone I consider a brother more than my first cousin. As you all know by now my cousin Marcus is the one who sold a fake story to TMZ. Not only am I the godmother to both of his daughters, I'm also best friends with the mother of his children. Someone asked which side of the family he belongs to? He is my dad's nephew. How was he able to make it go viral someone else asked? He tagged an ex fiance I haven't seen since I was about six weeks pregnant with MJ. My son is now four months old so you all do the math. He did all that to make sure his little video went viral. A lot of people are saying I'm wrong for suing him and causing him more embarrassment. To those that are trying to flip this on me, all I can say is I don't give a damn. He took it upon himself to bring a camera in a venue where it was prohibited. He then sold it to a blog and uploaded it himself on Facebook, Twitter, YouTube and Instagram. Yet you all want to act stupid on my live and blame me. Telling me to let it go when I'm being harassed by blogs. Typical of you all to blame the black woman."

"I see some of you are asking her about me. You want to know why she is not going after me as well since I'm in the video too. Yes I'm in the video but I didn't have anything to do with it being sold or uploaded. Hell at the time I didn't even know I was being recorded. I know my reaction to what was going on made it seem that way, I honestly didn't know. Some of you know me and you know I'm very outspoken and move differently from Reign. I will curse your ass out and give zero fucks on what I said when I said it. I can be just as ratchet and disrespectful as you all are trying to be on this live. Let's not try me, I feel like shit enough already and I don't mind taking my frustration out on you no life having trolls. I will be a z lister sweetie but you are here in my best friend's live stream so what does that make you? Obviously we are popping and entertaining enough for your ass to join this live. Yeah continue sitting your simple ass down and hating with your thumbs. You are a thumb thug, bitch I'm so scared. Bet you won't pull up to Queen City though. I pay for your flight and put you in first class for this first class ass whipping. DM me your flight information. Yeah that's what I thought shut the hell up simpleton. Anyway like I was saying I hate that my sister's reception was made into a sceptical. When she did everything she possibly could do to ensure her wedding stayed private for family and friends. I am really embarrassed that the father of my girls is acting like a scorn baby daddy. This is out of character for him and I'm disappointed."

"Okay you all we are going to get out of here before Jasmine stays in Jazz mode. Thank you all for joining us, see you all later. Damn Jazz did you have to get in that person's ass like that?"

"You saw it was being rude as hell to me first. I was trying to ignore that person but they kept at it. That's what happens when you troll me I'm going to pull your card and see are you bout that life or are you a thumb thug. All of a sudden he or she says I'm aggressive when I match their energy. Nah you are fake and I just proved it."

"I tried to keep a straight face when they typed that. Really bitch? You were on here being disrespectful  first. You shut them down though that was hilarious. So many people started trolling that person after that.  I was trying to keep it together while you were talking, I came so close to laughing.The comments did it for me, so many people had your back."

"I have to go back and read those comments. I stopped reading them once I got started. These people online are some bold individuals."

"They really are and it's hard to ignore them sometimes."

"I give them all the attention they need because clearly they don't have a life of their own."

"I'm just glad we got this over with and our story is out there too. Now I'm done with it and it's time to move on." Reign reaches over and hugs her friend and walks outside to join the family. Charlene was still bringing out food to the table and Montez was with their son sitting down. Moments later Jazz emerges from the house and joins everyone outside.

"It's over with," Montez asks.

"Yes our version is out and that's all I really wanted at the end of the day. Hopefully Marcus will do right and tell the truth. Even if he doesn't, we all know what really happened and at the end of the day that's all that matters," Reign answered.

"Are you sure you want to drop the lawsuit, baby?"

"I'm sure mama Lillie. It's time to move on and be family again. Jazz is right, all this is not worth losing my cousin. It will take a lot of work to get there but eventually we will."

"Alright let's move on from that topic. We had enough of  that drama. Let's get into this food. Baby will you bless the food," Charlene asked.

"Everyone close their eyes. Heavenly father, we come to you this evening to ask that you bless this food. Please let it nutrient our body like you meant for it to do. In your name we pray. Amen."

" I can't wait to get that shrimp pasta mama Lene," Montez said rubbing his hands together.

"I made that just for you baby, I hope you enjoy it."

"You know I am."

"You all went out for us, we really appreciate it. We are going to have leftovers for days. Sean and Jazz make sure you all take some of this home too."

"Now Reign you know you didn't have to make that announcement. We were already going to do that."

"Thanks for offering though sis."

"You are welcome Sean."

"Are you all staying tonight or heading back?"

"Montez is driving. What you want to do baby?"

"We can stay the night. I wanted to go to ya'll church tomorrow. That way MJ can see everyone again."

"Well that settles it, we are staying. Do you need to head to Target after we finish eating?"

"Yeah I can grab a button down shirt and some khakis. Are y'all riding with us Sean or ya'll heading back?"

"I will leave that up to Jazz and her parents."

"Sean now you know you two don't even have to ask."

"Right, Dad. Yeah let's stay and be church bound in the morning. After today and the way we all showed out. I think it's safe to say we all need Jesus."

"Amen to that," their parents agreed.

"Why must you all be like that," Reign asked laughing.

"The truth shall set you all free," Lillian responded

"The truth did just that," Jasmine agreed. Before they headed to Target. The women cleaned up the kitchen, while the men made plates to go for everyone. As they wrapped everything up. The grandmothers took the girls to Marcus while the grandfathers volunteered to watch MJ until everyone returned. It's been awhile since all four hung out together. After they finished shopping at Target, they decided to hit downtown Charlotte and walk around. It felt good to get caught up with each other. It felt like they haven't seen each other for a long time, in reality it had only been three weeks. They split up for a second just so they could catch up individually. Reign let Jazz see some honeymoon pictures and told her about how being married was better than shacking up. How she felt the difference on the first night. That she couldn't explain it but it had her so emotional. The journey her and Montez took to finally become one was worth it. Jazz then filled her in all she was working on business wise while she was on her honeymoon. She also told her about the aftermath of the reception that the cameras didn't pick up. How she had to damn near beg Sean for forgiveness because of her delay of giving Marcus an answer. The guys were talking about everything sports and business moves they were about to make. Montez talked a little about his honeymoon and all the sightseeing places they hit up. Sean was telling him where he wanted him and Jazz to choose for their honeymoon. They were still in disagreement but had at least narrowed it down to two places. As he spoke on his dilemma with his fiancee, Montez knew what his and Reign's gift would be to them. Whoever didn't get their way they would make sure they did. It was only right since their honeymoon was both gifted by their grandparents. Once the conversation felt dead to them. They hussle up and caught up with their ladies and sat down with them to watch the waterfalls.

"This is when I miss Queen City the most. They just don't have this type of scenery in Greenville."

"I know that's right sis, why do you think I'm up here just about every weekend?" No matter where I move, Charlotte will always be home."

"Queen city will always be home to us queens, that I will never argue with you about. I'm glad you wanted to stay an extra day babe, I really do miss my family. I didn't know how much until my wedding day."

"We have to do better with coming back frequently. I never want you to think or feel as if I'm trying to keep you from your family. I know how much your parents means to you, especially your dad."

"Speaking of fathers. We should get back to the house. Lord knows what MJ has them into."

"We already called, your mothers are back and they said they got it. If we wanted to hang out we could. I was thinking we hit up a club or bar that has a dance floor. We haven't done that in a minute."

"I'm with Tez. Come on Reign when the last time we showed these bitches how it's done on the dance floor. Jazz said as she got up and did a little dance."

"Hey! You know you don't even have to convince me. I love going to the clubs that haven't changed because I'm married. We are still young and far from an old couple. Ain't that right hubby.

"Damn right!"

"Okay newly weds let's go bring the sun up," Jazz said as she pulled her friends to leave.

# *Chapter Seven: Black Wall Street*

It's been a few days since the craziness that went down in Charlotte. Before it was back to business. We had to put our personal lives back on track. Hanging out at the clubs and praising God the next day is exactly what we needed. I was back to work looking for new houses to renovate and sell. Reign was still on maternity leave working part time at home and in the office when she felt like it. School was back in and they haven't hired anyone to keep MJ yet. They had to come up with a schedule that benefited both of them while they continued to look. When Reign had to travel out of town, MJ would usually stay with Montez's parents til his father got off. We would also step in, if the grandparents weren't available. The routine was working but they knew soon they would have to hire someone part time. In the meantime, I would continue holding down the office while also handling my own business. Reign has an awesome team, I wasn't needed much unless papers had to be signed and Reign wasn't available to do so.

"Jasmine, Mrs. Trina Johnson is here to see you."

"Please send her in Tamara and thank you."

"Hey Ms. Butler, how are you doing today?"

"As well as could be expected and you?"

"I'm doing well myself, no need to complain. As I told you earlier this week in an email I have some properties for you that I think you would be interested in. I would like to run some ideas for that property that would make you a lot of money. This also could be good for the black community."

"I must say I was intrigued when you reached out to me with this property. I haven't seen anything like this in Greenville and I especially haven't seen it for the black community. A lot of Hispanics and Asians have a lot of business here and I rarely see any black owned businesses all in one place like I see for other nationalities. Makes you wonder sometimes why it's like that."

"Exactly. If you do see a black owned business it's usually restaurants, clubs, or clothing stores. I think Reign coming here has shown some of our people that we are more than just cooking, clubbing and fashion. Also you are making a lot of noise yourself or I wouldn't be here presenting you with this opportunity. I saw you buying homes  in our neighborhoods and making them affordable for black families or single parent homes. You are stopping gentrification and I respect that. When I saw this abandoned commercial lot, I wanted to bring it to you because we shared the same vision. Rebuilding black community and putting our own back to work for ourselves."

"The rebuilding of black wall street. One community, one city, one state at a time. You are right, I am ready to venture out and get my own office space for my realtor company. This commercial lot can help me do that and employ more black people that are ready for real change like we are. I can see us doing just that with this property."

"Okay now that we are on the same page, are you ready to go look at this property?"

"I wouldn't have agreed to this meeting if I wasn't. I'm all yours today Ms. Johnson."

After Jazz finished up her business with Trina and signed the papers to own the lot. She stopped by Total Wine and More to pick up an Ace bottle. She was headed over to Reign's house to celebrate. She couldn't wait to tell her bestie about how one of her dreams were about to come true and she knew only Reign would understand. Since she has been in Greenville she saw how the Hispanic and Asian community stick together and hired their own to run their own. How no one batted an eye or gave them grief by them not hiring too many blacks or whites as employees. She also saw how black people would go spend their money at any of these establishments and not caring about it. On social media black women were getting treated badly in these hair places owned by Asians and it still wasn't stopping other black women from supporting them. How many black women you knew were going to give up their wigs and weaves because a few sisters were being mistreated? Boycott lasted for a minute and they were back in the stores buying bundles like there was no tomorrow. Why because black people don't own their own hair stores. Just about every store in America beauty stores are run by Asians and they are all set up in the black communities. Reign had started marketing more black owned hair stores that she could find in different cities and states. She was given black women who were tired of it, new ways to support their own. She even reached out to black own nail spots to get them out there to the black community. While she was in the wine store it hit her. She was going to use one of the spaces to open up a wine and liquor store. Selling more owned black products instead of a small section she always finds when she walks into these wine stores. She had so many different plans for the lot that she couldn't wait to get to her friend's house so they could brainstorm. As she was checking out she made sure she paid attention to the store's layout and how she was going to make hers even better. She wanted to make sure she was in competition with the biggest stores in Greenville.

"How late are you staying Reign," Tonya asked.

"I have no clue. Hopefully I'm out by ten."

"You want me to stay with you?"

"No girl, I'm good. Please go home, don't you have midterms you need to study for? I will see you tomorrow."

"I do but if you need me I can stay." Reign shook her head no. "Okay, well have a great evening and I will see you tomorrow."

"I will Tonya. You have a great night as well."

"Boss lady are you really staying that late?"

"Tam when I tell you Lucas is a distraction for me at home. Girl I am behind on a lot of our major accounts. I have to leave for New York next week to meet up with my old boss to give him my pitch for a Nike commercial. When I tell you I have nada I mean I have nada. I have to stay here a few nights to get my juices flowing. Lucas' cute face has me tending to him all day. Mersades comes home and gets him for a little while and I'm in the guest house chilling with them."

"Aw Reign you got it bad. Well I can help you. I have no plans for later, my boyfriend is pulling a double tonight."

"Grab your laptop and come on then. Shoot if you have nothing to do I'm not turning down your help."

"Girl I will be right back."
"Thank you Tam, I really appreciate it."
"I'm about to get out of here Reign if you don't need me?"
"Andre are you offering your service because I can use another brain."
"Yeah I can stay and help you out."
"Thank you I really appreciate it."
"What you need my assistance on?"
"The baby nike commercial. Nike is trying to increase their promotions on their newborn and toddler shoes. They want to shine some light their way."
"They called you because of MJ?"
"You can say that, also my reception going viral caught his attention too. He called and asked if I needed a distraction so here we are."
"Man, you must have a great work ethic and reputation for him to do that. You really left your mark out there with them. A beautiful intelligent black woman doing her thing and she's my boss."
"Keep pumping my head up like that and you will find yourself with a raise," she said with a smile.
"Okay I'm back and ready to brainstorm with you two."
"Hold on this is Jazz. Let me take this real quick. Here is what I came up with so far," she says as she turns her laptop towards them. "Hey Jazz girl, what do you need?"
"Your damn location. I'm here with your family and they say you went back to your office to get some work done. Are you still there?"
"Yes I'm her with Dre and Tam working on this Nike campaign."
"Dre?"
"That's what I said."
"He in your face huh?"
"Jazz is there something else you needed besides my location?"
"I sure do, but I need to see you in order to get it accomplished."
"Come to the office then I'm here."
"Already in the car headed your way. See you all in a bit."
"Alright team what you all think about what I have so far."
"I think this will work if you added kids from across the globe."
"That's a dope idea Tam. Show every household in popular countries with babies of all ages from newborn to five."
"Yeah I like that too Dre. Dang you all came up with that while I was on the phone? I really miss working with you all like this. I have been having a mommy brain with little imagination here lately.  I had to come in this evening and be around adults who understand me. Thank you two for staying late to help me."
"We are here for you boss lady. Now let's work on our pitch," Tamara said, getting excited.
"Andre while we are working on that, see can you get intouch with Juan from our web design team. He's a sneakerhead and our best bet for the presentation part. He sent MJ some dope custom-made air forces. I think I still have the pictures, look. How adorbs are those shoes?"

"Those are fire and he had them done in a bigger size."

"Yeah it's a size three. I just hope MJ doesn't skip a size and will be able to wear them when he gets a little older."

"Hey Reign, what Nike's brand did you want to concentrate on."

"Good question Tam. Dre, also see if you can get in touch with someone from their team to run you those numbers. I want to focus on the top selling shoes, but I want to start with the ones that are struggling first. That way  we can boost those sales and keep the top sellers, selling."

"I'm going to head back to my office and skype with him. When we are done I will bring you back what we came up with."

"You guys are going to have me out of here in record time. I thank you and my family also thanks you."

"Where's the gunshots at Andre?"

"My bad Jasmine I have an idea and I'm trying to head back to the office before I lose it. It's nice seeing you again and sorry for running into you."

"No worries Andre. What's up ladies? Look what I brought!"

"Ace! Girl, what are we celebrating?" Tam asked, grabbing the bottle.

"I am an owner of a commercial lot. Where I can open up new businesses in the black community and give them job opportunities. I secured us new office space for one another too. You are to move out of this or what!"

"I am so proud of you sis that's great! Let me see this lot of yours, I know you have pictures."

"Here you go. Whatever you do please don't swipe back."

"Ew! Why don't you delete those after you send them?"

"That's a good question. I don't know why I don't."

"Jazz you are so funny. There's never a dull moment with you," Tam said laughing.

"This is amazing Jazz for real. I can see you having this place packed out."

"That's why I came here to strategize with you on some businesses we can put out here."

"Oh babe I can't right now. We were just about to come up with a pitch for Nike that is due next week. Remember I have that meeting in New York?"

"Dang, that's right. Well how about I help you two with that and then we can work on my stuff for a little bit."

"Sure that works for me." A couple of hours goes by and the girls are having a good time working and catching up with one another. They had order take out and were eating and drinking. They wrapped up the Nike presentation and came up with different business ideas for Jazz's new commercial lot. Time was flying by, that they didn't even realize what time it was. It took her phone ringing and Montez 'voice on the other line for her to remember.

"Hey Tezzy baby!"

"What's all that noise?"

"Just Tamara and Jazz."

"Hell are y'all working or having a party?"

"Both. Why?"

"You don't know what time it is do you?"

"I didn't but since you said it like that. It must be ten."

"Hell yeah! Now do I need to come drag you out of there or are you packing it up and coming home?"

"I'm coming home Zaddy. What is my little man doing?"

"Taking his first nap before five."

"Dang it. I missed putting him down for tonight."

"I tried to keep him up but nine thirty hit and he was trying to box me. His whole fist met my eye. You know baby punches hurt like hell especially when they catch you slipping."

"That shit hurts even when you see it coming," she said laughing at him.

"True. For real baby, are you wrapping it up? I'm missing you."

"Yes baby I'm about to call it. I will be home soon, give me about thirty minutes okay?"

"I'm timing you. If you're not here in forty five minutes. I'm there getting you."

"Stop being overprotective Tezzy, I'm coming."

"Alright baby I am waiting on you. I love you."

"Tez said get your ass home!" Jazz said laughing.

"Nah chick he asked when I was coming home. Don't try to play me Jazzy."

"Mm hmm whatever you say, so we're leaving?"

"Kill the sarcasm Nicole. You know damn well we were wrapping it up way before he called," she said as she pushed her out the way.

"Hey Reign can I run this by you real quick?"

"No Andre because that will get my brain back into work mode and I will never leave from here. Show me tomorrow."

"You're coming back tomorrow," Tamara asked.

"Yeah so we can put this all together and make sure it's tight. I will come back a couple of more times this week."

"Cool. Plus with Tonya here the dream team will be full in effect again."

"Yes, so that works for everyone?"

"That's fine with me boss lady" Tamara says as she packs up her stuff and heads out.

"Yeah me too. Let me grab my stuff out of the office and I will see you all tomorrow." Dre says as he exits the office.

"Alright girl what time is your curfew? We don't want your daddy to come up here and show out."

"I can't stand you! You really get on my nerves. But I have to be home at eleven or he's calling the FBI, the CIA."

"Damn right! Now come on because I don't want to be the reason you're late and his ass being mad at me."

"I'm right behind you, just have to grab my laptop."

"Damn!"

"Is that Daddy Sean," Reign asked laughing.

"He's only calling me because your man called him, your whole family gets on my nerves. Hey Sean baby."

"Are you on your way?"

"Yes we are leaving now. Reign just went to grab her laptop real quick."

"It's just you two?"

"Yeah everyone else just left."

"Jazz, go ahead I have to reset the alarm."

"Are you sure I don't mind waiting?"

"Yeah I'm sure. Damn! Hey what's up?"

"Alright Sean I'm coming. I think that was Tez calling her back and she told me to go ahead and leave."

"Alright see you when you get here."

"Are you coming right now?"

"Yeah, as soon as this light changes I should be there less than two minutes."

"Okay I will wait for you. Dang it where did I put my keys, that's right it's on Tamara's desk."

"Sorry about that Reign. I grabbed the wrong laptop."

"I did the same thing, don't even worry about it."

"Okay let me go grab it so you can get home."

"I will clean up my office while you do that. Oh shoot Jazz left her Ace! I'm taking you home with me buddy. Jazz slip up is my gain."

"You girls had fun in here tonight, huh" Dre asked as he looked at her talking to the bottle. It startled her a little but she responded.

"No lie we did but we also were able to get work done. It's always fun when you are doing something you love with people who love it just as much as you do."

"That's true it's not work anymore it's just passion."

"Yeah, so you got the right laptop this time?"

"Yeah and you?"

"Yes right here."

"Okay I will walk you out and make sure you get in your car."

"I'm good, you can go ahead. I have to set the alarm."

"Reign can I ask you something?"

"Depends? Personal or Business?"

"Both."

"How could it be both?"

"I was just wondering if we would have met before you were engaged and after working with me. Do you think you would have gone out on a date with me?"

"I'm going to be honest. I don't do what ifs. Things happen how we make it happen. I wouldn't have dated my husband if I didn't see forever with him. As a matter of fact that's what I told him the second time we tried this."

He walks closer to her and she steps back. "Dre what are you doing," she asked with concern in her tone.

"I'm not going to hurt you. Just want to make sure you're not lying when you say there's no chemistry between you and me."

"Not on my end there's none. Dre enough already this is feeling uncomfortable "

"I'm not going to hurt you. Just wanted to make sure."

He grabs her face and brings her close and kisses her. Stunned at what just occurred. Reign pushes him off and they stare at one another waiting on someone to break the silence that took over the room.

# Chapter Eight: His Reality, Her Dreams?

As they stare at one another, Reign couldn't believe what just happened. What was he thinking and why she didn't stop him before his lips touched hers? He did it so fast that it caught her off guard. When she was able to snatched her head back from his hands, it made him bite her bottom lip. He could tell by her face that he was about to lose his job.  Reign takes her hand and wipes her mouth and sees that her lip is bleeding a little.

"Andre! What the fuck was that," she yells as she goes to her desk to retrieve a mirror.

"I have tried Reign, I really have. I know I may be out of a job but I don't regret what just happened."

"In other words fuck my marriage and fuck my family? I'm going to kiss my boss and take my chances? Did you really think I was going to throw all that away for you?"

"No. I just got caught up in the moment. It won't happen again."

"I know it's not because you are no longer employed here."

"Reign hold on."

"Please clear out your office and leave the company's laptop."

He walks up to her and tries to reason with her. How letting him go wouldn't be in her best interest or the company's. Before she knew it he had pinned her between the table and she couldn't move. She fought him trying to get away but he was stronger than she was. He ripped her t-shirt as he snatched her back to pull her close to him. It felt like a bear hug and she couldn't break loose. He ripped the rest of her shirt and started licking, kissing, and biting her where he could. The more she punched, kicked, and scratched him the more he got turned on.

"Yeah baby fight, pretend you don't like it. You feel that? That's about to be all in you. You want to fire me well I'm about to release all this fire in me. Letting me go is going to cost you and I can't wait to receive my benefits. Damn I wanted to do this from day one when I hugged you. Remember how hard I was then and you didn't tell him. I knew then that deep inside you wanted me too. Let me see how wet you are. Stop acting like you don't want it Reign."

"Andre please stop. I will stop fighting if you would just leave. Dre please don't do this."

"Shhh. Baby it's okay I got you. I'm going to show you what nine inches of hard black dick really feels like. Dame and Montez have nothing on this. Then I'm going to nut all in you baby. Yeah this is about to be something you will remember for a long time. When I'm done with you jail won't even matter to me."

He grabs her by the neck and starts choking her. Reign is fighting him off with all she had until she felt light headed. She could feel him trying to pull down her pants. She moves her hand down that way. She tries to stop him one last time, all of a sudden her body goes limp and she blacks out. When she awakens she is no longer in her office, instead she is back with Montez. They are taking a walk with Lucas and Storm after dinner. She's pushing the stroller while he walks the dog. They were talking about their future and where they see their marriage in ten years. How excited he was about opening up his own tattoo shop. They also talked about her new office space that she wanted to purchase since her team was expanding.

"Jazz is looking at some commercial lots. Hopefully she was able to close the deal on it today. She was so excited when she called and told me about the new property."

"Yeah that would be a smart buy on her part."

"I'm so happy for her she has been doing this for other major companies. To see her put faith in herself and making major moves here is great. I doubt she would have tried this in Charlotte."

"Marcus was wrong. She is not your shadow and you don't overshadow her. That's just a bond between you two that can't be broken and shouldn't be made to be broken."

"I couldn't believe he said that to her, that was so fucked up. Jasmine has always been her own woman and did her own thing. We were not always velcro. When we went off to college our friendship took a hit. I was playing wife and she was out living life. He said that shit to hurt her and I can't forgive him for that."

"Hopefully you two will be able to work this out. I hate to keep whipping his ass. Family or not he's not going to be disrespecting my wife."

"My husband the protector."

"Damn right! I don't play that bullshit when it comes to you. If they hurt you they hurt me. I'm not the one for all that talking so I'm going to fuck them up physically."

"Damn baby you feel so good. We should have done this a long time ago. There have been times I wanted to come in here and make love to you. Now look at us. What took me so long to get you like this. That husband of yours doesn't deserve you and after tonight you will realize that. Mmm baby this pussy of yours is so wet and warm. Damn you are going to make me nut in you early. Next time we do this I want you to ride me baby. I want your sexy ass looking down at me. Riding me with passion making sexy ass moans while taking my pipe. Let me turn you around and get it from the back, damn your ass is perfect baby. Did you let Montez enter this hole? Hmm baby? You let that weak muthafucker back here in my ass? Let me see if he's been back here, baby. Mmm I love how you are not fighting me baby. I knew you wanted the black stallion. Damn I can't wait for round two, baby. Yes this ass of yours feels good baby I'm going to release in here first. You like that, hmmm, you like when I smack that ass and go balls deep in? Talk to me baby let me know how good this feels."

"Baby do you mind if I go to the office for a little bit. I really need to get this Nike account completed."

"MJ distracted you again today? How long are you going to be there?"
"It's six now so no later than ten. Ten thirty and if your wife is not home please come and drag me out of that office."
"If you're not here by ten I'm already at the office in fifteen minutes."
"You are so serious too."
"Oh you know I am."
"I will make sure I call right when I leave. Let me jump in the shower and be on my way. You two stay out of trouble while I'm gone."
"MJ is sleeping from our walk. Let me lay him down and I will join you in the shower."
"Let's make that a bath then, I want to relax a little longer with just you before I go in."
"Alright let's switch. You lay down our son and I will prepare my queen's bath."
"How can I turn down that deal?"
"I mean you would be a fool if you did."
"Now you know my mama raised no fool." Montez goes into their bathroom and lights the candles. He ran more hot water than cold and put her favorite bath bomb in with the running water. He asks Alexa to play his Gerald Levert playlist. Reign walks in and watches her husband
set the scene. He was so attentive when it came to her and she loved him for it. She rarely had to ask him, her Tezzy knew what she needed before she did. "See now. What are you up to Mr. Santos?"
"What? I just want my wife relaxed and have ideals flowing out quicker when you get there. That's all your wonderful husband is up to. I promise."
"What is that supposed to be? Scouts honor?"
"Yeah I think that's what they do. Now let me help you out these clothes so I can get you relaxed."
"Baby, listen in order for me
"I got you Reign. I promise, I got you."

"Damn girl round three is better than the first two. Next time when I tell you not to fire me you will listen or I'm going to have to teach you this lesson again. What I'm saying this wasn't a lesson, this was passion. This is something we both wanted and needed. You are so wet baby I'm about to cum again. What's that? You want it on your face this time? Baby are you sure? Okay, I got you. I'm going to put it right there on your lips. Then I'm going to open your mouth and let you lick and suck the rest. You love how that sounds baby? Yeah I knew you would. Damn you so nasty, keep talking to me like that. Make me nut baby. Here it comes, ugh here I come. Yes baby yes. Damn those lips of yours getting me aroused again but I have to run. I will be back Reign. I promise baby, I will be back."

# Chapter Nine: I Made My Choices

Yes 911! Yes I need an ambulance quickly my wife has been raped and beaten! She's barely responding! 290 Laurens Rd! Please hurry!

"Sir how do you know she's been raped? Did she tell you this?"

"She didn't have too there's semen all over her!"

"Oh my God, okay sir! I have an ambulance and a unit on its way! Did you interfere with the crime scene, sir?"

"Only my wife when I tried to wake her."

"You said early she was barely responding, is she still that way?"

"She's in and out! How far out is that damn ambulance?! I'm about to take her myself!"

"Sir please do not do that, we want to reserve the scene as much as possible."

"Listen lady! That son of a bitch that did this, left enough semen for the cops. If that ambulance is not here in the next minute they will have to meet us at the hospital!"

"Sir I promise they are like two minutes away!"

"Too bad I said one! I'm taking her myself!"

"Sir listen to me please do not do that! You should hear the ambulance, they just told me they are almost there."

"Yeah I hear them. Let me go run out here and flag them down."

"Montez.... baby.... I'm.... so... sorry"

"Sir is that her?"

"Yes it is! Baby it's okay this is not your fault. Baby come back! Reign!"

"Sir!

"Hey sir let us through! Sir please move."

"She's not responding! Help her!"

"We got it sir."

"Baby I'm here, stay with me."

"Sir, how long has she been like this?"

"When I arrived here a few minutes ago, this is how I found her. It's 10:53 now so subtract some minutes from the 911 call.

"Hey I'm Chante Haughton of the special unit and you are the husband right?"

Yeah Montez.

"I noticed cameras when I walked in. Do you know where I can find the security tapes? I know you're going to leave with your wife. If you can tell these officers where we can find it."

"Um it's in the door on your left."

"Thank you so much Montez. Is it locked?"

"Yeah it is."

"Anyone have a key to it?

"Just me Reign and the security guy."

"Can I get your copy?"

"Yeah. It's this one."

"You said this one right?"

"Yeah that's the one."

"Any ideas on who would want to hurt your wife this way?"

"No. Not right now, no one is coming to mind."

"You wouldn't be lying to me right now would you? From the looks of things it seems to be more personal than random."

"Again no one comes to mind. Listen I need to call family and ride with my wife. There's a hidden camera in her office so whoever did this will be seen. I will answer all your questions at the hospital. If you don't mind I have some difficult phone calls I have to make, starting with her parents."

"Sure thing Mr. Montez. He is a little too calm for me, make sure you follow him and the ambulance to the hospital. I think he may know the person who did this and we need to find him before he does."

"I'm on it Mrs. Haughton."

"Sean. Where's Jazz?" Montez whispers on the phone.

"Laying down. What's up?"

"Listen I don't have much time. When I arrived at Reign's office she had, she um

"Tez. Hey man what's going on?"

"It's bad Sean. Someone has raped her, she's been raped."

"What!?"

"Man listen! I don't have much time but I have a feeling it was Andre."

"Say no more fam I'm on it. Fuck! How the hell am I going to tell Jasmine. You know she was just together, right?! Got damn it man! We are going to kill this muthafucker!"

"Damn right. I need you to find him before the cops figure it out. I have to go, I need to call her pare....

"Dude I can't imagine what you are going through right now. Tez?"

"Please find this niggah for me man."

"On everything man I'm on it! Jazz! Jazz baby!"

"Sean what is it?! Something happened with the kids!"

"When you, um. When you left Reign tonight did she close up with just you?"

"I left before she locked up, remember? Why are you asking me that? What's going on? Sean?!"

"Babe just real quick was it just you two? What I'm asking is when y'all were closing up. Tam was gone?

"Yeah she was gone."

"Dre was gone too?"

"Yes! Everyone else had left and Reign and I were in the parking lot. Oh wait she realized she grabbed the wrong laptop and she went back to retrieve her personal one. Then you called and I left before she came back... Wait. You didn't answer my question: what's going on? Why are you asking who was with Reign and me? Sean?"

"I don't know how to say it."

"Say what? Sean you are scaring me! Let me call this girl."

"Baby hand me your phone."

"Sean I swear for God if you don't tell me what the fuck is going on

"She was beaten and raped in the office," Montez just called me.

"What? What did you just say to me!"

"She was raped, Jazz."

"What? No! That's not possible! She just went back to get her laptop. She wasn't staying no later than that or for that to happen. Are you sure she was raped at the office?"

"Montez wouldn't  have called and played with us like that. Jazz, I know you are upset but right now baby

"Upset! You just told me my best friend was raped. I am clearly passed from being upset!"

"I know. Shit is not coming out right now baby. My bad."

"What did he say?"

"I need you to pull it together real quick and think. Any cars in the lot? Anyone suspicious you may have missed? The cops are going to ask you this when we get to the hospital."

"No. No one, no other car, nothing. She did receive a phone call, now that I think about it. I know it wasn't Montez."

"How do you know?"

"Because when he calls she always says Yes Tezzy or baby. I remember her answering and saying what's up before disappearing into the building. Wait! Oh my God! I think it was Andre because he left a few minutes before we did! If that bastard did this to my sister he is good as dead!

"Montez thinks it's him too. What was his mood tonight? Did he seem off to you?

"Just his normal self. He was under Reign for a moment before Tamara said that Reign had to put him on another part of the project to get her personal space back. We laughed about the shit. I never trusted his black ass. I kept telling her Sean that he was obsessed with her, but she wouldn't listen. I swear he better pray it was someone else because if it was him. Montez or Rome about to catch a murder charge.

'Who are you telling? He didn't sound good over the phone, I knew him for a long time this just pushed him over the edge. He wants me to find his ass and I promise him I would. Do you have an address on Dre that you can give me? We can't go back to the office because it's a crime scene and flooded with cops."

"Call your mother to watch the kids. I'm on my way to the hospital. I will get that information for you. I just have to get in touch with Tamara. Once I have it I will  text you the information. Sean, if Andre did this"

"He just signed his own death certificate."

  Jazz hops in her car and rushes to meet them at St. Francis hospital. She kept trying to replay what happened earlier that evening. How Dre stayed in his office for the majority of the time and that seemed weird to her. He was usually all in Reign's face but that night he kept his distance. Then she remembered he tried to convince Reign to stay when they were wrapping it up. He had to be the one who called her. She remembers being in the lot and no other cars were there except her and Regin's car. She scans the parking lot again in her head and still only remembers their cars being there. She also remembers Reign putting her phone to her ear as she went back in. Guilt took over her thoughts and she was mad at herself for not waiting for her to come back out. If she would have just stayed and helped her close the building this wouldn't have happened. That's all she kept saying as she entered ER trying to locate Montez. Finally she spots him and runs towards him. They embraced one another with a hug before he collapsed to the floor.

"He beat her up pretty good Jazz, but my baby fought back too. She has broken nails and bruises on her hands that shows she did. She was out of it when I arrived, the marks on her neck the paramedics believed she was choke unconscious."

"Tez, this is all my fault."

"Don't do that Jazz. There's no way you could have known this would happen."

"But if I would have just waited for her to come out this wouldn't have happened."

"Still not your fault Jazz. Besides Reign wouldn't want you out here blaming yourself. If anything I should have told her no, about going back to the office that late. But Tam was there and then you came so I was cool with it. When eleven o'clock came and she wasn't picking up her phone. I knew then something was.... Fuck man, he yells. I should have left beforehand. If anyone should be taking the blame it's me! Jazz I think she was pregnant. We had a doctor's appointment schedule for next week to find out. If this bastard," he pauses as tears just flows from his eyes. Jazz brings him closer to her and tries her hardest to console him but it wasn't working. She could tell he had so much guilt on him more than she had and it was weighing on him hard. Just when she was about to say something to ease his conscience,  he jumped up and headed towards the emergency doors. That's when an officer emerges and makes his presence known. He walks in front of the doors that Montez was headed to and stops him.

"Montez, right? Is everything alright?You look like you are about to do something you regret."

"Man I don't have time for this shit for real! Get out my face!"

"Just trying to make sure you don't go anywhere and do something stupid. I'm sure your wife wants you close by when she awakens. I'm sure she wants to see you here and not visit you in jail."

"Montez please chill. This shit is real fucked up but you do not need to get arrested right now. Think about your family! Lucas needs you more than ever."

"Am I allowed to go outside or what?!"

"Just don't leave this hospital sir."

"How about you go find the sick bastard who did this to my wife and stopped treating me like I did it!"

"That's not what I'm doing at all. I'm just making sure you will be here when she asks for you. If you need to step out by all means do so. Just don't leave these premises Montez."

"Can I take a piss first?"

"You are free to do what you need to do sir."

He walks to the restroom and throws water on his face. When he looked in the mirror all he saw was his wife lying on the floor with semen all over. He throws more water on his face and closes his eyes tight trying to block the image. Nothing was working; he felt as if he would lose it at any second. He walks out the restroom and pulls out his phone, he realizes he has missed a call from mama Lene. He called her back and she barely could get any words out. Charlene was a wreck and kept asking him questions he already answered. Romaine was blaming him with so many words. He could tell he was disappointed that this happened to his daughter. He couldn't believe this shit was happening. All he wanted was to wake up from this nightmare, as he ended the call with her parents. Montez looks around before looking towards the nightly heavens, he saw this happen to other women. Never in a million years he thought it would happen to his wife. They were just enjoying each other earlier. Laughing and carrying on like newlyweds, and just like that their world came crashing in. He keeps playing their last phone conversation but he can't recall her ever saying Andre's name. Maybe this was just a random attack and they're wrong about Andre. Jazz said he left before they did but she also remembers Reign getting a phone call and he knows that call wasn't from him. He never talked to her again until he found her in the office. He walks back into the hospital and finds Officer Harper.

"I just remembered something that may help you all find the man responsible."

"I'm listening Mr. Santos, what have you got for me?"

"Jazz said that when they were leaving my wife was on her phone heading back inside. I never talked to my wife again after ten oclock. Maybe the person she was on the phone with heard something and could help."

"We can't find your wife's phone sir. It wasn't in the office. We searched."

"My wife goes nowhere without her phone. Did you search the whole building or just her office?"

"As of right now your wife's cell phone has not been recovered."

"Well check her phone records then!"

"We need a warrant for that."

"I'm her husband and I'm giving you permission to check the damn phone records! Any other damn time you all would be on it the fuck is y'all problem?! Black young woman so you really don't give a fuck who did it!"

"Montez!"

"Fuck out my way Jazz!"

"I can't do that, Montez come on please calm down. They have protocol"

"Save that bullshit Jazz! Protocol my ass! They have their own black protocol right now. I tell you this officer Harper you better pray that your department finds him before I do!"

"Montez is that a threat?"

"Threat, promise, fucking guaranteed if I figured out who did this to her before you lazy muthafuckas"

"Mr. Santos?"

"Yes."

"I'm Dr. Rice and I'm the one who examined your wife. Can I speak to you over here in private."

"Ma'am, can her sister Jasmine come with me? I can't hear this by myself."

"Yes sir that's fine."

"Um we were trying to conceive another child on our honeymoon were you able to find out if she's pregnant or not?"

"Let's do this, let me start off with some good news before we get into the tragedy of what your wife suffered tonight. We did send blood work down to see if she was pregnant and she is pregnant. We wanted to do an ultrasound but we will wait on that for now. As of right now she has no STDs, she is cleared from Aids and HIV but as you all know we have to wait for that test another week or two to be certain. I can also discuss that more with you two later. As of right now she is cleared of that. From the rape kit we can confirm that she was raped. The rapist wanted to be known because he left traces of semen and bite marks everywhere possible. The police shouldn't have a problem charging him with this hideous crime once Reign is strong enough to let us know what happened. Now let me tell you what I examined. She has noticeable bite marks on her body. There's two on the back shoulders, one one the buttocks, three around the vagina area and one on her right breast. He also left semen in her buttocks, vagina, and her mouth. Honestly I don't know how much your wife will remember until she speaks to us. Right now she is conscious. The trauma that she has endured, she's not telling me or the nurses anything. After what I examined I really don't blame her. You have every right to go through the emotions you are displaying because you found her in this condition. I can't imagine what you are going through right now. Just know we have a grief counselor here if you need to speak with her or Reign. Reign is up and we helped her showered. I gave her some sedatives to help rest. You two can go back and see her now."

"Can you just just give us a mom mm moment Jazz," stammered out softly.

"Of course honey. Take as much time as you all need. She will need to see you two at your strongest. I don't know her personally but I do know that she wasn't who she was twenty-four hours ago. No woman should go through what she went through. Excuse my language but I'm going to do all I can to help nail this sick bastard."

"Montez listen to me, please hear me. I know you are ready to kill whoever did this but please think. She needs you more than ever now and you can't do a damn thing for her if you are sitting in county. MJ needs you as well and your unborn is counting on you also. I will hire a hitman to take this muthafucker out before I let you do it. I need your mind to be focused on being here to help her through it. Montez? Montez, you hear me?" As Jasmine tries her hardest to calm him down. She knows physically she's going to need some help. He had anger in his eyes as the tears flowed down his face. She knew he already entered the rage stage and her words were not connecting. She looked around the room trying to figure out what she could do. She reached in her purse and called Mr. Lucas.

"Hey how far are you guys."

"We're here, where are you all?"

"In the ER hold on I will step out and see if I can see you. Okay Mr. Lucas look over to your left."

"Okay I see you Jasmine."

"Please hurry! I have never seen your son like this before. I'm scared he's going to kill someone," she said crying.

"I got him. Son?" Montez? Look at me son. Montez?"

"Montez baby your mother is here. Son listen to me. You have to control your emotions right now. Do not do something stupid where it takes you away from your family! Right now Reign and your son need you to be smart and not stupid. Let the law enforcement do their job. Boy do you hear me?!"

"Let the law handle it? My wife is the complexion this fucking country hates. She is the most disrespected woman in this fucked up world and you want me to sit back and continue letting them disrespect her?! I failed my vows I wasn't there to prevent this shit from happening! We haven't been married two months and I let my wife get beaten and raped. Well I be damned if he breathes another day!"

"Montez," his mother yells. He pushes past his father and  runs out of the ER. Outside Sean was waiting for him, he hops in his car and they take off. Mr. Harper runs out trying to get a license plate number but Sean removed the plate already. He calls in the description of the car and comes back into the ER.

"Where is he going?"

"I don't know?"

"Do not play with me! Who was that and where are they going."

"I didn't see him hop in any fucking car so how the fuck will I know. Jasmine says getting frustrated."

"You were in here with him alone before they arrived and you are telling me he said nothing to you?"

"I don't like what you are insinuating but we just received the report. I was trying to calm him down, I was not in here plotting on him to get away. How stupid do you sound? He has a wife that's going to be asking for him why would I help him leave? When I know she needs him the most!"

"Montez please come back son. Do not do this. The police officer has called in the car you are in. Montez, do you hear me. Pick up the phone sweetie."

"Reign is asking for her husband. Did he step outside?" Dr. Rice asked

"No. Let me see if I can get in touch with him. He left shortly after you told us."

"It was a lot. See if you can get him back. This is the first time she spoke since she arrived."

"I'm on it. Montez I'm not saying this just to get you back here. Dr. Rice is here and she said Reign is asking for you. This is the first time she spoke"

"May I?" She asked as she reached for Jasmine's phone.

"Hey Montez, this is Dr. Rice. I just left your wife's room and she is asking for you. This is critical as you know she hasn't spoken since she's arrived. If you could please come back, I would appreciate it."

"Thank you for doing that. Now maybe he will do the right thing and come back."

"He will. He seems like the type that doesn't want his wife to worry. Now with him knowing she's asking for him and only him. I pray that will make him turn around and come back."

"God I hope so. Can I go see her or she only wants him?"

"As of now she is only requesting him."

"Okay. I will get him back here, excuse me. Sean, do you have Montez with you?"

I found him Jazz and we're about to end this piece of shit life!"

Put it on pause and bring him back.

"Why?"

"Reign is asking for him."

"Jazz for real?"

"She won't speak to no one but him. She's not even asking for me just Montez. Bring him back Sean. Now!"

"Okay baby. Turning around now."

"The fuck are you doing!"

"Tez they say Reign is requesting you and only you. Man I have to take you back."

"Jazz just saying that! Keep going to that bitch house!"

"Tell him to check his VM but Sean, I'm going to need you to turn that car around and bring his ass back!"

"Okay baby! She said check your VM."

"Tell Jazz I don't believe her or the doctor. Let me hear Reign my damn self!"

"Put his ass on the phone, Sean!"

"Jazz I "

"Shut the fuck up Montez Lucas Santos and get your black ass back to the hospital and tend to your wife! If you are not here in the next three goddamn minutes. I'm giving officer Harper the tracker number on Sean car. Play with me Montez and both of your black asses will be in jail! Waiting on me to decide when to bail y'all asses out! Hospital now! You now have two minutes!"

"We are almost there, just going to stop by Bojangles and make it seem like we went to get food for everyone. Okay babe?"

"Don't be fucking with me Sean. You better be on your way back."

"I swear we are, just chill for a few minutes."

"Okay play with me if you want to. See you in a few and I mean in a few." Moments later Sean and Montez emerge with boxes of chicken and drinks for the family. He finds Dr. Rice and she takes him back to see Reign.When she realizes it's him, her eyes light up and she smiles at him. He tries not to break and smiles back at her. Dr. Rice rubs his back and whispers words of comfort to him. He walks over slowly to her bedside and kisses her forehead.

"Hey Tezzy bear," she whispers.

He looks away because his eyes start to tear up and slowly wipes his face and slowly exhales.

"Hey baby. You have been asking for me?"

"Yeah, where did you go," she asks him, maintaining her whisper tone.

"Just went to get food for the family when they get here to see you."

"Oh that's sweet of you. Have you spoken with the doctor yet?"

"Yeah I have. Do you know why you are here?"

She looks at him and just from those words her happiness was gone, her smile disappeared, and tears flowed down her face. "I tried to fight him off, I really did baby. But he was choking me that I felt my whole body get numb and that's all I remember. I blacked out and when I awakened my body was sore and my face and body was wet. I just remember seeing you and the fear in your eyes. I didn't know exactly why you were like that but it's like in the same way I kind of knew why. I just wanted you to know that I didn't ask for any of this. I didn't do anything that made him think I wanted any of this. I'm so sorry that I didn't fire him like you asked me too. The choices I made is the reason why I'm now broken inside."

"Andre did this to you?"

"Yes."

"Baby is there something else you need from me? I have to get some fresh air."

"I'm scared and I just wanted you to hold me until I fall asleep," she said barely getting the words out. Montez takes off his shoes and walks to the other side of the room and lays behind her. His thoughts were racing, his heart was aching. He should have made Sean keep driving to Dre's house. They knew they had the right person but then he wouldn't have been here. His wife needed him to be here physically and he couldn't disappoint her again. As they laid there in silence just the sounds of their breathing filled the room. He places his hand on his wife's stomach and he remembers the doctor saying that she was pregnant. He didn't know how to tell her, in a way he didn't want her to know. He was terrified of what her reaction would be. Of course he wanted to keep their unborn but would she? They had created this one out of love on their honeymoon, but would she still see it that way. This horrendous situation would probably make her feel a certain way and she probably wouldn't want to keep it.

"Who has MJ?"

"Mersades has him with her and my Aunt Gene is on her way there. My parents are in the waiting room with Jazz and Sean. Um, your parents are on their way."

"Please let the cops handle this Tezzy. I know you, my dad, papa Lucas and Sean want to take the law in your own hands. I want you to promise me that you all will let them do their job."

"Baby close your eyes and try to get some rest. I'm here so you can."

"Hey Mr. and Mrs. Santos. I'm nurse Katie. Can I get you two anything? Extra blankets or food?"

"I'm fine thank you Katie," Reign responds.

"Okay just hit that button if you change your mind."

"I will and thank you. When is the detective going to get here? I'm ready to leave."

"They are looking over the security tapes."

"If they would come here I would tell them who did this to me. Ugh I just want to wake up from this nightmare. Why did this happen to me!"

"Baby please calm down."

"I can't, as she sobs. I'm trying so hard to act as if this doesn't bother me but I'm not okay. I'm in so much pain internally and externally. I didn't do anything to provoke this. Just asked him to leave the laptop after I fired him."

"Wait. You fired him? What did he do?"

"He made a move on me and I rejected him. When he tried to kiss me again that's when I terminated him. That's when he really got aggressive. I tried real hard to stay calm and not escalate the situation. He just wasn't taking no for an answer. That's when he grabbed me by the throat and choked me until I blacked out. I don't remember anything after that."

"You weren't conscious during the attack?"

"No."

"They took pic"

"I don't want to see them. Please don't make me look at them. I don't want to see it."

"I promise you. Just tell them what you told me and we will leave it at that."

"Reign!"

"Mommy!"

"I'm here baby. I am here! Tez baby have they spoken with her?"

"We are waiting on her now."

"Get her on the phone, so she can get her statement. I'm getting my baby out of here tonight."

"Yes ma'am, I will do that now."

"Son let me speak to you out here. Tell me you know the sick bastard that did this?"

"I do but they have an off duty officer on me watching my every mood. I know they are going to use my cell phone against me. I have been careful making sure not to use it or have it on."

"That's good son. Just give me the info you have, my brothers are here. We have it from here, that way you are here with Reign. I know you want to do this yourself but think about them. You are no good to them locked up."

"What about you? How am I supposed to look her in the eyes and say I let your father get arrested

"Montez, remember Damien? You know who your mother in law is right? We know how to use this injustice system to get justice. Just give me the information."

"Sean has it."

"Good. When we are done with him, he's going to be begging us to kill him. That I promise you."

"They have you on camera already, though."

"Son you are wasting time. Don't worry about me, I know exactly what I'm doing. Let me go in here so Reign can see me. How is she? Any noticeable bruises."

"A couple of bite marks and a swollen lip." Rome takes a deep breath and slowly exhales. He walks into the room and Reign eyes light up for a second then sadness takes over. He walks slowly to her and she quickly wraps her arms around his neck. Tears were flowing from everyone's eyes because you could fill the love between daughter and father. The bond these two shares can't be matched. Montez and Charlene know it all too well. Yes, Reign loved them both and cared about them but make no mistake about it. She was the true meaning of daddy's little girl."

"Dad I know you and I'm asking you to please let the police handle this."

"Of course I will. I'm not in Queen City baby and that bastard is lucky just because of that. So tonight he gets to sleep.

"Montez told you who he was?"

"Of course he did and you will tell the lead detective. Where is the detective anyway?"

"She's on her way," Montez responds.

"Good and they do know once they are done asking her questions that she will be returning back to Charlotte, right Montez?"

"I haven't had the chance to tell her that."

"No worries. We will when she arrives. Lillie is here too, and we have it all worked out."

"Tezzy you are coming too right?"

"We all are going baby. I'm not leaving you alone. I promise."

"Dad where's uncle Shane?"

"He's still in Virginia sweetie. He said he will see you back in Charlotte."

"You really want me to believe your twin brother is not here? Dad come on you promised me"

"I haven't broken any promises and your uncle is still in VA."

"What about the rest of your brothers?"

"Reign I came with your mother, I didn't bring them. You have been through enough today. Just rest baby girl."

"That's what I have been telling her. Maybe now that you said it she will do it."

"Tezzy," Reign reaches out her hand to him. He walks back over to the bed and gets in with her. He holds her in his arms until she falls asleep.They set their plans into motion and Rome leaves out to take care of Andre. In Charlene's purse was his cell phone turned on. Outside in the parking garage is Shane ready to make the switch. Although Montez wishes he could be there to do it himself. He realizes his in-laws were right. He was right where he needed to be.

<h1 style="text-align:center">Chapter Ten: Adjusting</h1>

It's been weird seeing Reign back home with her parents. Montez thought it was best for her to stay in Charlotte until he finishes her new office and their new home. He got rid of all her stuff and purchased new items. They worked on her new layout together and he helped design her a new sign. He has been busy going back and forth from her new office and their new house. Plus holding down his own business and working on finishing his tattoo building, which both businesses are a part of my new lot. It's been bittersweet watching it all come together. Sean has been doing his best to be the supporting fiancé and fill the shoes of my bestie but it's not the same. I love him for trying though. Reign has slowly begun to trust men around her again. It's been hard on her but she knows it has to be done, if she ever wants to gain control of her life again. She has been doing the work by going to group therapy. Also her and Montez are receiving counseling from Pastor Dennis. I call her at least twice a day and see how she is doing. Today I am waiting on a potential business for renting out one of my spaces. As soon as I'm done with them I will call her up and see how everything went today. It's Friday so I will be in Charlotte later spending time with her and then hitting up my family like I always do. Right now I'm looking forward to this meeting and hoping they have a fresh but smart business proposal. I personally don't want the same old thing with this lot. I want my black people to think outside of a restaurant, shoe store or boutique that will only stay open for a year. I made sure I put that out there, that way they wouldn't waste their time or mine. I'm looking to open businesses that they can say in twenty to thirty years they owned their establishments for decades. That they were able to pass it onto their kids or loved ones. That's my vision, that's the goal. A black owned grocery store. An abandoned motel that we turned into an affordable apartment complex helping people get back on their feet and giving homeless people shelter and jobs. This is what I'm looking to do first with this lot and hopefully be able to open up another one with the black own boutiques that you see on your instagram feed. I would love to get them in a shopping center in Greenville, Columbia, Charlotte and Atlanta. I want Noire Ddétenue Par Jasmine in all black major cities first, that is the goal and I was starting in the south first. As I continue to wait for a potential client and put my thoughts in my notebook. I was soon interrupted with Mersades calling in. I decided to answer it and prayed that the talk wouldn't last long.

"Hey Sades."

"Hey Jazz, are you with Reign?"

"No. I'm still in Greenville. I'm leaving after this meeting though."

"Can I bum a ride? I miss MJ and her."

"Sure. Where are you at?"

"My mom said to ask you that and she will bring me to you."

"Well good, have her bring you to the lot."

"We are on our way."

"If I'm not in the car that means I'm in one of the buildings."

"Okay see you in a bit."

Reign and Charlene just finished their walk at the park and decided to rest on the steps as they catched their breath. It's been a few weeks since the incident and they were trying to move on from it and heal. Reign still had visible scars and scars that you couldn't see. She hasn't been intimate with her husband and it was more of him then her. On top of that she was pregnant again and they hardly talked about the good news. She was just in with her therapist earlier that morning and the session was working on regaining oneself. That's what they told them in the group session. She was trying to do just that and decided to take her and MJ to the park. It started off fine until flashes of that night triggered her brain. She sat down on the steps and called her mother to meet her at the park. As she waited for her mother she held MJ tight and was humming some of his favorite lullabies. She hated when she would go through these episodes. All she wanted was her life back and no longer feeling like a prisoner in her mind. She couldn't understand why she was having a hard time with it. She doesn't even remember the actual rape. She remembers the fighting and getting choked out. Then waking up to Montez being frantic and that's it. Dr Green said she has blocked it out and that the only way she can get closure is to look at the photos or watch the tape. Everyday in their session he tells her that's the only way to free herself from it. She didn't want to remember and she sure in the hell didn't want to watch herself being raped. She told Pastor Dennis that God blacked her out for a reason and she wanted to leave it at that. How were these men trying to tell her what's best for her? She told Montez she wanted a woman therapist because she was tired of getting advice from an old white man. He promised they would find another one. She is in week three and still with Dr. Green. It was frustrating but her mother had convinced Montez that he was the best and that Reign had to put in the work. Montez was stuck in the middle; he knew his mother in law was right but he also understood where his wife was coming from. He was looking for her but every woman therapist he spoke to said that Dr. Green was the best. That they would take her in and were confident they could help her have a breakthrough. The thing was their method was no different from his and it would be in her best interest that she finish the work with him. When he told her what everyone was saying she told him to keep trying.

"Reign? Hey baby I'm here. Where did you go just now?

"I was thinking about my sessions with Dr. Green and Pastor Dennis. I'm really trying. I just don't understand why I'm still like this."

"You will become yourself again. Those memories that you are blocking. It's hindering you baby, it's holding you back on your recovery."

"I really don't remember the rape part and if I'm blocking it. Like I told Dr. Green over and over again that I'm not doing it intentionally."

"Do you think seeing the pictures of the way they found you will help?"

"I'm not ready for that mommy."

"Okay baby. I'm not going to pressure you on it. But Dr. Green thinks

"I know mama."

"Okay, well um MJ seems to take interest in the sounds out here."

"He's such a curious baby or just nosy."

"That's good that he is developing that skill so early. He gets so excited when he hears the birds. The way he moves his arms up and down."

"He is too adorable when he discovers new things. I can't wait when he's old enough for the aquarium and zoo."

"Reign, I know it's difficult to talk to me or Montez about certain decisions and I hate when I have to ask you. I would rather you volunteer to tell me versus me asking.

"You want to know if I'm keeping the baby?"

"Yes."

"He or she was created out of love so I'm keeping my unborn. I just don't know if my husband wants to as well."

"All you have to do is ask him. He's not going to push for the subject because he doesn't want to pressure you on it. Actually none of us wants to rush you on discussing anything. We are giving you time and space to work through it and be here when you do you need us."

"Yeah."

"What's wrong?"

"I just don't want you all to do that. It's hard to get back to normal when your family is not acting normal. I'm going through it and there are hours where I just want to scream and fight. There are minutes where I want to cry and not speak. There have been seconds where I questioned God and asked him why he just didn't let me die. Mom there's times when I wished he did, so you all wouldn't have to keep looking at me broken." She looks at her mother with tears flowing down her face. There's a brief silence and Reign gets up and leaves her mother and son on the steps. She grabbed her car keys and decided she needed to take a drive. Charlene asked her when she would be back but she didn't respond. Once she was in her car she put in Rihanna's Rated R album. As Mad House plays, she lets the top down on her new Range Rover Evoque. Montez had bought her the latest release for a Push Gift. He also wanted to get rid of the last thing that reminded him of Damien. She knew the old one bothered him a little so when she came out of the hospital and saw her new custom made car. She didn't second question it and was ecstatic on the newer model and the interior of the car. This time the car was black and the inside was purple and black. She thought she  was going to miss her white car with the white and purple interior. But after a few days in her new car, that car was a distant memory. On her drive she stopped by an ABC store and purchased her a bottle of Svedka Vodka Rose. She then went next door to the convenience store and bought her some Pork Rinds, Snickers, Reese's cups and Hannah's Hot Sausages. She drove to her favorite country road and parked her car at an abandoned parking lot. She decides that she wanted to sit on top of her hood. Once on top sits Indian style with her goodies she bought and watches the horses in the fields with Ri still playing in the background. Time slowly passes by for her as she dances and sings around her car. Other times she would just sit in her car and cry, moments she would laugh, and moments where she would be quiet and listen to God's music. Crickets chirping, birds singing, or the gentle sounds of the breeze. She had made several trips back to the liquor store, she was pretty much wasted at this point. She turned on the radio and let the quiet storm put her to sleep. Back at her parents house everyone was in panic mode. She had missed her appointment with Jazz and the wedding planner. Montez was back in Charlotte after working all day to come and find out his wife had been missing for five hours. He wasn't happy that her parents didn't call him to let him know what was going on. They all said they thought she would have been back by now.

They couldn't get a location on her because she left her cell phone in MJ's bag and there was no tracker on her car.

   "Damn where is she?" Jazz wondered "We all know she likes to take these long drives but damn we don't know where. What if she went back to Greenville?"

"Man she better not be back in South Carolina. What was the last thing she said to you Mama Lene," Montez demanded to know.

"She just wanted things to go back to normal."

"What does she mean by back to normal? Damn she was raped less than a month ago. It's going to take more time than a month. Are you all sure these therapy sessions are working? Montez maybe she's right about having a woman psychiatrist. Are you still looking?"

"Yeah Jazz, I am. I'm doing everything I can to get my wife through this."

"I know you are. I didn't mean it like that."

"Charlene is that all she said? Nothing else? Why does it feel like you are leaving something out?"

"Montez she was tired of me and the rest of the family handling her like a broken person. That's when she got up to leave, before she left she kissed MJ. I asked her when she would be back, but she ignored me and kept going."

"It didn't cross your mind to call me after that? I'm leaving her messages thinking she's asleep or not near her phone and the whole time she has been MIA for hours. We can't do a missing person report because it hasn't been 24 or 48 hours. What am I supposed to do? Wait around and do absolutely nothing!"

"My bad son. I thought she would be back before you arrived. I know my daughter will not harm herself. She wouldn't do that to us, to you, or to her son."

"That was before she went through what she did. I want to believe she wouldn't either but I'm with Montez something ain't right. Why leave your phone behind? What if something happened to MJ or any of us. She would've taken her phone so we could reach her. Leaving it makes me think she doesn't want to be found."

"Damn it! Why didn't I let them put a tracker on her car!"

"Don't start doing that to yourself. There's no way you could have predicted this."

"I should've had it installed after she was raped, but I didn't Jazz."

"Ugh! This is not your fault Tez stops beating yourself up over shit that is out of your control. You are not responsible for any of this!"

"Hey! Reign just pulled up," Rome yells from outside.

"Oh thank you God for bringing my baby home," Charlene shouted.

"Montez, she's stumbling, come and help me," Rome yells again from outside.

He rushes out the door and picks Reign up. Jazz grabs her keys and her shoes out of her hands and he takes his wife in the house. Jazz searches her car where she retrieves three empty bottles of Svedka Vodka Rose. She feels her body getting heated and she tries to calm herself down. The more she thinks how she could have been in a terrible car accident. The harder it is for her to calm down. She's pregnant and acting real reckless. Pissed, she leaves her shoes in the car and grabs the empty bottles instead. As she walks in the house and sees the worrisome on everyone's face she loses it.

"What the fuck is wrong with you Reign!" As she throws the first bottle at the wall. The loud crash wakes up MJ and he starts crying. Charlene leaves the room and goes to tend to her grandson. "I mean I get it sis you have been through a lot over these four years but damn it! You have to stop fucking doing this!"

"I have to stop," a slurred Reign responded. "Yeah Jazz let's blame the victim sis..... let's blame the victim."

"Jazz chill!" Montez demanded

"No I want fucking chill! I knew her way longer than you. Step the fuck off Tez! I'm not blaming you for being cheated on. I'm not blaming you for being beating on and you know damn well I'm not blaming you for being brutally raped. But damn it Reign these choices after these tragic events is all on you! Did you not think about your son today! How about the unborn you are carrying! Three fucking bottles Reign! Really? Three?" She throws the second bottle on the floor at Reign's feet. At this moment Rome had enough of the dramatics and took the third empty bottle away from Jazz reach.

"I am not drunk Jazz. You see I made it home," she says as she stumbles to the sofa and lays down.

"I'm about two seconds away from whipping your ass Reign! Let me take my ass outside and calm down before I kill your ass!"

"Baby help me understand why you drink three bottles of Vodka. Reign. Baby you don't want to have this child? Reign? Answer me damn it!"

"Our baby is fine Tezzy. She's fine, she says as she dozes in and out."

"How do you know? Baby! How do you know?!"

"Because I'm carrying her that's how I- I- know."

"We need to get her to an emergency room," he said to Rome, scooping her back up.

"I will get Jazz to move her car."

"Tezzy just let me go. I'm tired baby, please just let me go."

"Don't do this to me right now. I need you to stay up baby and stop talking crazy. I'm not letting you go baby. I love you too much to let that happen. Reign you hear me?!"

"My memories are coming back from that night"

"That's good baby, that will help you."

"I don't wa--- I don't wanna rem"

"Reign! Baby wake up! Keep talking to me baby we are almost there. Reign?"

"Just let me sleep it off Tez, I just wanna sleep."

"Reign listen to me. Did you take something? Is it me son or is her words too slurred?"

"She's definitely on something besides alcohol. Let me call Jazz, keep talking to her, Rome. Jazz, can you check her car?"

"I already have, there's nothing else in here."

"Okay."

"Are you all at the hospital yet?"

"Almost."

"I know I went off just now but I'm really concerned about her Montez. This is too much."

"I agree. I will get a handle on it. This won't happen again. Listen, we are here, call you back when we know something."
"Okay."

After they pumped the alcohol out her system and it was just the two of them. Montez told her that he felt she needed to get real help that he didn't feel the therapy section once a week was enough. He was really concerned and scared that he was going to lose her. She didn't respond, just stared into space and let the tears roll down her face. Deep inside she knows the outcome of her actions could end not only her life but their unborn as well. She didn't want to be apart from him or MJ but she knew he was right that she needed more help. She wanted her life back and in order for that to happen she had to check herself in.

*Chapter Eleven: The Past Is The Past*

I had the pleasure to sit with Dr. Reed Reign's new psychiatrist today for her last day of therapy. It's been forty five days and I can finally see the old Reign is back. She had us scared after that night, poor Montez had no other choice but to have her admitted. Once the doctor's were able to remove the alcohol, Dr. Williamson pulled him to the side to talk with him. Once Montez explained what happened to her, he suggested letting her stay at Dr. Reed's facility so she could fully do the program. After her first week there Dr. Reed then suggested that the first week wasn't enough time. That she thought a month would give her enough time to heal and address the night she was raped. Reign wanted to come home and wanted to be with her family. That's when Dr. Reed decided to be brutally honest not just with her but the rest of us. We were her enablers, we had her spoiled, and she knows with us she wasn't going to be pushed. Well I told her that she wasn't talking to me because I give it to Reign every time she does this bullshit. I'm the only one out of the family to give her tough love. She gave me a look and laughed. That didn't go over well with me so I asked her expensive ass, "what was funny?" She told me I would get my time before dropping a bomb on me. She brought up my relationship with Marcus, and then said my tough love was nothing but puppy love. Usually I have a comeback but now her overpaid ass had me rethinking our friendship and sisterhood. Damn all these years was I really an enabler to her? After that day it was clear that she needed to be admitted. The ultrasound they gave her, showed she was still pregnant and they weren't too concerned about the baby's development because she was just a little over a month pregnant. They did tell him that her doctor will probably want to see her more often. Just to make sure she will go full term and to see if the child's development was compromised. Next thing we knew those thirty days became forty five days. For the last two weeks she was let out. They allowed her to travel to Greenville to see her original doctor, Dr. Morales and also to spend time with Montez and Lucas. Now here we are on the final day of her release and Dr. Reed wanted to include me in her last session. Once I was in her office I had one question for her that I was dying to ask since she said what she said.
"What did I do?"
"Nothing Ms. Butler. You are the last important person in her life that I wanted to have a session with."
"Last important? According to who? You?"
"That's not what I'm saying. I always start with the parents and siblings if the patient has them."
"Not to cut you off, if that's the case then I should've been here with her parents."
"You two are alike in so many ways that's the same thing she said. Not only her, the parents and the husband. I'm going to tell you what I told them. I'm looking for DNA related,that helps me understand why one sibling acts differently than the other sibling or siblings. I understand how you two grew up together, still you two don't have the same DNA running through the veins. My job is to get to the root of the problem, that's why I always start with family, spouse, and then friends."
"Okay I understand now. When will Reign join us?"

"After our thirty minutes."

"Okay so um how does this work?"

"You say you and Reign grew up like sisters. What was that like?"

"I can only remember certain things. I mean we got along for the most part."

"Let's start with boyfriends. Who had the first boyfriend?"

"Reign did. We were in the third grade and his name was Jermaine. You could not separate those two. They sat with each other at every assembly, field trip, and recess. They broke up in fourth grade though."

"I know you two were little but did you feel anything at this time. I mean your best friend has a boyfriend and you don't."

"No I didn't."

"Let's move on to middle school."

"I rather not. Seems as if you already know enough about him."

"I want to hear from the one she told everything too."

"He was an asshole who broke her heart. The end."

"You know she told me you were going to be short about this subject and I thought she was being funny."

"Nope she wasn't."

"What about the family? Did her parents approve of him."

"I guess in the beginning they did."

"Did you also like him at first?"

"No."

"Can I ask you why?"

"Sure.

"Why didn't you like him?"

"He took my best friend from me."

"How? I thought you and Reign were inseparable?"

"We were then and still are today but that doesn't mean a new man can't change a person's daily routines. He made sure if we spent time together he was there. Any trips we took, he had to be a part of all of them. While the whole time he had all these different girls around. He was the perfect man during off season and a cheater during the season. Reign would act like she didn't see it and that would pissed me off."

"Maybe she didn't see it, I mean could that be possible?"

"He was a charmer but she knew. She caught him a lot flirting with those groupies, hell she even fought one girl."

"You are making my point. Maybe she didn't see him as the problem and just saw the girls were the problem."

"Is that what Reign told you?"

"Actually you did. You just said she fought the girl and not him. Did she even check him about the girl?"

No, not that time. Alright maybe with her, she felt that way. The other ones though, she did see he was the problem."

"Tell me how she was to you when she finally did see it?"

"Numb is the best word I can come up with. She couldn't understand why he couldn't stay faithful especially since she was doing it for their relationship."

"She never cheated on him?"

"Hard to believe huh? Bastard had groupies that he had sex with and she stayed being faithful to his ungrateful ass. I would have felt better if she did the same but she didn't and I for one didn't understand it. Especially when he got one of them pregnant."

"Why do you think she did that?"

"You know what I don't know. I would ask and she would just say I didn't understand. She would never tell me why really."

"The best friend you shared everything with never told you that? Are you sure she didn't or could it be possibly she did and you weren't listening?"

"Is that what she said?"

"That's not how this works Jasmine. I'm asking you to go back and try to recall those conversations. I'm not here to tell you what she told me. Only she can do that."

"Okay? Let me think back. It was the year he proposed and she said yes. I was pissed at her for taking me out to celebrate, especially when I found out why we were celebrating."

"It was just you and her?"

"No, she invited me and the crew. A few friends from high school and college days. Also a few basketball and football wives and girlfriends."

"Once she made the announcement while you all were there, how does that make you feel?"

"I told you. Now who is not listening?"

"No I heard you, you said you were pissed when you found out why you were there. My question was as soon as she said hey ladies, Damien proposed and I accepted. What did you feel?"

"Pissed!"

"Do you want to elaborate?"

"Dr. Reed piss is piss I don't know what else you wanted me to feel."

"Just want to know how you really felt besides pissed. Your best friend, your sister, your confidant. Just announced that she is marrying a man, that you not only disapprove of but also the one responsible for coming between you two. Close your eyes and go back to that moment. Are you there?"

"Yes."

"Before she made the announcement what were you two doing?"

"You want to know about Reign and I or everyone that was there?"

"Just you and her. What was it like there when it was just the two of you."

"We didn't have too many one on ones. She was busy making sure everyone was having a good time and I was helping."

"You were playing co host with her?"

"I guess you can say that."

"I'm simply asking you, I'm not telling you. Did you feel as if you were co hosting the party?"

"Actually that night I felt like an outsider looking into my best friend's new life. I watched her laugh with the different sports wives and girlfriends trying her hardest to become a part of their world. While the one she knew the longest was being treated like an outsider."

"Did you ever tell her that?"

"My first time ever admitting it."

"Interesting. I remember when we first met and you said to me and I quote, "I'm the only one who gives her tough love." Do you remember saying that to me?"

"I recall. I also recall you calling my so-called tough love, puppy love."

"Why do you seem upset right now?"

"Truth hurts."

"That was a feeling you never told her? She was engaged to an all star rookie and now was part of this circle and you felt like an outsider. Why couldn't you tell her that back then?"

"I didn't want to seem like a hater or being jealous of her new life. I just continued being the friend I have always been."

"Do you see now why I said that you all are her enablers?"

"I actually realized it as soon as you said it. We rarely didn't  have each other back, nine out of ten times we always sided with one another. The black version of "

"Thelma and Louise."

"She told you that?"

"You know she did."

"Yep. We would metaphorically ride off a cliff for one another, us against the world."

"Nine out of ten times and that night of what became an engagement party was the one time

"You jumped out of the car."

"Damn your good."

"My expensive ass better be."

"I really need to talk to Reign about holding water," she said laughing.

"You want that bucket to leak with the money they are paying me right," she asked laughing with her.

"I guess Dr. Reed."

"I'm going to keep it one hundred with you. Don't look at me like that, I know some hip hop lingo. I talk to people younger than you all who don't mind being themselves sitting in that chair."

"I am being me."

"You are being Jasmine, I only seen Jazz twice so far. Everyone I have talked to have me thinking Jasmine rarely shows up. Only time I would see her according to them is when she is in business mode. Jasmine is politically correct and Jazz is the alter ego. I'm still waiting on Jazz."

"The two coexist, there's no alter ego to me. Jasmine is Jazz and vice versa. I don't show my ass unless I have too."

"Understood. Let me ask you this. Do you think Reign has relationship issues?"

"I think we all would if we gave one hundred percent to the wrong person for years."

"You may be right about that. Well Jazz that's our hour, how do you feel?"

"The same with a little more knowledge about myself and Reign."

"I'm going to tell you like I told everyone else although she is free to leave today. The work with her doesn't end. She still has appointments with me on Thursdays and she is welcome to bring any of you when she comes."

"I'm good Dr. Reed, I will keep you up on your offer if my status ever changes."

"That's all I ask from you. Do you have any concerns or questions you want to ask me before I bring her in?"

"I'm good."

"Okay, I think she's ready to tell you now. The question I have is, are you ready to hear it?"

"If it has to do with me. Then yes I would love to hear it."

"I know you felt like you and Reign were close and you told each other everything. I just want to prepare you that you didn't and neither did she."

"I did tell her everything."

"So you told her everything that was happening with you and Marcus?"

"Wait, she talked about that to you? You know what, it doesn't matter. My situation is different."

"How so?"

"It's different because. Well it's different to me because. Aw hell I guess there is no damn difference."

"Now that you have acknowledged that. I will bring in Reign. Tracy can you please tell Reign she can come in now."

"Yes. She is on her way."

"Thank you. As we wait for her, would you like another bottle of water?"

"No I'm good, thank you for asking."

"No problem. If at any time you need one just let me know. Hey Reign. How are you today."

"I'm doing good. Hey Jazzy! I missed you sis!"

"I missed you too babe. You look refreshed, Montez said that he could see the old you coming back."

"I don't know about the old me but the prison me is gone. Thanks to you Dr. Reed."

"You put in the work. I just brought you out of it so you can see where the problem was."

Am I the problem?

"No Jazz, you are not."

"Okay Reign and Jasmine let's see how well you two really know one another. Jazz do you know how Reign handles negativity?"

"By drinking or taking long drives."

"Did she ever tell you what alcohol and long drives do for her when she can't handle certain things in her life."

"No, now that you asked me that. I always assumed why she does it."

"What were your assumptions?"

"It helped her escape her problems."

"Reign is she right?"

"No. Before I could drink or drive I would take long walks by myself and talk to God. I started doing it when I was eight years old, maybe. I would live in this fantasy world a lot of times by myself. This started when Abs was born and our time together wasn't that often. My parents never gave me a sibling. That when Abs was born, it was felt as if the only sister I knew was slowly being taken away from me."

"I thought you said I wasn't the cause of this?"

"You are not the main cause, our parents were. You couldn't come see me as much anymore and that wasn't your fault. I just found myself alone a lot during that time."

"I lied. I'm not ready to hear this Dr. Reed."

"You two want to take a break?"

"If that's what Jazz needs."

"No, I don't. Go ahead, I am listening."

"I realize I started dating Dame because I was missing my sister and I needed to pass time away when you were busy with Abs. You know that I met him at the park the same day you were supposed to meet up with me. But you couldn't because your parents needed you to babysit. I was watching the boys play ball and he approached me and we were inseparable from then on."

"What are you telling me is, Damien was more of a replacement than a boyfriend?"

"At the beginning he was but of course as we grew older he became more of a boyfriend and later fiance. After talking with Dr. Reed I realized I let a lot slide with him because we were friends first. It felt more like giving my friend a pass instead of my man."

"Then reality finally hit and you handle it like you did as a child."

"Yes. Instead now I use long drives and alcohol to help me deal with pain. I would never take my own life but I do realize that this time I could have. Not just mine but the baby too. That made me realize I needed help and I was out of control. I had to come to reality that I was a rape victim and now a survivor of rape. It was time to face it and take an emotional rollercoaster ride."

"I'm here for you sis all the way riding these emotional rides with you."

"She is so blessed to have a strong family. I don't get this too often but it makes my heart smile knowing she has a strong circle. Reign is there anything else you want to tell Jazz?"

"Just thank you, as she begins to get teary eyed. I needed that wake up call that night. I needed that anger and disappointment from you. You are the only one besides my mother that gives me tough love or swift kick in the ass. If you weren't there that night I wouldn't have been here going through the program. I would still think long drives and alcohol would help me through it. I know I took our friendship plenty of times to the end of the cliff and I'm so sorry for that."

"I took you through a lot of shit too, there's no need to apologize to me. I just didn't want to lose my sister that way. I want us old and cripple, pulling each other's life support chords at the end of this life."

"Oh Jazz," Reign said with a slight laugh. "Only you would have the perfect way to die. I love Jazzy."

"I love you too Reign drops."

# *Chapter Twelve: Daddy's Little Girls*

   Things have been beyond weird between Marcus and I ever since the reception. Not to mention the lawsuit, the live stream, and Reign being raped. We still have to be cordial around one another for our daughters and that is no easy task. The girls haven't picked up on it yet and I keep telling Marcus we need to fix it before they do. He's still pissed and really doesn't care if they do. He wants them to know that I'm the reason we are not a family. In the past that would have scared me but Sean and I finally have the kids getting along. Marcus is mad because that plan has now fallen apart. It's Friday and it's another drop off day with him. After this I meet up with Reign and my wedding planner. I decided to go with Miss Janice, since she did a wonderful job at Reign's wedding. I decided to have a beach wedding somewhere in North Carolina so she will be bringing me different locations. I can't wait to start planning and picking out colors and decorations. Sean said whatever I want for our special day was fine just as long as he had complete control of the reception. I agreed for now but he should know by now I'm going to add my two cents. I'm just going to let him take the lead and make him at least think that for now. As I continue to wait for him to arrive, I decided to get on Twitter and see what the latest trend was. Well that was the plan until Marcella interrupted me. "Mom I have to go," Marcella yells as she gets out of the car.

"Hold on baby. Yasmine, you get out of the car too. We are all going in together."

She grabs Marcella's hands then walks to the driver side of the car and opens the door for Yas. She forgot to put Marcella's back doors on safety. She made a mental note to do that when they came back to the car. Yasmine steps out of the car and follows behind them, just as she opens the door to the restaurant, Marcus pulls up.

"My bad. I had to stop and fill up the tank."

"Daddy! Daddy," Yasmine says with excitement as she runs towards her father.

"No problem. Marcella really has to go or she would be running towards you right now as well."

She holds the door while Marcus scoops up Yasmine and follows behind them into the restaurant.

"Can we eat here please mommy and daddy we're hungry? Yasmine asks both parents, giving them her puppy eyes."

"Yas, I don't know"

"It's fine with me Jazz. If you're not in a rush," he says, interrupting her.

"Let me take her to the restroom and think about it."

She picks up Marcella and does a quick jog to the restrooms. She grabbed the wipes from her purse and wipes down the toilet seat and then adds toilet seat cover to it. While she was doing that, Marcella was pulling her leggings and panties down.

"Good to go baby girl. I'm going to be right out here okay?"

"Okay mommy."

As she waits for her daughter to finish up. She thinks about what Marcus said and tries to figure out his agenda. He was either trying to set her up as the bad one if she turns him down and leaves or he was being genuine when he said he wanted her to stay. She wanted desperately for them to get back to normal but so much had been said and done after the wedding. He was hitting low over the Moore's house and those words still stung. She could forgive but she would never forget. Looking at her engagement ring she knows she made the right choice and Sean was definitely the one. She decided to text him and let him know what was going on.

*Hey baby. The girls wanted me to stay and eat with them. I'm going to say yes if that's okay with you?*

*Just you and the girls???*

*Marcus too........*

*Who's idea was this? The girls him.... or you???*

*Definitely not mine. Yasmine suggested it.*

*I'm about to VC you. Pick up.*

She looks in the mirror and makes sure her face is straight as she waits for him to video chat with her. Marcella came out of the stall and went to wash her hands. Jazz lifts her up so she could get some soap then let's her down so she could wash her hands. As she finishes up Sean calls.

"Hey baby give me a second I'm in the bathroom with Marcella."

"Okay."

"Hey Sean!"

"Hey baby girl! You had to use the bathroom?"

"I had to do one and two but I'm all done now."

Sean laughs and says, "You unloaded in public? You are your mother's child."

"When you have to go you go," she said smiling at him.

"That's right baby girl! Don't hold back, release it."

"You so silly Sean. I'm going to eat now! Bye Sean!"

"Bye baby girl. Hey beautiful."

"Hey."

"Yas and Marcus ambushed you huh?"

"Yeah you can say that. Hold on again, okay?"

"Yeah."

"This is Sean. I will be back."

"That means you are staying? He said it's okay?"

She lets out a slight laugh at his sarcasm and she knew exactly what he was doing. He was trying to bait her but she saw the hook and the worm. "I will be back."

"See now I want to say no because that muthafucker is up to something."

"I will leave, if that's what you want?"

"Jazz I'm telling you this is exactly why he did that shit just now. If you go back in there and say you can't stay. He's going to use that to make me the bad guy. If you stay it still makes me the ass because it's like I gave you permission to stay. Lose, lose for me so do what you feel you need to do. Is Reign with you yet?"

"No she is still at her parents house. I'm on my way over there after I leave here."

"They should be home soon. Montez almost has their new home finished. Just have to knock out the wall in their bedroom. She doesn't know about that surprise right? "

"Listen if I can keep her engagement a secret from her, this master bedroom she's getting is a piece of cake. I just need Montez and his crew to move a little faster. I miss her in Greenville but I understand the move."

"I still can't believe they are still going through this legally. She needs closure and his lawyers are dragging this case."

"Ugh let's not talk about it. I'm keeping her distracted with planning my wedding and the commercial lot. Plus her own work and MJ."

"She's blessed to have you for real baby."

"I don't know about all that but that's my sis and I got her no matter what."

"Mommy are you staying to eat, Yasmine," asked pulling on her mother's shirt.

"Yeah baby, let me finish up with Sean, okay?"

"Okay mommy. Wait, the lady wants to know are you thirsty?"

"Tell her yes and I want a cherry Pepsi."

Pepsi with cherries got it mommy.

"No Yas that's not what, dang it! Sean I have to go. I love you, talk to you later."

"Good ol Yas," he said laughing. I love you too baby talk to you later."

"Hey how are you? My daughter just came in to order my drink. I just want to make sure she got it right?"

"Your husband corrected her, so we have it coming."

"Oh good thanks. Wait, my husband? That's not my husband."

"Oh I'm so sorry. I saw the ring and the girls calling you two mom and dad I just assumed."

"That's fine. I'm engaged to someone else. He is single."

"Okay. You two are doing the co parenting thing. That's always good to see. Well your drink is coming out. Did you want an appetizer?"

"I might. Let me go see how far they got. Thank you again."

"No problem ma'am be right back with your beverage."

"Okay did you all get an appetizer yet?"

"We were waiting on you,"Marcus answered.

"Let me see what they have, how about the chilli cheese fries?"

"Yes!"

"Marcus?"

"Whatever my girls want is fine with me."

"Chilli cheese fries! Chilli cheese fries!"

"Okay how much soda have you two had? Shhh chill."

"Sorry mommy."

"What are you two now? Twins?"

"Mommy you are funny," Yas chuckled as she went back to coloring her paper.

"Here you go ma'am. Are you guys ready to start with an appetizer or ready to order?"

"Both," Marcus and Jazz responded at the same time.

"What are you two, twins?" Yasmine said laughing.

"Go ahead Marcus, she said as she swiped her daughter hand messing up coloring."

"Okay my baby girl will have the kids spaghetti with extra meatballs and my princess will have the kids cheese pizza. Their mother will have steak medium well sauteed with mushrooms, loaded mash potatoes with broccoli for her vegetables. And I would have a rack of ribs with loaded mash potatoes with collard greens. For our appetizers the girls have chosen chilli cheese fries with extra ranch dressing."

"Okay, coming right up sir and I will have that appetizer right out."

"Thank you," they all said in unison.

"Where are you headed after we eat?"

To my parents house to meet up with Reign."

"I just saw her yesterday. She seems to be doing better."

"Yeah she is moving on the best she can."

"I feel bad that it took that, for me to reach out. I should have done that but my ego and pride wouldn't let me."

"You know God always makes a way for us to see our wrongs before it's too late. At least you had a chance to do it while she is still breathing. Some people don't get that."

"That's true. I owe you a sincere apology as well. I never wanted to disrespect my girl's mother like that. I was tripping hard that day and a lot of that was coming from a hurt place. It won't happen again and I hope you can forgive me."

Apology accepted. I have to get out of here before I'm late. Excuse me Miss, can I get a to go plate for my food?

"You sure can. Anyone else needs one?"

"No we're staying for dessert right daddy," Marcella asked.

"How can daddy say no to that face. If you could bring us a menu so they can see what sweets you have."

"Coming right up."

"Thank you."

"Alright ladies you all have fun with daddy. Mommy will see you Sunday."

"Bye mommy love you!"

"Bye Yasmine and Marcella, mommy loves you two"

"To the moon and back," they all say in unison.

# *Chapter Thirteen: Beach Theme*

I finally arrived at my parents' home and of course Miss Janice beat me to my own wedding planning. As I got out of my car, I noticed Reign"s car wasn't here yet. As I was walking in I called her to make sure she was still coming. To my surprise when I walked in everyone was sitting in the main room and they all were waiting on me.

"Took you long enough friend. Why are you calling me? You thought I wasn't here?

"Shut up Reign! You get on my last nerves. I apologize for being tardy, the girls convinced me to eat with them and their daddy."

"Oh…. Are you okay baby? That had to be rough even though my grandbabies were there."

"It actually went well mom. It was the past that we were accustomed to before the bad break up. It was a nice dinner, with that being said I need some of that champagne you all are drinking."

"While you are pouring yourself a glass, Miss Janice has come up with some great locations for your wedding," said Charalene.

"Alright Miss Janice, show me what you have for me."

"Have you two decided how many you are inviting?"

"Fifty on both sides of our families so no more than a hundred. As of now thirty people have already RSVP, with that being said I only want to see intimate venues. I don't want anything lavish, let me change that not too lavish but memorable"

"Jazz I was about to say who the hell did you think you were talking too."

"I came to my senses quickly, hush Reign. Anyway, Miss Janice, do you have anything like that in your portfolio?"

"I have five locations where I can make work. Did you want to do everything at your wedding venue or did you want the reception to be somewhere else?"

"All at one venue. It's bad enough people have to travel a little to attend, I wouldn't want to move them after the wedding."

"Then I have the perfect two places. You can have a beautiful wedding on the beach with the sun setting in the background that you two requested. This place also  has a beach home where the groom bridesmaids and groomsmen can stay. Depending how many you will have, you would also have enough room for your parents and the reverend. There's a hotel nearby where you can have your family and friends who want to stay."

"That sounds like a winner to me. What's the name of it? I want to send it to Sean.

"Bald Head Islands, here's the link to it. Are you still letting him do the entertainment part of it?"

"Yes, you still have his appointment for tomorrow. I already told him my little input, but the rest is on him."

"Alright have you all decided on the food?"

"He will have all of that for you tomorrow as well. Now does this place have an alcohol license or will we have to get one?"

"Good question, I will check on that tomorrow and have the answer for Sean. Are you ladies ready to look at the flower arrangements, plate settings and tables arrangements?"

"This is my mothers' expertise. All Sean and I want is black and red decorations with a splash of cream. Wait hold on, this is my mother law to be. Hey Ms. Grey, did you get lost?"

"I don't think so, is this your car out here in the driveway."

"I am coming out now. Yes ma'am you are at the right house come on in. You are right in time to help us pick out these decorations. Can I get you something to drink?"

"Water will be just fine sweetie. Hey Lillian and Charlene, how are you ladies."

"We are doing well so glad you could join us today. We know how busy you are with your daycare."

"Which will be having a new location thanks to your daughter. I still can't believe in a few months I will own my own building and my son made it happen."

"We carried them for ten months, gave them life, and raised them. That's the least they can do is treat us every once in a while."

"I know that's right Charlene. I know that's right!"

"Don't mind us mama, we are not sitting here while y'all ridicule us."

"Right Reign! I mean damn they act like we haven't shown gratitude."

"Aw our babies are still sensitive Charlene."

"Alright, alright you three, could you just pick out the dinnerware. Miss Janice charges by the hour."

"Well that's true, but your mother has been multitasking. They are almost finished with the decor. I love working with you all, especially your mothers. It's always professional and fun with you all. I know I am about to experience another beautiful wedding filled with love."

"Aw Miss Janice thank you. After seeing how Reign wedding turned out, I knew I was going to hire you. I can't wait to see the end results in June."

"I love doing weddings, especially outdoor weddings. When you called and told me you two had settled on a beach wedding. I was looking at all kinds of locations in North Carolina.This is going to be another beautiful wedding and I'm glad I am a part of it."

"We only work with the best and that is you ma'am."

"Thank you, that means a lot coming from my people. I love seeing black love and the unity of it in holy matrimony."

"Amen Miss Janice, we love to see it!"

# Chapter Fourteen: My Son's Mother

I would be lying if I said that everything went back to normal after being raped and going through the therapy. That it was voila magic and just like that, the shit went away. It wasn't that easy at all. There are still nights when I wake up in cold sweats or times when we are making love that flashes appear and we would have to stop. Moments they would leave for work and I would lock the doors, I would make sure all windows were secured, checked security cameras every five minutes. I knew he was locked up but his terror was present like he wasn't  then there was the fear of being raped by someone else. That was just my first trimester living with my parents and my family. Once Montez had our new home upgraded in the master bedroom we finally moved back to Greenville right in the middle of my second trimester. I am still paranoid being here in the city where it began but at least the scenery is different this time around. Although we had our best moments in Montez's old house, he thought it would be safer and wise to move and upgrade. We were expanding our family and a three bedroom was no longer going to be big enough. So we bought land in Simpsonville, the country part of Greenville and built our dream home. What we designed together was perfect but Montez had an inspiration moment and decided to knock down a wall and expand our room. And when I walked in and saw what he did, I wasn't mad at him. My walk in closet is every woman's dream. I felt like a black Paris Hilton in my closet space. I now don't have to give up any shoes to make space, that's how much shoe space I have. I don't do too many bags but if I wanted to start I had plenty of space for that too behind my shoe wall. I'm not even going to brag about the clothes space you have to see for yourself, I have no words to describe it. When we were in that cabin in Tennessee, my hubby loved the fact that the jacuzzi was out on the balcony so he made sure in our new house we had it. The bedroom itself was simple. Just a California King size bed, tv that comes down from the ceiling. My baby and his toys, listen he can have whatever he wants after giving me my dream walk- in -closet.  MJ room design stayed the same and we are waiting for the baby reveal to start on this little one room. God I hope and pray it's a girl, I want to do My Little Pony theme so bad. I'm in the kitchen right now making hubby some breakfast before he goes to work. I'm still trying to get acquainted with everything here, especially this kitchen.

While Reign was in the kitchen Montez finally woke up to see that his wife was already up and doing her own thing. He stretched out in the bed and wiped the sleep from his eyes.The sun was shining through their blinds and he could hear the birds chirping. He sat up in the bed and grabbed the baby monitor and noticed MJ was still sleeping and he wished he could switch bodies with him. He did the one thing he didn't want to do and that was get up and get dressed for work. He had a big day today from interviewing people to rent out space in his tattoo shop to doing new landscape work for the new condos they were building downtown. He landed his business another major client that would keep his employees busy for a while. It felt good helping others and he has been doing that a lot more when Reign entered his life. Together they had both built an empire that they both were proud of, not just for themselves but for their children. As he stepped in the shower and let the warm water run through his hair.  He thought about his wife's journey and how through it all she stayed strong and fought. She could have just given up on life and went to a dark place and never returned, but she didn't. He made sure he was there every step being the husband she needed. He was at every appointment even when the sessions  weren't meant for him. He made sure he was there when it was over and she saw his face. It's been hard some days holding her when she cried out, rubbing her hair til she was able to fall back to sleep after a nightmare. They both have been waiting patiently for the trial to begin but the muthafucker keeps changing lawyers and the judge keeps moving the date. It would really bother him if the dude was out on bail, but bail was denied. So if his bitch ass wanted to stay in there and continue delaying they were not stopping him. As he turned off the water he could smell the breakfast that his wife was cooking for him. He couldn't wait to get in there and throw down. He wrapped a towel around his waist and grabbed his brush to redo his man bun. Reign walks in and they stare at each other through the mirror.

"Good morning sexy," she says as she hits him on the butt. "Do you need some help with that?"

"If you don't mind beautiful."

"Not at all because you my dear are struggling. I love doing your hair. It gives me extra practice for our daughter."

"That's another boy baby don't get too excited."

"No it's not. We are not about to start this argument this morning. It's a girl's end of discussion."

"You can't just end it like that."

"It's already been done babe.How many interviews you have this morning?"

"Five."

"What do you have after that?"

"I was thinking about getting my haircut. What do you want, me to keep it or cut it?"

"Why do you want to cut it, fall and winter are coming up? Don't you think you need hair on your head for that? What was the point wearing all this hair during the summer if you were going to cut it in the fall?"

"Just say you want me to keep it because you love messing with it."

"That's not the only reason sexy," she says as she follows him back into the bathroom. She sits on the sink and watches, while he attempts to get dressed for work. Seeing that his wife was now in a giving mood. He removes his towel and moves her panties to the side. She takes her fingers and starts massaging her clitoris while making sexy moaning sounds. She had him so turned on he started slowly ejaculating his hardness. Now she was really turned on as she removed her wet fingers and placed them in his mouth. As he tastes her sweetness he places it in her giving her hard but slow strokes as he loses himself in her. She wraps her legs around his waist, wraps her arms around his neck and pulls herself up. They are now in their favorite position. He is slowly guiding her up and down his hardness that it made her body shake. He felt her warm cum flowing down on him and now he had her kitty talking. She grips him tighter and moans "oh my God baby please don't stop, keep her cuming." Now she was making his body jerk by slightly biting and kissing his earlobe while tightening her muscles around his penis. Now he was moaning "damn baby you say don't stop but you trying to make me explode all in this wetness. Come here baby girl," he whispers as he carries her to the bed and lays her down. He wants to make sure when he leaves the house today. That he leaves her desiring him all day while he's gone. He removes her panties and places his tongue inside her. The breakfast she made for him was going to wait. He was about to enjoy his favorite meal.

Reign was in the kitchen making her favorite drink as she took a break from work. When her doorbell rang, it startled her a little because she wasn't expecting company. She walks to the window and looks out the blinds. When she saw it was Tonya, she opened up the door.

"Hey Reign I hate to bother you at home. Tam and I have been calling you and you weren't picking up. I just dropped by to make sure everything was okay."

"Aw damn I forgot to take my phone off silent, MJ was sleeping and I didn't want to wake him. Come on in, while I grab the phone and put it on vibrate. Thanks girl for coming all the way out here and checking on me. That was sweet of you to do that."

"No problem. You at least call us once to check on us. That when one o'clock came and went and we didn't hear from you. We were a little worried."

"Sometimes I forget that you all

"You don't have to finish that Reign."

"Thank you. At some point though we have to move on from that and put trust back out there in the universe. Anyway have you all had lunch yet?"

"No, I was going to grab us something on my way back."

"I have a better idea. Let's go to Red Lobster, my treat. I will call up the crew and have them meet us there. That sounds good to you?"

"Free food always works for me."

"Let me get MJ ready and I will meet you all there."

"I will call everyone for you while you do that. Anything you want me to order for you?"

"Um just order me water for now and for my appetizer order me the stuffed mushrooms. Tell everyone to go ahead with their order of drinks and appetizers

"Sounds good boss lady see you in a bit."

Sean was sitting in his car staring at Dana's door trying to get his mind right while listening to Mobb Deep. He was praying a little prayer as he did often before knocking on her door and picking up his son. He never knew which Dana he was going to get so he trained himself for all of her mood swings. As he finally steps out of the car he notices a figure staring at him through the window and it wasn't Dana. The closer he got to the door he realized it was a man that would be opening the door for him and he was right.

"What's up man I'm Sean and I'm here to pick up my son."

"That's what's up man come in, he ain't here right now. Dana took my car and went to Wal-mart with him. They should be back soon."

"I will stay out here til they pull up."

"Yo, can I ask you something?"

"I mean you can but don't look for me to answer if I don't think it's any of your business."

"Aye dude fair enough I don't want no problems. I just noticed you were in the driveway a long time before getting out. I was just trying to figure out why? I was about to come out and asked you but I remembered Dana telling me that you might beat her back here."

"Do you have any kids?"

"Nah man no kids."

"Well there are two types of mothers our generation knows that fathers call them. We either say baby mama or the mother of our child. I call Dana my baby mama. Do you know why?"

"Let me guess she's drama for you?"

"Damn right, every chance she gets! Now she knows I come and get my son every Thursday at seven p.m. It's been a court order like that for months. She pulls this bullshit at least three times out of a month. Now if I complain to my lawyer about it then I become baby daddy to her. Do you know why?"

"Man I just asked what I thought was a simple question. I wasn't expecting all of that."

"Good luck with that homey."

"Oh were good you don't have to worry about that."

"Good for you. Just know you touch my son or any harm comes to him. I'm coming with an AK7 to you and everyone you love. I don't give a damn about who she has blowing her back out. SJ has a father and that's me. We understand each other......"

"The name is Blaze Atkins and I hear you loud and clear Sean Gray."

"Good. I will wait outside to get my son."

"Yeah you do that."

"Fucking ridiculous!" Sean says as he leans on his car waiting on Dana. She has had him every since 4pm and she waits until it's time for me to pick him up. Before she decides to make a run to Wal-Mart. She was always doing everything she could to get under my skin and I am tired of it. Now why couldn't she drive her car to do her errands? Another game she's playing is that she just wanted me to know she had a new dick in her life. As if I give a fuck. While waiting for her ass to pull up, let me call my baby and let her know what's up.

"Hey baby can you stop by the store and pick up some flour? I'm out and I need to make these homemade biscuits for SJ, he's been asking for them. Where y'all at anyway I thought you would be here by now."

"I'm still here waiting on this girl to bring him back."

"Bring him back? Sean it's almost eight oclock why did you let her take him somewhere?"

"I didn't. She left out before I got here. She is playing games again. She has some new dude here and I guess this is her way of introducing us. She made me think she was here and took SJ in dude's car."

"Let me get this straight. She left her car and you thought they were both there? Instead she takes the guy car and you think she did that in order for you to meet her new man?"

"Yeah."

"I think you are putting way too much thought into it baby, don't you think. If you would have just knocked on the door as soon as you arrived then you would have known that."

"You know I have to go through my routine before going to her door."

"Well have you called her to see what's taking so long?"

"Jazz, come on, we have been doing this for six months. Ain't no point in me calling that damn girl. She pulls a stunt like this all the damn time. If I'm making a phone call it's to your mom because I'm sick of this shit!"

"Okay baby calm down. Give her fifteen minutes and if she's not there I will call her. I'm going to run to the store myself and grab some things. You want me to stay on the phone with you?"

"Don't go to the store, me and Junior will do it as soon as I have him. I don't want you and the girls out this late. He can get his biscuits in the morning. It's fine. Don't we have some cornbread you can substitute for the biscuits?"

"Yeah I will do that and make the biscuits for tomorrow."

"Man here this"

"Sean don't you dare call her a bitch. Now I don't like her either but I'm not gonna sit here and listen to you being disrespectful. That's still SJ's mother."

"If that's what she acts like then why can't I call her that?"

"Chill and be nice. We are going to act like the Obamas and aim high."

"I feel like being Donnie and not giving a fuck what comes out my mouth."

"My bad Sean the lines were long at Wal-Mart. SJ wanted that game to play with you and I had to pick up food for next week. That's why we are late. You know how it is when you're in Walmart time goes by and that's what happened."

"Hey SJ man! What game do you get for us," as he ignored her.

"Tekken seven."

"Aw cool man can't wait to play you and beat you. Here talk to Jazz and put your seatbelt on."

"Okay daddy. Hey Jazzy! I have a new game!"

"You do?! What game do you have?"

"Next time you pull this stunt with me get ready to head back to court."

"Sean I'm not lying that's what happened. Dang I didn't do it intentionally, time really got away from us. Take the bass out your voice and help me take the groceries in. Please."

"Get your little boyfriend to do it. I have to get our son home to dinner. That we are now late because of you."

"That's not my boyfriend, he's just a friend."

"I don't give a fuck Biz Markie! Get him out here to help you!"

"Really? You are doing all this in front of our son? Okay I got you Sean."

"I don't give a damn Dana! This was your last time being late, I mean that!"

"Bye baby. Have fun with daddy I will see you Monday," she says tuning him out.

"Okay mommy! Love you!"

"I love you too."

"Didn't I tell you to chill before she was out of that car," she asked in a serious tone.

"You didn't hear her bullshit just now?"

"Actually I didn't but I could hear you yelling, was that necessary to do in front of him?"

"No."

"Right. Damn baby I asked you not to do that. You have to learn when to pick your battles with her. Now you are looking like the bad parent in front of SJ. Okay I'm done. I will see you two when you get here. I love you."

"I love you too baby."

"See you in a bit."

"Yeah alright."

"Daddy don't be mad at mommy. I couldn't make up my mind."

"I'm not mad anymore son, I promise. Dad just didn't want to get you home this late and then have to wake you up early for school. It won't happen again. I promise little man."

"Okay daddy. Jazzy said she's making me biscuits in the morning for breakfast and I can have all the maple syrup and milk I want."

"Jazz setting up your teacher for failure tomorrow," Sean said laughing.

"How daddy?"

"Dad just joking around."

"Oh. You think Uncle Tez will come by and play with us? I miss him and MJ."

"You know what let's call him and see."

"Okay daddy!"

"Whats up man?"

"I can't call it, what are you doing?"

"Just fed Lucas and we were chilling watching some preseason football. Panthers looking good."

"They always look good. The question is will they maintain it?"

"I don't know man, our backends haven't been the same since they let Josh go. That's my only concern for the defense. Cam is Cam how he goes is how the offense goes. If Panthers don't do their thing this year my Chiefs are looking good too."

"Same thing with Chiefs but I let you live. It's Eagles all day over here."

"They're playing each other this year in Charlotte we should catch it."

"When?"

"It's on a Sunday. We can go see the in-laws that weekend and make it a men day on Sunday."

"Too bad Lucas is not of age he could have gone."

"Yeah I have plenty of games to take him to, so it's all good. I will call Romain and you hit up David?"

"Bet. Hey I was calling you for something else though."

"What's that?"

He taps SJ on the shoulder and on cue the little boy with excitement says," Hey Uncle Tez!"

"Junior man what's up! You were quiet this whole time I was on the phone with your Pops? How did that happen?"

"I was waiting my turn. Miss Martin is teaching us that."

"Miss Martin?! That's your new first grade teacher?"

"Yes and she's pretty."

"She pretty huh? What makes her pretty?"

"I don't know, she's just pretty to me."

"I hear you man. I hope Miss Martin teaches you a lot more. That's good she is teaching manners. Every young man should learn that."

"Uncle Tez?"

"Yes?"

"Can you and MJ come over this weekend and play my new game?"

"You have a new game? What are we playing?"

"Tekken Seven."

"Of course dude we will be there Saturday and you can show your little cousin how it's done!"

"Yay! See you Saturday!"

"Alright lil man. Okay Sean I holler at you man."

"Alright."

"This weekend is going to be so much fun. Can we go to the park too daddy?"

"Whatever you want to do, it's fine with me."

"Cool. I'm hungry, why are we stopping at the store?"

"I have to pick up some things for us this weekend. Jazz said dinner is ready you can eat as soon as we hit the door. Here want some goldfish to hold you over?"

"Yes sir. Can I get some chocolate milk too?"

"Are you trying to get Jazz to kill me? Um how about some two percent milk?"

"It's okay daddy I wait until we get home."

"Are you sure?"

"Yes sir."

"Alright let's get you home my fly guy."

# Chapter Fifteen: No Regrets

The weekend was crazy once again with all the kids being here but we had a ball. We took them to the park and wore their butts out. We taught them how to play kickball. It took a minute because they kept confusing it with soccer. But once we taught them how to play they had so much fun. It started out with the girls vs the boys. Next thing we knew more kids joined us and even some adults. I felt as if we were back in the nineties when social media wasn't popping and this was all that mattered. No lie, all though we were all having fun, your girl was so happy to hear the ice cream truck coming. I saw a lot of parents with the same face of appreciation when they heard it too. That only meant break time and gave us a moment to come up with something else to entertain them with. After they ate their ice cream they ran over to the park and played on the playground. Sean and I took a seat on a nearby bench and watched them play.

"Look at you, your little self is turning all red."

"Shut up Sean! You get on my nerves. I can't help it. I'm not all chocolate like you. I need extra help with the sun tan lotion."

"You need for me to put more on you?"

"No I'm actually good thank you. Look at our kids, it took them awhile but they are finally getting along."

"You mean the girls finally accepting Junior and sharing their mommy with him."

"I said what I said, we don't have to point out that my two were the problem with their possessive selves."

"I wonder where they get that from?"

"Duh, their daddy side of the family. My side does not act like that."

"The daddy side huh?"

"Clearly," she said as they both laughed.

"Do you ever wonder what it would be like if we never met or hooked up?"

"In the beginning but not recently. I didn't want to be permanent with you in the beginning."

"I remember because of Reign and Montez."

"Right. I thought it was going to be the same situation with Marcus and Dame all over again glad it wasn't. We all have separate lives that hanging out with one another a lot wasn't really possible. Especially with our kids' routine and the co parenting schedule."

"I appreciate you and your mom for making that happen for me. Dana was only giving me Junior when she had stuff to do or needed a break. Lillian made sure that stopped once we were solid."

"Listen I'm a daddy's girl and I know how important it is for the father to not only provide financially for his child but also be a presence in their lives. Especially when the father wants that then we as mother's should give him that without being all bitter or vindictive. We can be complicated too, that's because we realized too late we opened our legs and got pregnant by the wrong man. That usually happens though when community dicks impregnate us and leave us to be a single parent. Then goes to create more broken homes leaving us to be the mother and father. That's not my life or battle because thank God I open my legs to the right ones, twice."

"I might not like Marcus but he takes care of Yasmine and Marcella."

"That's not the second time I'm talking about babe."

"I don't get it."

"I see, she said laughing."

"What am I missing? You open your legs twice to the right man."

"Men."

"Men? They have different daddies?"

"Oh my God you can't be this slow Sean. Maybe I was wrong about getting it right twice."

"Oh shit! Are you pregnant? By me? Of course by me! We are having a baby!"

"Shhhh! Sean! Babe chill! You are the only one who knows. I haven't told the girls yet or my parents. Hell Reign doesn't even know."

"Say word! You told me before Reign!"

"Well in fairness she didn't impregnate me so I think the person who did should know first."

"Woman are you crazy! You are out here playing kicked ball with these heathens."

"Wait, now our kids our heathens?"

"Not our kids! These other little demons out here!"

"Wow babe really? Stop talking about these people kids. Our child is fine being active is good for the baby. It's not like I was out here playing dodgeball with them. It was a friendly game of kickball. That by the way the girls denominated the boys in."

"For the last time we let y'all win."

"That's your story?

"And I'm sticking to it! Now getting back to my unborn."

"I would like to think I had something to do with that. Our unborn you meant to say?"

"No I meant mine. It's because of my soldiers that you are pregnant with my daughter."

"Really? Let me get this straight, carrying it, gaining weight, mood swings, and stretch marks is light work compared to little white tadpoles entering my egg?"

"In three months it will be our child right now it is just my tadpole in there."

"You are lucky that you are cute when you are excited for one. And that my hormones and mood swings haven't kicked in for two."

"Yeah okay I'm ready for all that. So when did you find out?"

"I had a feeling that I was but it was confirmed Thursday during my doctor visit. We are four weeks pregnant next week."

"Damn baby I'm more excited than a mug right now."

"You want a girl?"

"Yeah. That shocks you?"

"Yeah it did."

"Do you want another girl?"

"It really doesn't matter but I think SJ might want a brother to even the playing field."

"It really doesn't matter to me either because this one will not be our last. Girl or boy I am hyped that my baby is carrying my baby, as he kisses her on the forehead."

"Reign and I have repeated our mother's and we didn't even plan this. The only difference is I am marrying her husband's homeboy and this is my third child and her second one."

"That is crazy for real."

"You wait until I tell her she is going to freak out. Oh my God our mother's are totally going to be the happiest grandmothers in the world. I hope they let your mother in, she said with a big smile."

"She ain't got a chance in hell do she?"

Jazz takes her hands and places them on the side of his face and brings him closer and whispers, "She really doesn't but I'm going to try my best to make sure she does."

"I really would appreciate it baby and so would my mother," he said with a nervous laugh.

"How do you want to do this announcement? Easy breezy or a dinner?"

"Let's do it at my mom's house after Thanksgiving, on the weekend?"

"That will work since my family is coming here for the weekend."

"Cool that works. In two weeks we will let the family know of our new addition to the Gray family. Dang babe you will be pregnant coming down the aisle in June."

"Thank God I haven't picked out my wedding dress yet. It's going to need a lot of altering. This also changes what I originally wanted. It's okay though I'm sure I can find something beautiful."

"I'm sure you will baby. You have made my day. I can't wait to tell the world that you are carrying my baby."

"Our baby."

"Not yet it isn't," he says as he brings her in for a hug.

# *Chapter Sixteen: Absalom*

High school football is a big thing in the Butler's family thanks to my big little brother Abs. Not to brag or anything but Deion Sanders has nothing on him. He plays that position and doesn't showboat. High school coaches run the ball against them because they are scared to throw against him. He has them terrified and we love it and so do the scouts. It's Friday and I'm back in Charlotte with the girls and Mersades. She wanted to come and  support her "friend." Reign and Montez are coming up later and he will have all his family and friends here. The Butler family do not come short with gear okay. We all have our Abs Clutch t-shirts and hats on. Of course we have the best poster boards made by his nieces and our family will be the loudest in the crowd. We shut it down every game and now that it's the playoffs it's really on.

"This has to feel crazy. All this hype how do you stay calm?"

"I'm not calm, trust my adrenaline is crazy right now. I just have to stay away from the family before they have me wilding out.

"You are conserving your energy?"

"Right. I'm glad you made it to see me play."

"I missed a lot of your regular season games no way I was missing this."

"My sister didn't bug you about us did she?"

"Actually no. We talked about everything but you. I was waiting on her to do it but she didn't."

"We are not in the clear though she most definitely is scheming."

"Well when we are ready to tell them we will. Until then we will continue saying friends which isn't a complete lie."

"It's hard when you're here though. You don't know how bad I wanted to hug and kiss you when you walked in."

"What's stopping us now."

"Nothing," he says as he pulls her by the waist and they embrace in a hug. "Damn baby I missed you. It's been a long week.

"Thanksgiving break is coming up and then we are on Christmas break. We have plenty of time for one another."

"Yeah but I don't know how much longer we can keep this a secret. Someone is about to discover we are more than just friends."

"Yeah your nosy ass sister."

"My dad and Sean think that too, not just my sister."

"Because she put it in their heads at the time that we were truly friends."

"Okay, my sister is a good PI, I can agree with you on that."

"Thank you. Call a spade a spade."

"Let's not take these few moments alone and waste it on that. When we could be doing this."

He pulls her closer to him and they start kissing. They were outside under the hickory tree in the backyard, being hidden by the leaves. They were really into one another that for those few moments there they had disappeared from the world.

"Abs ready to go for tonight, " Reign asked David.

"Yeah we put in some extra sessions in the gym last night after practice. He's as ready as it gets. I need to grab him and get out of here the coach wants them there an hour early to go over film. Have you all seen him?"

"I haven't but I'm sure he's with Sades let me call him," Jazz offered.

"What's going on sis?"

"Where are you and Sades? Dad is looking for you. He said you have to meet with the team to look at some tape."

"We are in the backyard. I'm on my way."

"Dad said to meet him in the front he already has your stuff."

"Alright I'm coming."

"Back to the real world?"

"Unfortunately. See you after the game?"

"Yes you will. Good luck baby."

"I don't need luck with you here, you're all the luck I need."

"I got you Abs, as she kisses him on the lips and heads back towards the house."

"Can I talk to you for a second,"Reign asked as she got closer to the back steps."

"Did you see that?"

"Did I see what?"

"Reign seriously, did you?"

"Did I see you and Absalom emerge from a tree that Jazz used to sneak her boyfriends too? The same tree she made out at so her parents wouldn't catch her. Is that what you are asking me?"

"Honestly we just recently became girlfriend and boyfriend. We haven't been lying."

"Recently? How recent?"

"A month."

"Oh that is recent. Did you wait a month after you and Dallas broke up?"

"More like six weeks after that."

"I see. He do know you are waiting to be married before having sex correct?"

"Yes. I also know he's not a virgin. We know each other pretty well since we were friends first."

"I will keep you two secret for now, it's not my secret to tell."

"Thank you Reign we appreciate it."

"No problem, just make sure you'll tell them soon. I feel bad keeping this from your brother and Jazz. Especially your brother who has no clue. I most definitely do not want to keep this from him. You know you just put Jazz back on high alert with the getaway to the backyard, right? That's her old stomping place. She knows all the blind spots and taught them to Abs."

"No worries sis, everyone will know soon. I promise."

"Alright, well  help me pack the stuff in the car. That way we can get you in those bleachers to cheer on your boo."

"Thanks Reign."

"No problem babe."

      The game was good, Abs team could go all the way this year. My brother is a beast out there, they really hate to see him coming. After the second quarter the coach refused to call a throwing play his way. That made his coach counter with putting Abs as a corner blitz. That QB was going to see him one way or another and the coach made sure of it. When the game was over my brother had two interceptions, four knockdowns, three sacks, and six tackles.

"Damn man! Now that's how you shut down a muthafucking offense! That defense of theirs are better than the pros almost," Montez yelled towards the fellas as they high five each other.

"Abs' is a special talent David. I know you are so proud, Rome said patting him on the back."

"He's special and I let him know every chance I get how proud I am of him. These scouts are on him hard, I don't like that and neither does Lillian. He's just a junior but they have been harassing us since eighth grade."

"Dang eighth grade that's crazy," Sean said, shaking his head.

"It's great for kids and families that are looking for a way out the hood. We don't want the NFL to be his only career or option."

"Still his skills are better than most professionals and you two have done a great job keeping him grounded and focus on his academics." Rome said

"Look at Lillian. She is so superstitious she has been doing this since little league."

"Leave my mama alone. Lord she can't help herself mama Lene," she said laughing.

"Your mama is crazy baby, she has been that way since middle school. Poor Absalom has been dealing with it since he was six years old."

"She really does this after every game? She goes on the field and checks on him before he can go into the locker room," Mersades asked.

"Every game," they all answered in unison.

"I remember his first game playing JV. He stayed on the field so she could do her regular routine. The defense coach yells for him to come on and be with the team. Mama Lilly looked at him then reached in her purse and told the coach to come here. She handed him her card and told him if she wasn't allowed to check her son after each game. Not only was she going to sue him, the school and the county. She was not only going to take them for every dollar they weren't worth, but the cents left over as well. Ever since then, no other coach had a problem with her doing this after every game." Reign told Mersades.

"A bad ass mom, I can dig that," Sades said laughing.

"Why do you think we call her for everything dealing with the law? My mama doesn't play when it comes to her children, family, and friends. She's a true rider or ride to the wheels falls off."

"She will still be pushing that car even with the wheels off. She will make sure we will reach our destination," Charlene added. "I thought she would leave that and join me on becoming a judge. But she was so serious about becoming Claire Huxtable. Girl get your butt up here that boy is fine! The rest of the team wants to leave sometime tonight!"

"Shut up Charlene! I'm coming dang!"

"Why do they sound like you and Jazz."

"Don't do us like that, Sades. It's a long ass walk from Charlotte to Greenville," Jazz teased.

"A long walk," Reign said laughing.

"Lillian come on! We are ready to eat," Rome yells from the bleachers.

"Rome I know you all can see I'm coming! Stop rushing me!"

"Lawd let me go help mommy before she causes a hunger riot."

As everyone makes their way back to the cars. Sades receives a text message from Abs asking her to wait for him at the bleachers. He let her know he caught  a ride to the restaurant so they could have some more alone time. Mersades asked Montez if it was okay for her to ride with him instead. He gives her a concerned look but with Reign's encouragement he breaks down and says yes. She watches them disappear to the parking lot and then turns her focus back to the football field. She was proud of Abs tonight he got two interceptions, four knockdowns, and three sacks. The defense coach uses him for everything, thanks to his dad training he's able to do it. She could tell that helps him stay focused when he's out there. Finally he emerges on the field with a guy and a girl and they all have bags. She makes her way down the bleachers to meet them halfway.

"Stay right there, Sades I don't need you getting hurt on my watch. Not the track star, your brother would kill me!" He yells as he comes through the gate.

"What?! How am I going to get hurt coming down these bleachers."

"I don't know but your brother has text me four times in the last twenty seconds and he said if you twist an ankle. He was going to end my football career! Hell at this point I'm carrying you to Antwan's car!"

"Are you serious? He sent you that many messages? He just left."

"I don't even know you or your brother but somehow he texted me and told me I better drive like I had Miss Daisy in the back of my ride. I text him back and ask who is Miss Daisy? He put in big caps GOOGLE IT!"

"I had to explain to both of these knuckleheads who she was, a girl said laughing. "Hey my name is Chantel and this is Antwan my boyfriend. It's nice to finally meet you Mersades. Abs talks about you all the time. I feel like I already know you at this point."

"I know a little about you two. It's finally good to put a face to the stories. Are you ready for basketball season?"

"Girl yes! We already started conditioning and with me almost done with cheerleading for the football team. Let's just say I can't wait to exchange these pum pums for sneakers."

"I hear you. Good game tonight Antwan. Four touchdowns is very impressive."

"Thank you. They are calling me the next Drew Brees with height," he said laughing.

"Okay I can see that she said laughing with them. "And baby you were amazing out there, you were straight killin them on the field tonight."

"I had to give my girl a show tonight."

"I thought you've been to his games before?" she asked.

"First time as his girlfriend but yeah you are right I have been to a few games. I just didn't get introduced until now."

"I can't believe you two are keeping up with that lie."

"Boo leave them alone they say they were friends. Leave it at that."

"I'm just saying I watched you two on YouTube it just didn't look like you two were just friends."

"Trust we got that a lot but we were truly friends. Just friends with incredible chemistry that we couldn't ignore anymore."

"Okay not to be nosy."

"Meaning she is about to be all in your business."

"Shut up Twan! Anyway is this why you and what was his name again? I know his name is a city, um"

"Dallas." Sades answers

"Yes Dallas. Is this why you two broke up because of the YouTube channel?"

"Um it had something to do with it but it wasn't the main reason. He wanted to date girls that were, how should I put it, sexual active."

"Oh you are nice. He was a piece of shit in other words. Got it girl. These boys think all we are supposed to do is spread our legs wide for them. Too much love and hip hop in their world. I'm not stretching my legs wide unless I'm getting ready for a game and if Twan wants to be a POS like boys like Dallas he can exit out at any time."

"How the hell are you throwing my name in this? I never once pressured you or will I ever pressure you into something you are not ready for. Now shut that craziness up and put on your seatbelt."

"Here let me get that for you baby, as he opens the door for Sades. Please buckle up, I have a feeling Tez is going to be in the parking lot waiting."

As they get on the road and make their way to the restaurant. They were being encouraged by Twan and Chante to go ahead and let the family know they were a couple now. While they had the  family together and in a great mood, plus they would be there to support them. Mersades agreed but Abs was dragging his feet for one person only and that was Montez. He was more afraid of him then he was of Papa Lucas.

"I'm just saying Abs man. Jazz already thought you two were together when you weren't. You really think her suspicion is not at an all time high at this moment," Twan ask him

"I know y'all right we should go ahead and tell them tonight. We just wanted her parents to be present at the time."

"Oh that's easy. Facetime them in."

"I mean I'm not scared to tell my parents. Montez Lucas Santos is who he is having a problem with."

"Well girl ater tonight I can see why, plus have you seen a mirror of yourself? He has a right to be in bodyguard mode at all times. You are looking like Apollonia sitting back there."

"Apollonia wow."

"You never heard that before?"

"Um no."

"Who they say you look like then?"

"Um no one famous that I can recall and most definitely not Apollonia. I get compared to a lighter version of my mother a lot."

"Your mother is dark skin?"

"Yes."

"Does she look like a dark skinned Apollonia?"

"Um I can't say I ever thought that about my mother. Now you are going to make me really look at her and compare her to Apollonia," she said laughing.

"I'm just saying everyone has a look alike and you are giving me Apollonia vibes especially with your hair wavy like that."

"I mean she's a very beautiful woman so thank you. Just no one ever said that to me before. You are the first."

"I swear baby you are crazy."

"She doesn't look like Apollonia to you either Twan?"

"Nah babe she doesn't."

"Abs what about you? Do you see it?"

"Well since I have seen her mother she does look like her mother. I'm with Sades now I'm going to be looking at her mother comparing the two. Because now I can't get the image out of my head."

"Anyway y'all get on my nerves," she said laughing. "Sades let's follow each other on social media."

"That's cool with me. Here is my @ it's the same for all the apps. Sades Benz Santos."

"Cute girl I like that. Mine is Chantels It All."

"Why are you all so creative with these names. Why can't you just use your names and be done with it," Abs asked

"Right man they are naming themselves like they are Social Media Famous. Mine is Simple AntwanQBJones."

"Right and mine is Absalom Abs Butler."

"Simple and boring," they both said at the same time laughing.

As they pulled up to the restaurant Montez was outside waiting on them like Abs predicted. He looked at Mersades with concern in his eyes and she held his hand to let him know that they had this. As Twan parked the car he turned to them and gave them the head nod. The boys get out of the car and open the door for their girls. Mersades grabs Abs' hand again as they walk towards her brother.

"Babe your hands are sweating badly."

"Did your brother grow the last time I saw him?"

"No Abs he hasn't. Chill he likes you."

"Yeah that was before I started dating his sister."

"What's this? When you need helped across the parking lot in sneakers, he asked in a serious tone.

"Tezzy, he's being a gentleman like you."

"Really? It seems to me it's more than that. Why don't you all go in and sit with the family. No not you, you stay out here with me."

"Tez this is his dinner"

"He will be there shortly Mersades, go in with the family. No voy a decirte otra vez!"

"No tienes que gritarme, me voy."

"Take a walk with me Absalom."

"Okay but um I think my sisters Jazz and Reign are waiting on me."

"Your parents too, I still need you to take this walk with me."

"What's on your mind?"

"I thought you said that you and my sis were just friends? What happened to that?"

"Um well we um"

"Absalom what happened to the "we are just friends" line you were giving me and the family? It's a simple question."

"At the time we were just friends. I wasn't lying about that. But when her and Dallas broke up I no longer wanted to be just a friend. I wanted to be her boyfriend, so I asked her if we could be exclusive and she said yes."

"I see. Here hop in."

"I thought we were just taking a friendly walk?"

"Now we're about to take a friendly ride."

"Montez man, I'm really hungry. Can we postpone this after we eat?"

"Nah let's go get this understanding now. Hop in amigo."

"Um you well yeah okay."

"Listen I have been protective over Maitea and Mersades ever since I could walk. Although I'm Tea's little brother I didn't play any games when boys wanted to be her boyfriend. Then Mersades was born and my big brother mode really kicked in because I had so much practice with Tea."

"I understand that. I'm like that with Jazz."

"Exactly you want to protect her as much as you can. Now you do know my sister decided to wait until she was married before having sex right?"

"Yes we have discussed that."

"If at any time it becomes too much for you, end the relationship. Do not try to pressure her into having sex with you."

"I will end the relationship."

"Are you sexually active?"

"I have had sex, yes. Actively doing it, no."

"I hear you Abs just know if I find out that you are trying to pressure her. I'm going to break both your wrist.We understand one another?"

"Yeah I hear you loud and clear."

"Good. Let's go in and celebrate your victory tonight."

"Right behind you"

"Well tonight was interesting."

"I told you all that they were going to end up together, and I was right."

"Now that they have announced it, shit feels weird."

"They live in different cities and can't really see one another unless we make it happen. This is the best thing for my brother and Mersades. It will be fine."

"Jazz, your brother has friends with cars and he is trying for his license during Christmas break. That alone should let you know two hours apart is nothing for them to see each other."

"It's still fine. My brother knows she is saving herself for marriage and he will not pressure her. Plus school is still in and they both play sports and do summer camps for those activities. I think you and Montez need to relax."

"I'm more relaxed than Tez, that's who you should be concerned about. Dallas was a virgin himself, your brother is not in that category. I know when I had sex for the first time. I became addicted."

"That's you, that's not my brother. He's not sexually active like that."

"How do you know? Because he told you that? You know teenage boys don't tell their parents everything"

"Let me cut you off right there. I'm not his parents, I'm his sister and we are tight."

"Yeah so tight he denied his true feelings he had for Sades and lied to not only us but you as well."

"Okay that's true only because of the situation. When it comes to these girls or  life in general he comes to me a lot and he's no sex addicted."

"You are a sex addicted that's the only person I care to know about," he says as he gets behind her.

"Aye and you know it," she sings as she begins to grind on him slowly.

"Let me help you out of this."

"See this is exactly how we made this one."

"Just know if you keep on being this damn sexy, we are going to make plenty more."

Nothing and I mean absolutely nothing is better then morning sex. Not just any kind of morning sex the three am kind that have you waking up and wanting it. Especially when your sex partner is smelling extra good. I mean ladies you know that cologne that had you sexing him all night and wake up and he's still smelling like it? Y'all know that cologne or aroma that stays on his favorite shirt you like to wear when he's gone out of town, or favorite boxers that have your scent and his because of extra activities you all do in public. All because he has on that damn cologne that drives you crazy. If your man doesn't wear a certain fragrance that makes you say in your Scorpion voice, "get your ass over here and drop dem draws." I suggest you find some and buy it for him. Now let me tell y'all about last night and him smelling all good. It made your girl ride him till he fell asleep. I  didn't give him a chance to put it on me. He had no problem with it either. He gave me some strokes that almost knocked my ass off, but you can call me rodeo girl. Because I had strapped that down and was not about to be thrown off. That was a few hours ago, it's about to be two thirty in the morning and that cologne has me licking him slow. I have him moving a little as I tease him. Massaging his scrotums before giving him his wake up blow job. As I take in the tip I can feel him becoming bigger in my mouth. He grabs my head slowly guiding me the way he wanted it. I love it when he holds me there for a few seconds until I gag on it. Yes my man loves for his dick to be wet and sloppy. It turns him on and he is ready to blow my back out.

"Damn Jazz you are going to make me pre nut."

"Me? This all you. I was doing you slow, that's you being aggressive this morning."

"I mean I was sleeping good and then woke up to some spectacular head and for a moment I thought I was still sleeping."

"That's the lie you are going with."

"Mm come here babe and sit her on my face."

Without any hesitation I squatted and balanced myself while he went to work on my wet lips. The way he was taking every drip like it was his last meal turned me on even more. Before I knew I was slowly riding his face. A few "damn baby right there and ohhh that's my spot" moments later he finally flipped me and was giving it to me from the back. When I'm in this position it's pretty much a wrap for me. Sean knows how to make my back arch and knees shake. He gets in so deep, I'm talking balls deep and all that has me having multiple orgasms that it makes me tap out. I literally lay flat out and beg him to hold me. We have come a long way from the first year of dating. I use to think Marcus was going to be the best I ever had in the sex department. But after finding out about my infidelities Sean has surpassed Marcus. As we lay in pure darkness with only a little moonlight peeping in from the window. I feel sleep about to take over as I try to stay focus on his after sex talk.

"Damn Jazz. Just damn."

"Damn Jazz? Hell I should be saying damn Sean! You know you took that round hands down."

"Did I? I don't know babe I think it was your wetness that made it a damn situation for both of us. Is this what it's going to be during your pregnancy? If so I need to hit the gym to keep up."

"She has been wet a lot lately huh? I think it's the foreplay that has her like that."

"Whatever it is I'm not complaining."

"I'm not complaining at least for now I'm not. Is it a supermoon tonight? The moon is really bright coming through the blinds or am I tripping?"

"It's just a full moon that has risen and the sun probably about to come up pretty soon."

"What time is it?"

"A little after four."

"We better get some sleep then, check out at eleven. Then pick up the girls from Marcus by one."

"Are you going to stay asleep this time, remember you woke me up."

"I promise. I will now go to sleep."

Check out time was at eleven and we both knew this. We discussed this before falling back to sleep this morning. In our minds we were going to do the right thing; wake up, shower, get dressed and head out. Two out three ain't bad we did wake up in time and we did shower. It was a wasted shower but it did take place. I don't know what happened to be honest. You would think we had never seen each other naked and wet before. We are acting like some damn college students this morning. The sex was on point and paying extra is going to be worth it. I took a shower first this time and dressed in the bathroom. Now he is in there doing the same thing. I guess it's going to be a fast food restaurant because I'm not going to be late getting the girls from Marcus. I don't give him any reason to talk bad about me when it comes to our co-parenting. That's one thing he couldn't say about me that I was a bad mother or I ever tried to keep his girls from him. I even put my move to Utah on hold from him. Although we are going to have to visit that topic again once Sean and I are married. We have been discussing franchising Noir Propre in unexpected places and places where it is needed the most. Midwest and the south is where my focus will be. I hate when my thoughts are stopped because someone wants to call at the wrong damn time. That's just great, it's Sean's phone. "Baby! Dana calling you!"

"Answer it! I'm still in the shower!"

Who the fuck said I wanted to answer it and talk to her. "Hey Dana girl what's up?"

"Hey girl! Nothing much, where ya man at?"

"He is in the shower. Do you want to just call him back?"

"I'm surprised that you are not there with him," she said laughing.

This bitch. "Well now we tried that earlier and we didn't get far, so this is actually our second shower. I'm pretty sure you don't want any more details then that."

"No, I'm good on that."

That's what I thought.

"I was just calling because SJ needs soccer shoes and I was seeing what time you all were going to be back here."

"Oh okay." Now she knows damn well we get back around four every damn time. "We should be there no later than four thirty. Did you want us to stop by the mall here or you wanted him to see if he could make Haywood Mall when we get there?"

"If you can get him and take him here. I think he will need him to make sure they fit right."

"Sounds good. We will call when we are close."

"Thanks Jasmine, I really appreciate it."

"No problem. See you later." Next time I'm going to let that go straight to voicemail. He never talks to Marcus when he calls and he was like that way before I cheated. I wish he would say differently. Now what the hell was I doing before she called. Oh yeah taking this stuff to the car. "Where are you going with that?"

"Um, doesn't the luggage belong in the car? I mean I could be wrong but I think that's where it goes baby."

"Smart ass! Put that shit down! Didn't I tell your hard headed ass I had it when I got out the shower?"

"I don't recall."

"Man, move. What did Dana want?"

"She wants you to take SJ to get some soccer shoes today."

"Damn! I forgot about that, glad she called to remind me. Is this everything?"

"Yes my chocolate baby, that's everything."

"Jazz did you grab the charges, I'm tired of buying new ones every time we leave Charlotte."

"They are in my bag."

"Are you sure?"

"Yes baby. When Dana called I grabbed them and put them in there while I was talking to her."

"Bet. Let's go get these babies of ours and head home. Did you want to eat in or out when we get them?"

"Let's do fast food, then when we get SJ we will eat at The Cheesecake Factory."

"Sounds good to me. What do you want?"

"BK."

"Are you sure?"

"Sean what do you want to eat?"

"BK is fine."

"No it's not. What did you want?"

"Five Guys."

"The girls are not going to want that. We will get BK and you can hit up the guys."

"Nah if we all are not eating there then I will do what the majority wants. BK it is. Why can't he ever beat us here?"

"Sean we are thirty minutes early."

"I know.Still he never beat us here, we are always waiting for him."

"Come here."

"Are you going to distract me?"

"Of course. Take a selfie with me, I'm feeling cute and you're sexy with those shades on."

"How many pics are you going to take for the Gram?"

"One more. Let me see your shades. I should have bought myself one. They look so good on me."

"Stop trying to steal my father's day gift from the kids. Give them back."

"I paid for them."

"I love you for doing that, now hand them over."

"Hold on let me get a pic by myself in them. Look how sexy I am, baby."

"You are sexy and even more sexy without them."

"You get on my nerves here."

"You love me though and that's all that matters." He leans in and they kiss. "Let me stop before we do the nasty in broad daylight."

"Right, especially the way you were kissing me. I almost forgot where we were."

"Always blaming me for your seductive ways."

"Excuse you bae? You kiss me. All I was trying to do was take some selfies with your shades. How did this get flipped on me?"

"You want me to distract you? Come here," he says mocking her voice.

She gives him a playful shove and says, "I did not say it like that. You play all day Mr. Funny man. Is that Marcus pulling up?"

"Yeah that's him. I will grab the girls and their stuff. I will be right back." She couldn't believe it Sean was actually getting the girls without her assistance. As she watched from the rear view mirror she saw him give Marcus the head nod and opened the backdoor. Yas was knocked out and he was carrying her to the car. Marcus grabbed Marcella and she could see that she was also knocked out. They strapped the girls in and Marcus headed back to retrieve one more bag and was bringing it to her.

"My parents took them to the waterpark this morning and tired them out. Here are some souvenirs they bought for them"

"I know they hated to leave."

"Actually they were ready to go. They were there for about three hours so they had enough."

"I'm glad. I'm about to join them and get me a nap in as well."

"Alright I will see you next Friday, you all be safe."

"You too. I'm so proud of you. I thought you were going to leave it to me."

"You are about to be my wife in a few months, I need to get over that, I thought today would be perfect to do so."

Thank you. That's all I ask, that you try." She kisses him on the lips and holds his hand as they head back home.

# *Chapter Eighteen: Unexpected*

Time has been flying by. I can't believe today is the first day of Andre's trial. It's been almost a year since he brutally raped her and seeing him in court made me sick to my stomach. Reign is officially eight months pregnant and Dr. Morales let the courts know that it was in her best interest that she sit this one out. He informed them of her high blood pressure and how it wasn't good for the baby for her to be there. He wanted her  to continue being on bed rest. The judge agreed, plus with the surveillance from her office camera and her statement to the police was more than enough. My mother had prepped Montez for months and he knew what was coming at him on both sides. We just had to make sure that he kept his composure during his testimony and didn't join Andre in a jail. I promised Reign that we wouldn't let that happen, well we were at least going to try and stop that from happening. My mom's plan was to ask the prosecutor to call him first and get his testimony out the way, she agreed and that's why he is up first. As everyone gets settled in they bring in Andre. He's looking around the courtroom and I knew then he was looking for Reign. I did a quick glance over at Tez and he had his eyes locked on his every move. I looked over at Sean who was towards the front and he gave me the okay signal. I closed my eyes and said a prayer to God. I ask him to give me the strength of one hundred men if Montez decides to get up and rush his sorry ass. I must have been praying for a minute because I can hear Montez asking me am I okay.

"Yes I'm fine. I just didn't know what my reaction was going to be once I saw his ass again."

"Do you want me to sit there so I can block his view from you?"

"Damn, you almost had me Tez. No I'm good where I am at and so are you."

"Jazz if I wanted to get up and fuck dude up, I would have done it by now. There's not one person in this courtroom that would be powerful enough to stop me. I promised Reign that I wouldn't get arrested. I'm not going to break that promise to her. I'm going to tell the judge and jury all that happened that day to the best of my ability. I'm going to let them know how this has affected her and our family after it happened. I'm going to let them know the only reason he is still breathing is because of my wife and my kids. I'm going to leave that stand and when I'm done I'm heading home to be with my wife. I promised her one million times this morning that I wasn't going to fuck him up. I'm a patient man and I know God will give my opportunity to beat the shit out of him. When that day comes no one will be able to stop me."

"Okay I hear you and totally agree. Just remember she can go into labor at anytime and

"Jazz! I'm good, I don't need a pep talk from you!"

Everyone in the courtroom now focuses on them. Jazz thinking to herself that maybe she should have just let things be after he said he was good. Now his mother Mia was making her way towards them and close behind her was Charlene, Romain, and David.

"Hey baby let's step outside for a minute before you have to get on the stand."

"Mom"

"Just for a minute Tez I promise you will not miss a thing."

"This would be a good time to make sure you are ready for the cross. Just a couple of minutes and we will be right back."

"Alright Charlene let's do this," he says as he gets up.

As he leaves he realizes that there were a lot of people crying in the courtroom. He figured they were all overwhelmed not only by his outburst but the way the women surrounded him to calm him down. How Romain and David stood there shielding them from people staring and trying to see what was going on. As they walked out of the courthouse Charlene handed him the phone."

"Hey baby. Are you okay?"

"You know I'm not."

"How can I help?"

"This is hard for me baby and I'm trying real hard to channel this rage but seeing him looking for you. I-I"

"Okay. Just come home then. I'm sure the prosecutor and Lillian can have you testify later today or tomorrow"

"Daddy."

"Yes MJ that's daddy. Hold on let me speak to him and I will let you talk to him in just a minute."

"I got him," Lucas says.

"Thank you Papa Lucas."

"No problem hija."

"So what do you think, Tezzy? You want to wait and go later?"

"No baby, I'm going back in there and get this over with. I love you and I will see you later."

"I love you too and I will be here eating and waiting on you."

That made him smile as he handed the phone back to Charlene and gave David and Romain the nod that he was ready to go back in. Before he could enter his mama pulled him to the side and she prayed over him. Once she was done he felt this calmness come over him that he hasn't felt in awhile. His mother knew of his hurt, anger, and frustration and she knew only of one person that could control that. She was not about to lose her son over that demon in the courtroom. She knew as well as he did that he was needed at home and not in jail. Let karma deal with Andre and let God deal with her son's emotions. As he walked back in, he had a new power over him and for once Andre was not in control. As the defense was giving their open argument Montez closed his eyes and focused on Reign, MJ, and Roman. He listened as the defense lied about what really happened that night according to Andre. He was not about to let that lawyer put him back in that rage. Jazz was holding his hand and her leg was shaking uncontrollably. She also was trying so hard not to have an outburst and get kicked out of the courtroom. She couldn't believe that niggah actually told his lawyers that they were having an affair and that she was looking for a way out of her marriage. That what the jury were about to see on the video is two adults having rough sex. He actually said that was what Reign liked from him and that's why he left her in the office the way he did. That was just their routine, he would leave first and she would leave after him. Did his lawyer really think after the jury watched that video that they really was going to see consensual sex between two adults? She looked over at the jury and they actually looked to be feeding into his bullshit and that made her furious. She was so pissed it made her squeezed the hell out of Montez's hand.

"I know Jazz. I know. Don't worry either way he has it coming to him. In jail or as a free man that muthafucker had it coming to him."

"I am praying for jail because God knows if he doesn't, you know what I don't even want to think that way."

"Is the state ready to call their first witness?"

"We are your honor."

"Okay let's begin with the state's first witness."

"Thank you, your honor. The state would like to call Mr. Montez Santos to the stand."

"Do you swear to tell the truth the whole truth so help you God?"

"I do."

"Can you state your name to the jury for me again Mr. Santos?"

"Yes I'm Montez Lucas Santos."

"And why are you here today sir."

"The victim of the case is my wife."

"How long have you two been married?"

"Not long. It's been eight months since last week."

"Do you know my client, sitting over there?"

"Yeah."

"How do you know him?"

"He is an ex employee of my wife."

"Okay Mr. Santos let's start from the beginning of how you two met. What was your first impression of him."

"I didn't like him."

"How did you know if you were going to like him or not if you never met him before?"

"My first encounter with him wasn't good. From day one I just had bad vibes concerning him."

"How did your wife feel about him."

"She thought his resume and his work was great and that he reminded her of a female version of her."

"How did she feel once she knew you didn't like him?"

"She just reminded me it was a business move and she hired him because he was a nice fit for her company. That if things got too awkward or if he was unprofessional again she would fire him."

"Again? What did he do that made her say that?"

"When she hired him she reached out her hand to give him a handshake and he instead grabs her and brings her in with a hug."

"Did your wife tell you this?"

"No, I walked in on it."

"You saw this whole encounter with your own eyes?"

"Yes."

"Where were you to see this happen?"

"I was stopping by to take her to lunch, as I walked up the door I noticed she was finishing up her interview with him."

"Can you describe how her office is set up."

"Sure the way her office is set up is when you walk in there's a receptionist that greets you. There are five offices in the building and my wife is the last one in the back. She has two chairs that sit outside her door. On each side of the door is glass where you can see in."

"Were you sitting in one of those chairs?"

"No, I didn't have time so I was going to sit there but when I was walking up. She was getting out her desk chair making her way towards him with her hand out.

"Okay as you were walking up to her door to sit down. You see your wife walking towards the defendant with her hand out like this. In your mind she was starting or ending the interview?"

"She was ending the interview."

"How do you know that, Mr. Santos?"

"Because when I walked in her receptionist told me she was wrapping up her last interview. She was the one who sent me back there to wait."

"Okay now you say your wife extended her hand for a handshake but the defended wanted a hug instead?"

"Yeah."

"How do you know that your wife wasn't reaching out for a hug?"

"Because that's not how she reaches out for a hug. No one I know reaches out for a hug that way, especially a female. Most guys might do that when we are about to greet one another. But I never saw my wife do that ever. When she wants to give a hug to someone she reaches out with open arms like this. She does not do this to give a damn hug."

"Is it possible that the defendant thought she wanted to hug instead of a handshake."

"The defendant just wanted to embrace my wife; he didn't mistake anything."

"Objection your honor! He doesn't know my client to make such outrageous claims."

"Sustain. The jury should ignore that last statement from the witness."

"Alright Mr. Santos tell the jury what happened next."

"I walked in the office and told him to let my fiance go."

"What happened after you did that?"

"He stepped back quickly and started stuttering as I approached him."

"Did he apologize?"

"Yeah."

"What about your wife?"

"She wasn't too happy with me?"

"Why?"

"The way I bust in and was acting didn't sit well with her."

"She didn't see anything wrong with the hug?"

"I didn't say that. I said she wasn't happy with the way I busted into her office. She told me she was about to handle the situation herself and that she didn't need me to do that."

"Did she say this with the defendant's presence?"

"Not that particular argument. He was there when she told me to chill and sent him to take his drug test."

"She was more frustrated at you and not him. Did that make you mad that she wasn't angry or upset about that?"

"Nah that's just my wife, she is professional at all times. I knew she wasn't going to show out and I know she wasn't going to stop me. She let me handle it to an extent and then cut me off when she felt like I was going too far."

"She knew you were reaching the point of no longer talking?"

"Yeah she could tell I was about to get physical."

"Yet she still hired him."

"She said she would handle that situation if it would ever happen again. That he was just excited because she hired him. She didn't think anything else of it."

"Did you?"

"Everyday  since that occurred."

"The defense says that she was actually having an affair with Andre. How do you feel about that?"

"I feel nothing, about lies."

"You don't think she carried out a relationship with the defendant?"

He laughs at her question before saying, "No."

"Why do you laugh at that?"

"My wife has been through a horrible relationship where he cheated on her multiple times and she never cheated on him. She wouldn't cheat on me because that's not who she is, plus she wouldn't have the time especially with him."

"He claims on business trips and during after hours at the office."

"I don't give a fuck what he's claiming I just told you she wouldn't had the time."

"Mr. Santos I know this is hard but let's try to stay respectful in the courtroom."

"My apologies, your honor."

"No problem. Please continue Mrs. Grant."

"Why are you so sure they never had an affair?"

"She has a hidden camera in her office and it has been there way before he was hired on. Not just her office but throughout the building. She only went out of town with him twice. Therefore this little fantasy of his is impossible. She never looked at him like that. Ever."

"Okay let's go to the day when you discovered your wife. What did you all do that day?"

"I left for work that morning and stopped back home for lunch. She was working on her proposal when I walked in. I had to make her put her laptop down so we could eat the food I brought home. It was a normal lunch. We talked and spent time with our son before I left again."

"When you were there for lunch was your son up?"

"He was. He was in his swing when I walked in."

 "When you left, was he still up?"

"Yeah but we tired him out so he was on his way to taking another nap."

"When you arrived it was just her and your son."

"Yes."

"When you left, who was there?"

"My wife and my son."

"Did your wife know your routine? Did she know when you would be home?"

"No because I never knew."

"Do you ever call and let her know when you are coming home?"
"Sometimes. If I think I'm going to be too late."
"Did you call her on that particular day?"
"No."
"Did you come home late?"
"No."
"Did you get home at your usual time that day?"
"Sure. It was a little after four when I called it quits for the day."
"When you got home what happened?"
"Reign and my sister was finishing cooking and setting the table when I walked in."
"Your sister?"
"Yes my younger sister stays with us from time to time. Permanently during summer occasionally during school. That particular week she was with us while our parents were out of town."
"Where is your son at this time."
"He was asleep when I came in."
"So everything was normal that evening. Nothing out of the ordinary?"
"Just our typical day."
"What happened next?"
"We sat down and ate and my sister was telling us about her training that day. I remember her asking Reign about a particular track shoes she wanted. Since my wife has a connection with Nike, my sister was asking her if she could get her a certain pair. After that we cleaned up and decided to take a walk."
"How often do you all take walks after dinner?"
"We rarely do that."
"Any particular reason you all decided to go that night?"
"She wanted to walk because she didn't walk any that week. She usually walks twice to help lose the baby weight she put on."
"Okay take the jury on the walk you guys were having."
"She was telling me that she needed to get to the office tonight because she had fallen behind on some of her major accounts."
"Did you know she was behind?"
"No."
"What time was this discussion?"
"We were walking around five thirty or a little after that."
"What did you say after she told you, she was behind?"
"I joked with her and said MJ got you off your game. She laughed and said he's not the reason. She asked me ``was I cool with her going back to the office to get caught up?"
"Why did she ask you that?"
"New moms think new dads are hopeless and we can't take care of the kids without them." The women in the jury started smiling and nodding their head yes as he spoke on it. "She was

concerned about MJ more than me, I told her I had it. I also told her not to stay in the office too long."

"What was her response to that?"

"She said she would be home around nine o'clock, ten the latest."

"Mr. Santos were you okay with that?"

"Yeah I had no problem with my wife going to her office to get work done. I joked and said if she's not home by ten thirty I was coming to drag her out."

"What was her response to that?"

"She laughed and said I will drag myself out if I stay past ten."

"What happened after this discussion?"

"We walked back home and I ran her bath water. We do what married couples do. She then got dressed, and before she left. She kissed me and MJ goodbye and left."

"Did you and your wife have sex any time that day."

"Yes."

"If the DNA test shows your semen in her that day. That would be accurate and not suspicious?"
Correct.

"Let me ask you this. Did you have to wear condoms with your wife before you two were married?"

"In the beginning of the relationship."

"When did she make you stop?"

"When we were engaged but she stayed on birth control."

"Somewhere she stopped with the birth control because she was pregnant before you were married right?"

"I wouldn't say she stopped. She probably just forgot to take them some days. I know she wouldn't take it during her menstrual. She hated how she felt when it was the time of the month."

"If your wife was having this affair would she be reckless and not make him use condoms?"

"My wife was pregnant when she hired him. That was the whole purpose of the mass hiring she did that month. She wanted to start working at home and travel less. Reign would never put her unborn child at risk." His defense is nothing but lies!"

"Objection your honor!"

"Sustain. Mr. Santos please stick to answering the prosecution questions. The jury is to ignore the last line Mr. Santos said about the defense."

"I will move on your Honor. Mr Santos do you remember what your wife was wearing that day before she left the house?"

"Yeah she had her laidback clothes on. Nike t-shirt, jogging pants, and tennis shoes. She also wrapped her hair up in bond. She didn't look like a woman going to work when she left."

"She didn't have on her regular work attire?"

"It wasn't any point too. The office hours are from eight thirty am to five pm."

"Do her employee's be in the office after those hours?"

"Yeah if they have a heavy workload."

"It wouldn't surprise you if some employees were still there?

"Not at all."

"On that particular day to your acknowledgement was anyone in the office when your wife arrived?"

"At the time she left no, I didn't know who was all there."

"When did you find out Mr. Santos?"

"When we spoke later."

"Who called who first?"

"I called her. It was ten o'clock and she didn't call to say she was on her way. I was a little concerned."

"Why the concern?"

"We always called each other if we were going to be out late so we wouldn't stay up worrying about one another. It's been like that since day one. When it was ten oclock and I hadn't heard from her I just called to see if she decided to stay later."

"Did she decide to stay later."

"No."

"Did she seem upset or mad that you called her?"

"Not at all. When she picked up you could hear laughter and people talking in the back. I could tell she was having a good time and figured that's why she hadn't called."

"What happened next?"

"I asked her if she was working or having a party?"

"What was her response?"

"She laughed and said both. I asked her if she knew what time it was and she said no. Then she said it must be passed the time I said I was going to be home and I told her it was."

"What did she say then?"

"That her and the girls were packing it up and heading home."

"She didn't mention the defendant?"

"Unless he's a girl then no."

"Did you ask her who was all there?"

"She told me before I could."

"What did she say?"

"She said it started out with her Tamara and Dre. Then Jazz stopped by with some news and that's how work became a party."

"Did she ever tell you that Andre was still there or not?"

"No."

"How do you know he was no longer there?"

"When I called and she said me and the girls."

"It could have been possible that he was there but not in her office?"

"Yeah. All I knew when I called her that was the whole conversation. They all were working on the Nike project. Later Jazz stopped by and before she knew it time had passed by and she lost track of it."

"Mr. Santos, was that the end of the conversation?"

"Once we discussed all that she said she would see me in a little while. I told her again if she wasn't back home in forty five minutes. I was coming to get her."

"Did she take you seriously?"

"I doubt it. I said it in a jokingly manner because she laughed when I said it. She said if she's not home by then she would drag herself out."

"Your honor is it okay if we take a break right here."

"I have no objection. Is that okay with the defense."

"It is your honor."

"Okay court is in a fifteen minutes recess. Mr. Santos you may step down. Remember you are still under oath."

"I understand."

"Alright court is now in recess."

"You are doing a good job, baby. Just keep your eyes on the prosecutor and not him."

"That's the plan mama."

"Well continue to stick with it and this will be all over for you today and you can get home to your family."

"I'm trying Charlene."

"I know you are sweetheart. I know you are."

"Do you want to grab something from the vending machine?"

"Yeah Sean let's do that."

"Jazz you want anything?"

"No babe you two go ahead I'm good."

"Man you are about to speak on finding Reign. I just wanted to make sure you were straight?"

"I feel like I'm about to go to jail. This muthafucker is going to make me break my promise. I know I'm going to look at him just to see his reaction. When I do tell the jury how I found my wife. I swear Sean if I don't like what I see I'm hopping off that stand and going straight for him!"

"Listen whatever you decide to do just know I got your back. On a hundred Tez man I got you."

"Preciate you bruh."

"No problem man. Let's get back in here."

"Are you coming."

"Yeah, give me a moment. My phone is vibrating."

"Okay I see Lillian coming my way. I will see you in there."

"Hey Reign what's going on?"

"Put Tezzy on the phone."

"He's not with me anymore. Lillian came and got him."

"Sean, keep it real with me. Do papa Lucas need to bring me up there?"

"Yeah Reign. I don't think he's going to be able to keep that promise to you unless you are here to help him. To be honest with you if he does decide to snap, I'm going to help him because this shit has been built up for over a year."

"Sean that's not what I wanted to hear. Instead of talking him down, you fan the flame on the fire?"

"This is hard on him Reign and he is trying but damn the muthafucker who raped his wife is feets away.

"Let me speak with my mom or his mother, Sean."

"They are in the courtroom. We are about to resume soon."
"Damn it Sean!"
"Let me speak to Mr. Lucas. I can fix this Reign."
"What's going on Sean?"
"Montez is about to snap and the only person that can stop him is with you. But she doesn't need to be here knowing her due date is coming up. So I was thinking if you bring MJ that would stop him from doing something stupid."
"And you couldn't talk him out of it?"
"It's not up to me Mr. Lucas. He said if he didn't like ol boy's facial expression he was going to get him."
"Damn it! Where is my wife?"
"They are all in the courtroom."
"Damn it! Alright, shit! I guess I'm bringing him."
"Get her here as fast as you can."
"Leaving now."
"Babe what's taking you so long they are about to get started again?"
"Montez is going after Dre."
"What! How do you know?"
"He just told me."
"Damn it! Come on let's get back in here!"
"There's more."
"What?!"
"Lucas is bringing MJ up here."
"You told Reign?"
"I couldn't talk him out of it, Jazz. The only person that can stop him is Reign but I know she is not supposed to be up here so Lucas is bringing MJ."
"Sean come on! She is not staying away from this courthouse after you told her that. Why did you do that? You know her blood pressure is easily triggered with concern or stress and you just put her through both. I have to let everyone know what's going on.Let's go!"

Is the prosecution ready to continue?

"We are, judge."

"Mr. Santos please come back up here. You do understand that you are still under oath?"

"Yes your honor."

"Okay Mrs. Grant you may continue with your direct."

"Thank you judge. Mr. Santos we left off with you and your wife finishing up the phone conversation. What happened after you two ended the call?"

"When I got off the phone with her. I went into our son's room to check on him. I watched him for a little while before leaving him and going to the entertainment room to watch ESPN."

"How long before you realized your wife still wasn't home."

"When ESPN did the same highlights again it was an hour or so later."

"What did you do?"

"I called Reign to see where she was at but her phone went straight to VM."

"VM?"

"I'm sorry I meant voice mail."

"Did that concern you?"

"Yeah it did. So I called Jazz and she said Reign should have been home because she just ran back in to grab her laptop."

"Tell the jury what's going on in your head after hearing her best friend telling you that."

"I just knew something wasn't right. I woke up my sister so she could listen out for MJ and I went to go look for my wife."

"Did you think she was having an affair Mr. Santos?"

"No!"

"Why are you in a rush to find her?"

"My wife's phone is going straight to voicemail and her best friend is telling me that she should have been home by now."

"Never once did it cross your mind that she was with someone else?"

"No. I thought about a lot of stuff while looking for her car but cheating on me was not one of them."

"You said you were looking for her car?"

"Yes. When I left the house I drove her route when she went to the office. I thought maybe she got a flat tire and was stranded somewhere."

"Did you see her car anywhere."

"Not on the drive to the office."

"When did you see your wife's car?"

"When I arrived at the office."

"How many cars were in the lot when you arrived."

"Just hers and mine."

"What happened next Mr. Santos?"

"I checked her car and nothing was wrong with it or the tires. So I figured she went back in and decided to continue working on her Nike proposal."

"What did you do next?"

"I calmed down a little and I went into the office and saw her laptop and purse sitting on Tamara's desk."

"Did that seem odd to you?"

"At that point I panicked again because it threw my initial thought out the window. If she did decide to stay late. She would have her purse and laptop with her."

"What did you do?"

"I took off running to her office screaming her name."

"Did she respond to you Mr. Santos."

"No," he says in almost a whisper.

"I'm sorry Mr. Santos can you speak up so the jury can hear you."

"I said no."

"Do you need a moment Mr. Santos." At this moment Montez had checked out. The prosecutor's words had turned into mumbles and his eyes were focused on Andre with so much rage. Andre saw that Montez was staring at him and decided to fuck with him. He blew him a kiss and smirked at him. Sean had his eyes on Tez and he knew that his friend was about to go after him. He glanced at the door to see if Lucas was able to make it there on time and saw that he didn't. Sean knew he had to do something before Tez did something stupid so he jumped and yell, "Montez man don't do it!" It was too late he had already jumped off the stand and had tackled Andre and his attorney out of their chairs. Sean, David, and Romaine were right behind him trying to pull him off but Montez had a grip on Andre's throat. He was trying to choke the life out of him. The more they pulled on him the tighter his grip got. Finally the police officer was able to move all the men out the way and taze Montez. Reign came in but it was too late they had her husband pin down and was escorting Andre out. The judge was banging his gavel trying to get some kind of order back in his courtroom. When Reign yells, "Please let my husband go!" That's when her water broke with all of the chaos going on no one noticed it. Until she yelled again, "my water just broke!" The family ran towards her and Montez was trying to break from the cops that had him. While Lillian pleads with the judge to have Montez detained later. She tried to explain how hard it was for her client today and he did his best to stay calm. But given the circumstances it was harder for him to restrain himself.

"Mr. Santos I know this wasn't easy for you being in front of the man that is being accused of raping your wife but you can not act like this in my courtroom. What you tried to do today was take justice in your own hands and it just doesn't work that way. Do you understand?"

"I do."

"Sir that's his wife back there and she's about to go into labor. I know you have to hold him for assault and contempt. All I'm asking that one of the officers goes with him so he doesn't miss the birth of his son."

"I will set his bail at 40,000 and if you all have the bail money to get him out. He can be released to see the birth of his child. If not he will sit there until he does."

"Thank you, your honor."

"I need the courtroom cleared out and bring the jury back in so we can dismiss them for today. We will resume with this case tomorrow."

"We have that four k Montez. Don't worry you will not miss the birth of Roman."

"Please hurry Ms.Lillian."

"I'm going to get that cashier check now."

"No! Please don't take him," Reign cries out.

"Reign baby I'm so sorry," he managed to get out before the officers escorted him out.

"Reign it's okay honey we have that four thousands dollars he will be out in no time the judge just promised me. We need to get you to the hospital."

"I have to get the money for you."

"Reign really? Girl I'm not worried about that money right now. David come on and let's see if we can find TD banks."

"Okay Reign you heard her, we need to get you to the hospital," her dad says as he picks her up and they head out the courtroom."

"I hate that I had to tase you man. This is the part of the job that sucks for me. If someone did that to my wife I would have reacted the same way. That's why I took my time doing my job. If you would have choked the life out of him he would have deserved it."

"Thank you officer for just using your taser gun on me and not shooting me."

"We don't have police officers like that here, at least I haven't seen any. The gun is my last option especially in a situation like this. I knew you weren't armed if you were, then our metal detectors sucks."

"Still as a black man with a white cop nowadays. I'm just saying as a black man I should have been smarter."

"Trust me when I say. Every man in that courtroom understood. That's why the judge was quick to set a bail for you. Does your family have it, to get you out?"

"Yeah they should be on their way to get it. Hopefully my son will wait for me."

"When was her due date?"

"Next month."

"The baby should be fine."

"I pray to God he is. Now looking back at it I should have remained my ass on that stand. Now I have sent my wife into early labor for unnecessary drama."

"Yeah it was. It's hard to let the justice system handle something like this. I'm just saying if I were in your shoes, I would have reacted the same way. Well let me get back out here. I hope your family comes through for you."

"Thank you officer"

"Michael Riley you can call me Mike."

"Thank you Mike for the talk while I wait."

"No problem sir."

      As Montez waited for his bond to be paid the rest of the family were en route to the hospital. Everyone seemed on edge and were dealing with different emotions. Sean and Jazz were arguing in the car because he called Reign and told her what was going on. He already felt bad because she went into early labor but he didn't think she would have shown up. He also thought that Lucas would have talked her out of it.  David and Lillian were arguing because Lilly was about to take out four thousand dollars to bail out Montez. He didn't understand why she didn't let Reign or her parents do it. She just kept telling him it's just money and it's not like they can't afford to pay them back. She knew the money would be back in her account from one of the Moore's or Santos's. She wasn't understanding why he was so upset about her doing this for her client and best friend. Meanwhile the Moore's had arrived at the hospital and Reign was placed in a room. It seems like she wanted updates every twenty seconds on her husband. They kept telling her as soon as they knew something, she would know. It still didn't stop her from asking them. Jazz and Sean finally arrived and headed to her room. When they entered the room, the nurse had just finished putting in the epidural. It was just a matter of time before she would be feeling good and relaxed.

"I am here sis and MJ is in the waiting room with Tea and Mersades"

"Good. I know he is super excited to see his little brother. I just hope Montez is out in time."

"He will be, my parents just text and said they are on their way back to the courthouse."

"Well Jazzy, Sincere should be here pretty soon."

"Girl I wish I still have almost three months to go. But I can't wait til he gets here just as long as he waits until after June nineteenth.

"Well I thought Roman would wait until his due date. As you can see he is ready to come into this world."

"If his mama would have stayed away today maybe he wouldn't have received the extra urgency to see it."

"How did I know you were going to blame me."

"Oh I just don't blame you, I curse Sean ass all the way out on the ride here."

"That she did. That's why my ass over here being quiet now."

"Leave Sean alone, he did the right thing by calling me."

"How? You are in labor and Montez still got locked up. How was that the right thing to do?"

"I needed to be there for my husband and I would have been if the traffic wasn't slow."

"Shoulda, woulda, coulda but you didn't. My little nephew is all early because of you two."

"You are lucky these drugs have kicked in."

"Whatever chica."

"Hey Reign. I see the little man all early and ready to see his beautiful mom."

"I don't know why he's in a rush to come into this world, Dr. Morales."

"He wants to meet his mama. Where's Montez?"

"He is on his way."

"Okay good he has time she hasn't dilated much, we are at three. How are we feeling pain wise Mrs. Santos?"

"Two," she sings.

"I see the epidermal has kicked in. Alright Reign I will be back to check on you two. Everything seems to be going fine with him. His heartbeat is strong and steady."

"Okay Dr. Morales. See you in a bit."

"I remember she was like this last year. It doesn't take much to get her in a happy place," Rome said.

"Yes she is still lightweight when it comes to that," Reign's mother said
"She sure is. Well I will be back later."
"Sean let's step out and grab some food. All this drama has us hungry."
"Jazz where are you going to get food at?"
"I was going to get a salad from Pete's. My bad mama Lene and Roman I'm so hungry. I was about to leave without asking if you two wanted anything. Did you want me to bring you all something back?"
"No that's okay we will go grab something out of the cafeteria. Reign is finally asleep so we'll sneak out with you two."
        As Reign's parents leave out with Sean and Jazz. Charlene receives a phone call from Lillian saying that they had Montez and were en route to the hospital. She explained that Reign and the baby were doing fine and that she had only dilated to three. That they were going to get some food while she rested.
"Well if you are about to eat we will meet you two in the cafeteria."
"Good. Then you can give me your bank information so I can pay you back for getting my son-in-law out."
"No need Montez and Lucas already did that. I wasn't worried about it. I knew I would get it back eventually."
"You had volunteered so fast that I didn't think to say I will help you pay for it."
"I knew my baby would go crazy if he stayed in there. You know how I hate to disappoint our kids. I just reacted as I would with any client."
"Thank God they have you as their lawyer this time around. I love Justin but he doesn't have a better instinct and quick thinking."
"Girl you know I am on it especially when it comes to our kids."
"I know that's right. We have to protect our kids and our grandbabies. Did you want me to wait in the lobby for you or you all not that close."
"No we have at least ten more minutes, go ahead and find us somewhere to sit. Lucas and Mia should be there before us if you wanted to wait on them."
"Just as you said that they walked in. We will see you all when you get here."
"Hey how is Reign and Roman doing?"
"They are doing great Mia and now that our son is on his way Reign will stop worrying about if he's going to make it on time to see his son born."
"I fussed at him for losing it like that. I asked Lillian would he be able to finish giving his testimony and she said they were meeting with the judge later today. What is your opinion on it?"
"The judge will let him finish because he would want the defense to be able to cross. I think they have to figure out if that bastard should be in the courtroom while he finishes his account of what happened."
"After what happened I pray the judge does not let him be in there. Montez said he was taunting him while he was up there. That  when he blew a kiss at him, that's when he lost it."
"I didn't catch that. I wonder if anyone else did? I'm sure Lillian will bring that to his attention today. Judge probably is not going to care either way, I know I wouldn't. Contempt is contempt;

he probably won't get anything just a court fine and a slap on the hand. I doubt he would put him in jail for it."

"I'm praying he won't but it's still going on his record?"

"Lillian will be able to stop that from happening. He would pay the fine and that should be it."

"God I hope so."

"Come on let's get something to eat, this will all work out in our favor. I really believe that."

As the women joined everyone else in the cafeteria. Montez and the rest of them show up and he rushes to be by Reign's side. While David and Lillian find everyone else at the cafeteria. When he is told what room his wife was in at the front desk. He gathers himself before walking into their room. When he walks in he finds her sleeping with her back turned to him. A smile hits his face as he hears his son's heartbeat on the monitor. He walks to the other side of the bed and he can't believe how beautiful she is and how lucky he was to have her as his wife and mother of his children. She had her hair up in a messy bun and no make up on but her dark skin melanin had a natural glow to it. He sat down and put his hands on her stomach and whispered "baby I made it." He lays his head down and closes his eyes to get some rest with her. He's been through one labor and he knows how it's going to go. He needed to prepare himself mentally and the only way to do that was to get rest.

# *Chapter Twenty:Bond*

Seven pounds three ounces and twenty inches is Roman Alexander Santos and he is all energy. He has been wide awake since entering this world. He is trying hard not to miss a thing, it's as if he knew he was a baby born from survival. He went through a lot with his mother and he wanted to show her that he was strong just like her. A little after his arrival the whole family had made their way from out of town. Except for Montez's grandparents they were still on a flight headed their way. Everyone else was accounted for and it felt like a holiday. The family's attention was given to Roman and MJ, their parents were in their own little bubble so they didn't mind. They preferred them to get all the holding, kissing and loving now. Because when they got them home all that was going to change. They were still going to receive it just with less hands.

"Now everyone will have to clear out of here because my sister will need her rest soon," Jazz announces, getting the room silent.

"Yes we will," Charlene agrees.

"Thanks Jazzy," Reign says softly.

"You know I got you girl and I'm going to need the same thing from you in three months or so."

"I got you sis," she says with a smile.

"He is so adorable and he's going to be a chocolate baby like his beautiful mama. Are you excited MJ," Mia asked

"Yes! My buda, my buda."

"Yes son, that 's your brother, Montez says as he gets up and walks towards him. This is your little brother Roman."

"Reign, if he wasn't early you probably would have pushed out an eight pounds baby," Maitea said as she walked over and took Montez's seat.

"Thank God he did his mama a solid huh," she said laughing.

"He did sis, he really did. I'm just glad my nephew is here strong, healthy and nosy as hell."

"Can you blame him, the whole tribe is in here."

"No, I don't blame him at all. Honestly how are you holding up? I know these months hasn't been the easiest."

"I'm getting there, one day at a time."

"Well I'm here for a while to help Montez and Jazz through this trial. I'm also here for you and my nephews as well. I see Mersades has been a big help as well."

"She has. The whole family has been great and well you know Jazz ain't taking no bullshit. It's been hard at times but my family wasn't going to let me check out."

"Damn right! We were not about to lose you, we love you too much sis."

"Ditto, Jazz chimed in.  Reign, you are looking sleepy, you need us to leave now?"

"If you all don't mind so we can have just a moment to ourselves. I love you all"

"But you want us to get the hell out, Lucas said laughing."

"Something like that Papa Lucas."

"Say no more baby girl we will be on our way," her dad says as he kisses her on the forehead.

"And thank you for allowing my name to be a part of my grandson's name."

"All my princes will have a representation of the strong men in my life, you do not have to thank me for that daddy."

"Still I'm honored and so grateful."

"You are welcome."

"Okay y'all seriously let's go so they can have their family time," Mia says as she hurries everyone along.

"Finally some peace and quiet. Do you want to hold him Reign?"

"Not right now babe I'm tired."

"Ok I will put him back in his bed."

"Mama!"

"Yes sweetie." Lucas reaches his hand out to her. Montez can you put him up here please?"

"Yeah sure thing." As MJ gets comfortable, Reign closes her eyes and drifts off to sleep. Not long MJ was sleeping with her and Montez buzzed in the nurse to take Roman out. He walks over and kisses Reign and MJ on the forehead and sits back in his chair and falls asleep himself. It had truly been a crazy day that ended with a blessing. He made it out in time to see the birth of his son and he was able to sleep with his family tonight instead of a jail cell. Many black men in his position couldn't have said that.

"Did Reign seem off to you?"

"She was a little quiet but damn look how much she's been through. I'm a man and I'm telling you now I would have been broke. It's true what they say about our black queens y'all are strong as fuck."

"We are but I'm really concerned. She barely held Roman."

"Maybe she just wanted everyone else to have their chances while she rested. To me she just seemed tired, Jazz."

"I really pray that's all it is. My mom is on her way back to court to see what they want to do with the rest of Montez's testimony. Then I'm next to be called and Sean I don't know how I'm going to get through this. You know my emotions are all over the place."

"I'm going to be right there with you to help you through it. Just focus on me and not him."

"I know what I'm supposed to do. We went over it a million times and I still don't think that's enough. It's totally different when you are up there and you see the bastard who brutally raped your best friend, my sister. He has a defense that's lying about a nonexistent relationship."

"You know that, don't let them get off your game and what your mother has prepared you for. She told you his lawyer job is to either trip you up or make you look like the guilty person. The last thing you want to do is make his ass the victim."

"Victim my ass! I don't care how much his attorney comes at me, I will never make him look like a victim!"

"Yeah we need to call your mother over. I see now how this will turn out tomorrow."

"I hate him! I told her not to trust him and look! Look what happened! Now it seems like Reign has a detach from Roman. God I pray that I'm wrong but it's like when she looks at him reminds her of the rape."

"Come on Jazz don't do that. She was probably just overwhelmed and tired, so let's not jump to that conclusion."

"I know her and I'm telling you. Montez needs to know this so we can get ahead of it and get her the help she needs."

"Let's hold off on that

"Last time someone told me to hold off and let's see, my friend got raped! I'm not sitting on this one. I would rather be wrong than to let postpartum step in and destroy my friend!"

"Okay baby calm down. We will let Montez know."

"Thank you."

"Listen I don't want to be responsible for sending another one in early labor anything to keep you calm."

"You know what else would keep me calm?"

"What's that?"

"Crab legs."

"Here I'm thinking you were going to say me."

"Food, then you babe."

"Okay. Well how about Red Lobster?"

"Yes baby and some cheddar biscuits and stuffed mushrooms."

"He wants all that?"

"Yes! Oh a lobster tail and loaded mash potatoes with broccoli."

"Is there anything left on the menu?"

"Shut up! Don't do that," she said laughing.

"You want to see if Mersades and Abs want to go?"

"You know they do just swing by and get them."

"Who are they with?"

"That's a good question, let me call him."

"What do you need, Jazzy?"

"We headed to Red Lob"

"Yep come and get me and Sades. We are at Tez's house."

"Damn! Can I get it out or nah? We are on the way, big head."

"Good looking out sis. You always take care of me."

"You know I got you for life."

"I know and I got you. Love you and see you in a bit."

"Love you too Abs. They are over Montez's house."

"Alright. I don't know why they didn't just come with us when we left the hospital."

"They probably thought we all were headed that way."

"Daddy I don't want red lobster."

"We don't want it either mommy."

"What do you all want?"

"Pizza," they all yell!

"And ice cream, Marcella added.

"Yeah and ice cream!"

"Lord. Okay we will order pizza and get you all some ice cream."

"Thank you!"

"What are y'all triplets now Sean asked laughing. When they start responding in unison?"
"I don't know babe, but I love it."
"Yeah they have most definitely come a long way, glad they are finally getting along. Let me call my mother so she can get them. We can stop by the store and grab their ice cream on the way."
"I will order online and have it delivered to her house. What do you want on your pizza SJ?"
"Pineapple and pepperoni."
"Mommy we want that too."
"Ew, okay. Sean I know your mother does not want that. Ask her if she wants us to bring her something back from Red lobster?"
"She said pizza is fine, but she wants a meat lover's with extra mushrooms."
"Anything else?"
"She said order wings too, babe?"
"Alright. Tell her everything has been taking care of all she has to do is sign my name. Alright Gray fam everyone head to the car, let's get this show on the road."

# Chapter Twenty-One: Day 2

It's day two of the trial and the judge has decided that Montez could finish testifying. The judge also allowed Andre to be present because he wanted to be. Lillian notified him of what else happened to set her client off and the judge said he will keep an eye on things. He said the defendant still had a right to be in the courtroom if they choose. After they were done with matters that didn't concern the jury. The judge instructed the bailiff to bring them in. Outside the courtroom Montez's sister was trying to keep him cool headed. He saw the birth of his son and the strength of his yesterday. He knew how important it was for him to find restraint. He knew he could not have another episode like yesterday. "I got it this time Tea I promise. I will not have a repeat of the last time."

"You better not. The judge will not be that understanding again. I know it's hard but he will get his. At this point you have to let go and let God."

"Easier said than done. I doubt I will ever let go. Today I will let God save him from a beat down."

"Good enough."

"Mr. Santos, they are ready for you," the bailiff said.

"Thank you.

"How are we this morning Mr. Santos?"

"Better judge thanks for asking."

"I'm sure your lawyer spoke to you about your conduct yesterday?"

"Yes sir she did and we all are on the same page. I want to apologize to you and the jurors on my actions yesterday. My emotions won the best of me. I promise it will not happen again. I just want to tell the court what happened and get back to my family sir."

"I accept your apology Mr. Santos and I'm glad to hear you are taking responsibility for your actions. Is the state ready to proceed?"

"We are your honor."

"Alright Mr. Santos come on up here and be sworn in."

"Good morning Mr. Santos."

"Good morning."

"I just have a few more questions for you."

"Okay."

"Yesterday you were about to tell us what happened when you discovered your wife."

"Yes I remember."

"Please continue from there."

"I just knew at this point something was wrong so I took off towards her office screaming her name. When I opened her door she was naked and laying on her side."

"She had no clothes on at all?"

"No clothes on. They were spread all over her office desk  and some were on the floor."

"In good condition?"

"No, her t-shirt was ripped."

"Mr. Santos is this the shirt you are speaking of?"

"Yes. It's my Nike t-shirt she had on."

"Your honor the state would like to enter evidence number twenty two in."

"Any objection defense?"

"No your honor."

"You may proceed."

"Thank you judge. Okay Mr. Santos, what happened next?"

"I was struggling to get my cell phone out. Once I did I called 911 and attended to her at the same time."

"Attended to her how?"

"She wasn't responding and she was bruised pretty badly. She had semen all over her and blood coming from her face. She didn't look like the happy wife that left the house earlier that evening."

"Do you remember everything you did to help your wife until the medics arrived."

"Yeah I wiped her down as much as I could with the shirt. I supported her head and I even took off my shirt and put it on her."

"What else did you do?"

"I stayed on the phone with the operator and talked to my wife as she came in and out."

"Did you notice anything else about her that was different?"

"She was weak, her hair was all over the place, she had bite marks on her and bruises around her neck."

"Anything else?"

"No."

"Judge Brown. I would like to now enter in evidence number 4. The 911 call that Mr. Santos made."

"Is there any objection from the defense?"

"We have no objection Judge."

As the prosecution set up the audio for the jury, Montez put his head down. He didn't want to give any eye contact to Andre. It was a few times he could feel Andre looking at him but he kept his eyes on the prosecutor or his sister. As the tape played the jury expressions were all the same. They were either listening with disgust on their face, others were shaking their head in disbelief. Especially when they heard Reign's moans coming through the call. One jury was crying when she heard her apologizing to her husband. It was the first time their parents heard the recordings also. To hear her in and out like that pulled on everyone's emotions in that courtroom. Even the judge had to turn away from the jury a few times. When it was over the prosecutor told Montez that was all the questions she had for now.

"How are you this morning Montez?"

"I'm great and you?"

"I'm feeling great, thank you for asking."

"No problem."

"Mr. Santos, would you say that you have an anger management problem."

"No."

"Yesterday was normal for you?"
"No."
"Interesting. Let me ask you this. You never liked my client from day one did you?"
"I didn't know of him to determine that from day one."
"You said yesterday that your first encounter with him, he was hugging on your wife, correct?"
"Yes."
"That made you what Mr. Santos?"
"Mad."
"Is your wife your property Mr. Santos?"
"No."
"That's how you treated her that day did you not?"
"No, I did not."
"Your wife felt that way did she not?"
"No, she didn't."
"She didn't tell you that Mr. Santos?"
"What part of no are you not understanding?"
"Objection your honor, can the defense please move on?  He has answered that question several times."
"I agree, get to the point or move on, counselor."
"Let's move on to a business trip your wife took with Mr. Sampson. Do you recall a Charleston trip?"
"Yes."
"Did you accompany your wife on this trip?"
"No."
"But you did show up unexpectedly on the trip correct?"
"Sure."
"This business trip they took, was that the first one with just the two of them?"
"I guess."
"Do you really want this jury to believe that you don't know about your wife's business trips?"
"I don't know if that particular trip was their first trip alone or not. She has and continues to have business trips. Some she does solo, some I take with her, others she takes with her employees."
"Okay Mr. Santos, let me ask you the question this way. On all your wife's business trips that she went with her employees how many did you pop up on?"
"Two."
"One was with Andre who was the other one with?"
"Jasmine."
"Who is Jasmine?"
"My wife's best friend."
"Why did you show up uninvited with her trip with Andre?"

"I didn't trust him by this time and I damn sure wasn't going to trust him to bring her home safely. When she told me she was riding back home with him after their business meeting. I left Greenville and drove to Charleston to bring her back myself."

"You didn't trust her in the car with Mr. Sampson but you had no problem with her being in a hotel room with him?"

"She was never in the same hotel room with him. They had separate rooms."

"Is that what your wife told you?"

He laughs and doesn't answer the question.

"Something funny about the question Mr. Santos?"

Montez just stares at him trying to control his anger.

"Mr. Santos did your wife tell you that she had a room by herself?"

"She didn't have too."

"That's not what I asked Mr. Santos."

Montez looks at Lillian and she motions with her hand for him to remain calm. He closes his eyes and slowly exhales. As he slowly opens his eyes he looks at the lawyer and says, "Reign did not tell me if she had a room by herself."

"Then she and Mr. Sampson could have a room together?"

Montez clenches his teeth together and doesn't respond.

"Your honor can you please tell Mr. Santos to answer the question."

"Mr. Santos are you able to answer the question?"

"No your honor because we never discuss it."

"Move on counselor he doesn't know."

"Yes your honor. Where did you pick up your wife, Mr. Santos?"

"At a restaurant."

"How did you know she was at that particular restaurant if she didn't know you were coming?"

"Social media can be a beautiful thing sometimes."

"You tracked her down through social media?"

"Sure."

"Mr. Santos you had a feeling your wife was cheating didn't you?"

"My wife has never cheated on me."

"The real reason you popped up in Charleston is because your wife and Mr. Sampson were having an affair and you discovered it on social media?"

"Nice twist but that's just not true."

"I would like to show defense exhibit number 262 to Mr. Santos your honor?"

"Continue Mr. Byrd."

"Is this a picture of Mr. Sampson and your wife at the restaurant?"

"Yes it is."

"Is this the beautiful thing on social media that helped you find the location of them?"

"Yes it is."

"When you saw this picture on social media how did you feel?"

"Nothing really. I take that back. I was glad my wife was still in Charleston and I had time to get to her before they left."

"It didn't upset you how close your wife was to Mr. Sampson?"

"You call that close?"

"Mr. Santos can you please answer my questions with yes or no."

"No."

"No what Mr. Santos?"

"You just asked me to answer you with a yes or no. I said no."

"Your honor. Can you please tell Mr. Santos to answer my questions."

"I don't consider that close."

"When you arrived at the restaurant where was your wife?"

"Sitting on the opposite side of the table."

"They were no longer sitting like this?"

"No."

"Are you sure?"

"Positive."

"What happened when you arrived at the restaurant?"

"Reign watched as I walked in and Andre didn't see me because his back was towards the door. I walked up and my wife got up and we hugged."

"Your wife was happy to see you?"

"Of course."

"She wasn't mad at you at all?"

"Shocked at first but not mad."

"Why was she shocked?"

"She didn't know I was coming and she at the time couldn't figure out how I found them. Til I let her know how unsafe it was to tag her location on social media and still be at the place she tagged."

"So you want me and the jurors to believe. That your wife wasn't mad at you for coming over two hundred miles unannounced and being a jealous husband?"

"I really don't care what you or anyone else believe about my wife not being mad at me. If she was mad at me trust me, she would have rode back with the defendant and not me. If she was having an affair and I caught her I wouldn't have let her rode back with"

"Your honor, can you please have Mr. Santos answer my questions with yes or no. We don't need the extra theatrics from him."

"Overruled, Mr. Santos you may finish with your answer."

"I was just going to say if I caught my fiance cheating that day she wouldn't have been Mrs. Santos today."

"She wasn't your wife during Charleston?"

"No."

"Why have you been saying wife this whole time if you two were not married yet Mr. Santos?"

"I'm speaking in the present. She's my wife now she wasn't during this business trip to Charleston."

"Let's move on to the night of the alleged rape." Montez felt his skin get heated when he said alleged rape and felt his temper about to get out of control. He closed his eyes and tried to calm

down. Maitea taps Lillian on the shoulder and whispers something to her. Lillian then taps the prosecutor and lets her know the situation. She nods her head in agreement and then asks the judge if they could take a break. Before the defense got started with their line of questions on that night. The judge agreed that this was a good time to take a break and asked the defense were they fine with it. They agreed and the court was dismissed for a fifteen minutes break.
"You are doing so well Montez. I'm not going to keep you long after the defense finishes their cross. Just keep your cool for a little bit longer okay? I will have you out of here before lunch."
"Thank you."
"You are doing good Tezzy."
"He is really digging in me sis. I don't know how much more of this bullshit I can take."
"That's his job to get to you like you were yesterday and your job is to not let him. You know your wife was raped and it wasn't consensual. You have to focus and make sure you get out of Reign's side as much as possible."
"The jury seems to be taking the defense side. Some of them look like they believe Reign had something going on with him."
"I don't think that's it all. That 911 call proves that they were moved and believes she was raped. What you are noticing from the jurors is that they are probably loving how you are defending your wife. While calling that piece of a shit lawyer out. Once that tape is shown no way will any of them still believe they were carrying on an affair."
"I hope you are right."
"I have a feeling that I am."
"Where's Jazz?"
"She had to step out and take a phone call. She's next to call so you know she's not going too far."
"I'm glad you stayed and didn't head back. Your presence and talks have really helped me."
"That's what big sisters are for and I got you til the very end. I love you Montez."
"I love you too Maitea."
"What about me? You love me too?"
"Yeah Jasmine I love your crazy ass too.
"I knew it. You are doing good up there. It was a few times I wanted to smack that man."
"You and I both."
"But you're not and you're going to calm down and get through these questions."
"I'm calm. Don't I look calm to you two?"
"Hell no but hey we know you are trying," Jazz says rubbing his back.
"Come on, let's get back in there."
"Montez let me speak to you before you go back in. You ladies can go ahead."
"What's going on Ms. Lillian?"
"I know you probably already know this but his lawyer is trying to make you react like you did yesterday. Just go back to answering yes and no to his questions. Let him do his defense. Please do not go back in there and go back and forth with him. I'm afraid if you do we are going to have a repeat of yesterday."
"I'm not going to lose it again. I will go back to yes and no from now on."

"Thank you. Remember you are out on bond that thirty six thousand is still pending."

"Thank you for the reminder of the 36k. Even more reasons to answer yes or no."

"Right. Are you ready to get this over with."

"Let's do this."

As they walk back into the courtroom they notice the jury is still out and the defense is requesting that Reign now appear in court now that she has had the baby. The prosecutor is arguing that it has already been decided that she didn't have to be here because of health issues. That just because she had the baby doesn't mean her health issues changed. The judge said for now he will stand by his first ruling and the victim will not have to come in. He did tell the defense they can file the motion again when the state has rested. He asked both sides if there were any more motions before he brought the jury back in. Both sides agreed they were ready to proceed.

"Alright Mr. Santos if you would come back up here and be seated. You do understand that you are still under oath?"

"Yes."

"Alright Mr. Byrd you may continue with your cross."

"Before we took a break. I was about to discuss the day you say your wife was raped. When was the last time you spoke to her that day?"

"Around 10:15 pm."

"What time did you make the 911 call?"

"11:07 pm."

"How long have you known your wife?"

"Three years."

"Mr. Santos, in your opinion is that enough time to know someone?"

"Yes."

"Did you know that your wife loves to role play?"

"Objection, Judge! May we please approach the bench?"

"Sustain. Mr. Byrd you are tip toeing the line sir. Jury you are to ignore the counselor question. Let's take a quick recess. Montez you may step down."

"What the fuck was that? Montez asked Lillian

"I pray he was not going where I think he was going. If he was, he is a piece of shit, right along his client!"

"So he was about to say that Reign and Dre was role playing and that's what the video will show."

"I believe that's where he was going Maitea."

"I'm going to fuck him up. When I see him outside this courtroom, I'm going to beat the shit out of him!"

"Montez please calm down! I'm pretty sure the judge is letting him have it. I'm sure he will not be allowed to ask you that."

"If he puts a strong argument that he has the right to defend his client and get his side out. The judge may not have a choice. You know that Lillian, we can't have them thinking the law will change because it's my daughter. Montez, just prepare yourself. The judge may allow that type of questioning, it's your job to answer yes or no as much as possible. Do not engage like you did earlier."

"Man y'all are asking too much from me right now, way too much!"

"When you answer yes and no it will get you off that stand faster son. The more you argue with him the more power you give to his theory."

"The judge is calling everyone back in."

"Thank you bailiff."

"Alright Mr. Santos if we can get you back on the stand before I let the jurors back in."

"Yes sir."

"I would like to apologize to the jurors for rushing you all out here. Hopefully there won't be any more breaks like that. Mr. Byrd, you make now continue your cross."

"Mr. Santos before the quick recess I asked you about your wife sex routine. Do you and your wife role play?"

"Role play? You mean dress up as characters before we have sex?"

"Is that what role play is to you Mr. Santos?"

"Your question is vague. Role play can mean different things, it all depends on the person."

"Did you and your wife act like someone else while having sex?"

"No."

"Have she ever asked you too?"

"No."

"Do your wife ask you to participate in sex fantasies?"

"No."

"Have you ever asked her to fulfil any of your sex fantasies?"

"No."

"Have your wife ever told you about rough sex she had with boyfriends before you?"

"We never discuss our sexual encounter from the past."

"Mr. Santos wouldn't it be fair to say that maybe your wife had another side of her that you didn't know about?"

"No. I know my wife and my wife knows me. She wasn't cheating on me."

"You said when you walked in the office. That your wife's purse and keys were on the receptionist desk, is that correct?"

"Yes."

"You didn't mention her cell phone. Did you see it there?"

"It wasn't out, maybe it was in her purse."

"Why didn't you call it again, when you saw her keys, purse and no cell phone?"

"It was going straight to her voicemail. Why would I call it again?"

"What is your wife's occupation?"

"She's a marketing strategist. She owns her own marketing company."

"Does that require her to have her cell phone on her a lot?"

"Yes."

"If you see that your wife's car is still outside. When you enter her building and see her purse and keys. Why not call her phone again?"

"I just wanted to find my wife, and my instincts were telling me she was still in the building."

"I see. Can I turn your attention to the police report and the statement you made concerning her phone."

"Sure."

"I would like to present state case number 3 4 and 5 your honor."

"Any objections from the state?"

"No judge, we have no objections."

"You may continue Mr. Byrd."

"The officer asked you about her phone and you told them you didn't see her phone. Is that correct?

"Yes."

"When you were at the hospital you told them that Jasmine remembered that your wife received another phone call as she went back into the building. Is that correct, Mr. Santos?"

"Yes."

"So from the time she went back into her office she had her cell phone correct?"

'Yes."

" Also in your statement you tell the officer that the phone call didn't come from you, correct?"

"Yeah."

"You then told the officer that whoever made that phone call did this to your wife, is that correct Mr. Santos?"

"Yeah man."

"Mr. Santos, are you telling these jurors the truth about the time you arrived at the office?"

"Yes I am."

"You didn't arrive earlier than that?"

"No, I didn't."

"Describe to the jurors again how your wife's office is set up."

"It's in the back of the building, directly behind the receptionist desk."

"If you are standing at the receptionist desk and you are looking back at the office can you see through her glass?"

"If you have great eye vision you probably could if the blinds are opened."

"Were her blinds open that night?"

"I can't recall."

'Will these photos refresh your memory?"

" If the photos show them close or opened, I would still say I don't recall."

"Okay Mr. Santos, I will let you know they were open when they took photos."

"My answer still remains."

"You saw your wife having an affair that night didn't you, Mr. Santos?"

"Your client wouldn't be sitting there if I walked in and caught him raping my wife! That I can promise you muthafucker! You are a piece of shit for defending that niggah

"Mr. Santos calmed down! Order in the court! Order in the court!

"I should have killed you yesterday Andre! I should have broken your fucking neck for what you did to my wife and unborn child!"

"Bailiff please get Mr. Santos out of this courtroom! I need order in this courtroom. We are adjourned for today. Jury I apologize for the outburst and that we once again are having a short day. You guys are dismissed until tomorrow, please remember not to discuss the case with anyone. I need the lawyers in my chambers now.

"Damn! Montez almost had his ass again if that undercover didn't come out of nowhere and tackled him. Did you see how fast the lawyer moved? He wanted another reaction but I know he didn't want that one."

"My son had every right to react that way. That defense lawyer was way out of line. What's going to happen now to him, Charlene?"

"I don't know what the judge is going to do. Lillian headed back with them, let's see if we can find them."

"We will wait out here while you all do that," Maitea said. "Jazz you are so crazy but I was thinking the same thing. He kept fucking with my brother and saw his life flash before his eyes when Tez almost connected,"

"He is probably going to file charges against him for attempted assault."

"You know he is. He almost lost his shoes the way he slid out the way. I think he is officially done testifying. No way they put him back up there tomorrow."

"That means I am next tomorrow.He lucky I'm pregnant because if he tries me the way he tried Tez. Like I said he is lucky I am pregnant."

"Just make sure you only use your hormones to cry and nothing else."

"You do not have to worry about me Maitea. I'm not trying to be locked in jail while pregnant and I damn sure is not coming out the bank to get bail out."

"I feel you. I know I told them we will wait on them for information. I really need to see my nephews before I head back to the A."

"Yeah and my curiosity is taking over. I need to know the tea."

"You and I both. Let's see what they decided to do with Montez."

"I am right behind you."

# *Chapter Twenty-Two: Easier Said Than Done*

When this trial began we tried our damndest to keep Montez in checked. For the most of his testimony my brother tried his hardest. Honestly how much can a man take at that point. Just imagine the love of your life and the mother of your children being raped and beaten. While I have you deep in thought, imagine the rapist just feet from you. Tell me you wouldn't take every chance you could to get to that bastard. I watched the jurors as they pulled him out the courtroom and they seemed to be understanding what he was going through. That was the last time on the stand the prosecution and defense said they didn't have any more questions for him. He wasn't arrested, they just took him to the back to calm him down before releasing him to his parents and mama Lene. They left and took him back to the hospital. That's how the court ended yesterday. The judge had no choice but to send us and the jury home. Now today I'm sitting on that chair and I'm trying different methods to remain calm. The prosecutor finished her direct and the Byrd guy was looking for papers. I knew exactly what he was trying to do, but I will not let him get to me like he Tez.

"Good afternoon Miss Jasmine, how are you today."

"I'm doing well."

"I just have a few questions for you. What time was it when you arrived at the office?"

"It was before eight."

"What time did you leave?"

"I am not sure the exact time without my phone records but it was around 10:10 or 10:15."

"Is this the time Reign left?"

"I thought she did."

"What made her stay?"

"She grabbed the wrong laptop and went back to retrieve the one she needed."

"Did you see her call anyone before she went in?"

"I saw her answer her phone before entering."

"You said in your police report and during your direct, that you were also on the phone. Is that correct?

"Yes."

"How do you know she didn't make the call herself?"

"Because I was talking to her and Sean at the same time. As she walked away, I heard her say "yeah what's up."

"How close are you and Reign?"

"Again Reign is my sister. We grew up together."

"Does she tell you everything?"

"Yes, eventually she does."

"What were your conversations on Andre?"

"He was a market genius like her, is what she would always say."

"Did she feel as if they had a lot in common?

"Business wise."

"If she felt more than that would she tell you?"

"She didn't feel that way about him."

"That wasn't what I asked you. If she had additional feelings for Andre would she have told you?"

"Yes she would have."

"How do you know this? I know you said you would ask her and she would deny it. How do you know this is something she didn't want you to know about?"

"If she was having an affair she would have told me. That I know for sure Mr. Byrd."

"Did she find my client attractive."

"I already said she did."

"Did she ever tell you that she would be with him if she wasn't married?"

"No, she didn't."

"Did she ever tell you about her business trip to Dallas?"

"I was there with her on that Dallas trip. As a matter of fact her whole team was there."

"Did you spend time with her the whole trip?"

"Not when they went to the business convention, I went sightseeing instead."

"Did her whole team attend that convention?"

"Only her, Tonya and Andre went. Tamara stayed with me to explore the city."

"What happened when the convention was over."

"Like I said earlier. She was about six months pregnant at the time and she didn't want to hang out. She stayed behind while we went to the bars."

"Where was Andre?"

"He was there for the first bar but then he headed back to the hotel."

"Did her and Andre hook up that night?"

"Hook up? No."

"What did she tell you again?"

"He stopped by her room to check on her. She let him in for a little while. They talked about the convention and he was telling her about the scenery downtown. Then Montez called and she sent him out so she could talk to her husband."

"I thought they were not married yet?"

"My bad. I'm talking in present time. Montez was her fiance at the time."

"Did she tell you that Andre was in the bed or sitting in a chair?"

"He was sitting on her bed and she was sitting on her bed too."

"Did she tell you how close they were on the bed?"

"No, we didn't have that discussion."

"Did she tell you that her back was bothering her and Andre gave her a massage?"

"Objection! Your honor if Andre wants to get on the stand and tell his side I am fine with that. But allowing his lawyer to do it is unacceptable!"

"Your honor I was just asking the friend what all Reign told her. I am no way trying to testify for my client. Prosecution opened this up when they brought up the Dallas trip."

"I will allow the question. Mr. Byrd if I feel like these questions are your way to get your client's story out. I will stop you, do we understand one another?"

"Yes your honor."

"Alright Miss Jasmine, if you are able to, please answer the question."

"She told me the baby was bothering her because he was on one side. That's all she told me."

"So she doesn't tell you everything?"

"Everyone knew about that on the trip. That was one of the reasons she didn't hang out with us. If he gave her a massage she would have told me."

"Jazz can you honestly sit there and tell this jury that Reign told you everything?"

"Something like that, yes she would. Did she tell me everything of course not. She always told me she didn't see him like that. We all saw he had a thing for her and she would always say it doesn't matter. It would never be more than an employer and employee relationship for her."

"Let's get back to their position on the bed. You said that she never discussed where they were positioned but they both were on the bed, correct?"

"Correct."

"Did she say how long he was in the room before Montez called."

"She didn't give me an exact time. Just that they were talking for a while and when Montez called she sent him out."

"But you don't know if he really left do you?"

"No, only what she told me."

"And you said you stopped by the room later before you called it a night."

"Correct."

"What time did you all get back to the hotel?"

"About two o'clock in the morning."

"Plenty of time for your friend to sleep with

"Objection your honor!"

"Sustain. The jury is to ignore that last remark. Do you have a question Mr. Byrd."

"I do."

"Stop with the side show Mr. Byrd and ask her a question."

"Yes your honor. You said that you and Montez had concerns about my client, correct?"

"Yes."

"But Reign didn't, is that also so correct?"

"Correct."

"That didn't seem odd to you?"

"No."

"Why is that?"

"You have to know my friend. She trusts people until they give her a reason not to."

"I have no further questions, your honor."

"State do you have any more questions for Jasmine?"

"Yes we do."

"Please proceed."

"Jasmine let's get back to this Dallas trip. When did you and Reign talk about the events of that trip?"

"Um we talked about it a little bit when I came to the room."

"What was the discussion?"

"She told me that Andre had dropped by earlier that evening."

"She volunteered you that information without you asking?"

"Well yeah. When I knocked on her door and she answered it threw me a little. I honestly thought she would be asleep."

"When she opened the door, did it seem like you woke her up?"

"No, she was on the phone."

"Who was she on the phone with?"

"Montez."

"Did she stay on the phone with him while you were there?"

"No, when I came into the room. She said Jazzy here let me talk with her before I call it a night. They did their corney goodbye routine and that's when she told me about Andre."

"How was she telling you?"

"When Reign wants to have a girl talk. She always starts it off with, girl you ain't going to believe this. I knew then she had something funny to tell me."

"What did she tell you?"

"She said Andre stopped by and it threw her off a little."

"Why was that?"

"She wasn't expecting him."

"What did she say happened next?"

"She said he was just checking on her before he called it a night."

"What else does she say?"

"She said she invited him in and paused the movie she was watching. They started talking about Dallas and she asked him about downtown, then she asked him why he wasn't still out with us?"

"What was his response?"

He said he didn't feel like hanging out either."

"Did she ever tell you that her and Andre were close that night?"

"No. She said he was acting weird so she texted Montez and told him to call her."

"Did she further explain what she meant by acting weird?

"That when he came in he just sat down on her bed. She didn't like that because there was a chair in the room he could have sat on. He was also trying to ask her personal questions about her relationship."

"What kind of questions?"

"He wanted to know if she had doubts about getting married. He wanted to know why they didn't do a lot of business trips together, just the two of them. That if Montez didn't trust her, why would she marry him?"

"Did Reign ever discuss her relationship with him?"

"No. He told her that's what he observed."

"Anything else you remember about that conversation?"

"She said when he asked about her relationship she wouldn't give him an answer and would change the subject back to business. She did that until Montez called and she got rid of him."

"You said when she opened up the door around two, she was still on the phone?"

"Yes she was."

"If I show you her phone records for that night. Will it shock you that she was on a phone call with him for five hours?"

"No, because she and Montez would binge watch old tv shows until one of them fell asleep. That's their thing they do when she has to travel out of town and he can't go."

"Did he miss a lot of her business trips?"

"I wouldn't say a lot. He probably missed four but no more than five. I mean she was pregnant and she didn't travel a lot. She trusted her team for the majority of the trips."

"How many business trips would you say she took last year, to your knowledge?"

"About fifteen."

"That seems like a lot."

"Actually that's low for her. She traveled out of town more than fifty times, when she first started up her company."

"The reason why she did a mass hiring that year?"

"She really did it because she was pregnant. We love traveling, but she was having complications with MJ that she had to cut back on traveling."

"I have no more questions, judge?"

"Mr. Byrd?"

"A quick follow up, your honor. Jasmine you said that Andre left you all after the first bar, correct."

"Yes."

"What time was that?"

"Around eight."

"The phone records the prosecution showed you. What time did Montez call her?"

"9:27 pm."

"No further questions your honor."

"Real quick Jasmine. How long have you and Reign been friends?"

"All our life."

"If Reign cheated on any of her boyfriends would she tell you?"

"Yes."

If you ever cheated on a boyfriend, would you tell Reign?"

"Yes."

"No further questions, your honor."

"You may step down Jasmine."

Thank the Lord this is over for me. Andre is really trying to sell this made up relationship between him and Reign. I'm not going to lie, his lawyer is good at creating reasonable doubt. At one point he had me going. I can only imagine what the jurors are thinking, I know there was no damn affair because I know my friend. These people do not, my stomach is in knots and I'm scared for her. What if they find him not guilty or worse a hung jury. If they have to retry the case then they would force Reign to testify. This shit sucks bad, I pray to God that when they watch the video. They will see it was rape and not consensual. I will not attend anymore court dates

until it is in the jurors hands. I did my part and now it's time to be with her and my family. Our parents are there and they will call us when it happens. Right now I am on my way to pick out Rome some new clothes and MJ some toys. Loud toys that will irritate the hell out of his parents. I mean that is the job of an auntie to spoil them rotten and annoy the parents in the process. I also figured this would help everyone to have their minds anywhere then the courtroom. I'm trying to get our lives back on track before this trial ever began. I know it will never be the same, I also don't want her back in that space before therapy either. She has come a long way from that awful night and I want my sister to continue moving on.
"Hey is there something particular that you are looking for?"
"No, not really. I will know it when I see it."
"If you need anything I will be over here."
That's code for I'm watching you. If Becky doesn't get out my face! Ain't nobody trying to steal anything out of this store. Now I know I'm about to head to Burlington Coat Factory and give them my coins. I was the only one in the store you would think she would have been a little less suspicious of me. Those prices were ridiculous anyway overpricing shit that I could get cheaper at Wal-mart. I'm going to make sure that my lot has a boutique with nothing but clothes designed by black people, that's how much I am tired of the bullshit in some of these stores. I'm not trying to brag or nothing like that but damn I know she saw me pull up in the Range. Just goes to show it doesn't matter to some of them how educated you are or how much money you have. They will always see us less than them not all but the majority of them will. I'm learning to be careless and spend my hard earned money somewhere else. I see so many cute outfits for Rome and since we found out that I'm having a boy also. I'm debating should I at least get them one matching outfit. I'm pretty sure we are going to have some professional photos once he is born. Sean wanted to name him Sincere Nicholas Gray and I loved it. He put my middle name in our son's name since his first born had his name. That was the deal we made, if it was a girl I would name her. He wanted a princess so bad no lie I was begging God for a boy. I told him I would think about trying for another one three years from now. This time I would secretly pray for a girl. I think carrying four kids is enough for me. I mean maybe my mind will change once I'm in my thirties but as for now, four is my limit. I see these celebrities having children late and I'm like God bless them. I am trying to get mine out the way earlier. That way when I retire I can go back to traveling with no worries. Looking at my cart I felt like crying, I went overboard with the clothes and toys for the kids again. Sean is going to kill me when he sees these bags. I feel as if I earned this today. I mean that was rough in there and although I had Sean with me. It still didn't make it any easier. My baby wanted to come with me after that but I convinced him to go back to work. I needed this me time without him asking me every two seconds am I okay. I also knew he wanted to discuss what happened and I just didn't want to. Not today anyway and I'm sure Reign will understand that too. At least I was hoping that it would. It's her first day home with Rome so I'm sure talking about what happened in court today is off the table. As I pull up their driveway, I realize Tez really has their ass in the country. I blew the horn to get his attention. The only thing my ass was carrying in the house was my purse.
"Why are you blowing the horn?"
"I need you to come and get the baby's stuff out the passenger side."

"Jazz? What baby stuff? I thought you had court today?"

"I was done around two. I left and did some shopping to free my mind from today."

"It took me two days and you are telling me. That you were done after a couple of hours?"

"Well I kept my hands to myself and didn't get held for contempt. Of course I would be done before you."

"You are so funny."

"I wasn't trying to be funny. How is my sis doing today?"

"Good actually. She was outside with me while I built their playground."

"How is that going? You know our kids can't wait to come over and play."

"I can't wait to have them all over either. Your man is coming through later to help me, he said he had to check on a new house you two bought?"

"Yeah this old two story house in Bellemeade that we bought a few months back. It needs a lot of work, once we finish it I know it will sell quickly."

"Oh you are not renting this one out?"

"No this one is going to sell double for what we paid for it. Sean got a great deal for this one 35k is what we spent. He can put it back on the market at 70k or more when we are done with it."

Damn you two are killing it in this market. How much longer before you build your team, I know eventually you two will be leaving here to expand."

"Yeah the plan is to wait a year and move."

"Are you still thinking about Utah?"

"I am."

"Marcus cool with that?"

"We haven't worked out all the details but yeah he is finally good with it. I mean it's not a permanent stay. Just want to get my business in some major cities that don't see me for my skin color, that's the only thing I have to pull off."

"My money is on you sis. If anyone can be a mogul is you."

"Thanks Montez, I really appreciate you saying that. Now can I go in or are you going to keep me hostage out here."

"Why are you blaming me? You stopped walking towards the front door, not me."

"Whatever man! Now move so I can get in this house. Now remember the bags in the front belong to your boys!"

"I got it Queen Jasmine!"

# Chapter Twenty- Three: Two Weeks

I had to sit there and listen to other people describe who they thought I was and give their interpretation on my relationship with Reign. I was attacked by the men in her family and my lawyer didn't want to bring that up. He said if it wasn't done by Montez he didn't see how that would help my case. He was trying to show that her husband had it out for me since day one because he was jealous. That as months went by I was still employed and the reason for that was this affair. I wanted to plead guilty when he came and spoke to me. That was my intent, I mean after her father whipped my ass that was my best bet. Then he started talking and I thought I could get off. When the trial began and Montez attacked me, my lawyer said we had him. So I sat there believing that maybe I could get off and I vowed if I did. I was going to apologize to Reign and let her know that I was truly sorry. I don't know what happened to me that night, I just snapped. I know she will never forgive me but I wanted her to know that if I could take it all back I would. That's when I decided not to take the stand and put my fate in the twelve jurors. I know what Reign's feelings are for me and she knows mine. I knew from day one that we belong together. My plan was to turn down her offer and start my own marketing company. Once I was in her office her beauty changed my mind. The pictures on the internet did her no justice, I tried not to stare when she was talking but I couldn't help it. The interview didn't last long although I wished it would have. We just had this chemistry and I knew she felt it. When he walked in and made it known who he was, I noticed she didn't look at him the way she had me. I really do believe if she wasn't carrying his child he wouldn't have been in her life. He blocked us from working one on one so many times that it was hard for her to get to know me personally. I know what I did to her that night was messed up, once I realized it. I had already taken it too far,and she felt so good I couldn't stop.I had time to think of a defense and this was the best one I could come up with. I sound crazy, I know. The moments that we did have were special. I don't care what anyone says. She was herself around me more than she was with him. He couldn't understand her skills and talents like I did. He was just obsessed with her beauty. I was in love with her mind, body, and soul. I was just late entering her world and she had to settle for him. If I would have met her right after her break up with that sorry son of a bitch. We would be one of the biggest marketing teams in the states. Instead she has to settle for less because of her sorry ass excuse of a husband. He couldn't even protect her in their marriage, he dropped the ball that night. No way would that happen to her if she was with me. He couldn't even handle me after that happened. He had to send other men to handle me. I would have beat his ass myself if I was in his shoes. I can't believe she is with that coward motherfucker, he has no clue on how to protect or love her. I know when the jurors come back they are going to find me guilty. I didn't know that she had a camera in her office. If I would have known I wouldn't have beat her like that. If I was in my right mind I wouldn't have done it all. That's God's honest truth, I didn't mean for things to get out of control. I wanted her to know that, looking around the courtroom I see she hasn't showed up again. I guess I will never get that opportunity now or ever. I wonder if she wanted to be here and he wouldn't let her. I know the doctor ordered her bedrest, she had her son though. I'm sure she is out of any danger and that just let's me know it's him still blocking. He knows his wife and I have something special and if she was here she wouldn't want me to be punished too much. I didn't mean to hurt her, I wasn't raised that way and the women in my life know this. I hurted them the most, but they promise to come and speak on my behalf if I'm convicted. The judge has entered the courtroom for the second time today. He must know something about the jury deliberation.

"The jury has reached a verdict, and since it is close to lunch I'm going to send them to lunch now. Court is now in recess until 2:00 pm."

Now we are on lunch break and I see the prosecution on the phone. It looks  like they are calling her family to let them know what is  going on. Maybe now she will show, God I hope she will. As they handcuff me to send me to the back it hit me. I could be going to jail for a very long time. They say when reality hits that ass it's a powerful punch to the head. I deserve whatever comes my way and unlike Montez I'm going to take that shit.

"How are you feeling Andre?"

"Relieved to be honest Mr. Byrd. I just want to thank you for all you have done considering the circumstances. I told you from day one that I never meant for any of this to happen and I meant that. I know if it wasn't for you talking to my mother and grandmother you wouldn't have taken the case."

"Everyone deserves redemption. You are absolutely correct your mother is the reason I took your case. Whatever the verdict may be, you make sure you tell that courtroom who Andre really is and don't hold back. You take accountability for your actions rather than the verdict is guilty or not guilty."

"I will Mr. Byrd, That I can promise."

"The jury is back in. Do you want to make an appearance now?"

"Yes. It's time for them to see me now. I mean my last experience with them had to feel like a movie. Rape victim runs in the courtroom and her water breaks as they try to get everyone out the courtroom."

"You know now that you said it like that, it did feel like a movie or a tv show. Some Law and Order type shit."

"We need someone to watch our kids, who don't want to be in the courtroom."

"You know your father in law does not like being there so we can get him."

"You are right Jazz, let me give him a call. I also need to call hubby and tell him I'm riding with you."

"I will call Tez, you get my nephews a babysitter. Montez are you headed to the courthouse?"

"Yeah, why?"

"Reign has decided she wants to be there

"Okay I will come and get her."

"I'm here, there's no need for you to do that, I will bring her."

"Who do you have to watch the boys? My sisters are with me."

"Papa Lucas said he is on the way."

"He doesn't want to be here for the verdict?"

"I guess not, Reign said he was on his way here."

"Alright we will meet y'all outside so we can go in together."

"As soon as your dad pulls up we will be on our way. See you all in a bit. Did you want to address the court or you just wanted to hear the verdict?"

"If he is found guilty, I do want too."

"I swear if that jury comes back with not guilty, it's on site for all of them."

"Sad thing is I know you are being for real. We can't be like that sis

"You continue playing peacemaker and let me continue being the hood ass friend. I said it's on fucking site for all their asses if they do not come with the correct verdict."

"My bad, do you. I mean what's another bail out for this family."

"Nothing. Just means one less lavish trip somewhere and whipping some of their asses would be well worth it to me."

"Calm down Sky Davis, I know you have hands. Let's try to keep our emotions in check. I mean I am the one he raped. If anyone needs to show their ass today if the verdict is not what it should be is me."

"Just in case you forget or you are  too stunned just know I am always ready."

"Thank God, Papa Lucas your timing is perfect! I was just about to slap my bestie."

"What are you two fighting about now?"

"Nothing, Papa Lucas, your daughter in law is being dramatic per usual."

"They are down for their nap. Rome has six bottles hopefully that is enough until I come back and MJ lunch is prepped in the refrigerator."

"Okay baby. I hope those jurors got it right and you get your justice. If they didn't don't worry, street justice will prevail for this family."

"Lord between you and Jazz.  Thank you Papa Lucus, love you."

"Oh he gets a Lord and love you. I see how it is Reign."

"Bring your ass Miss Gangsta I don't want to miss the verdict!"

      The courtroom was packed and I see that Reign did show, I guess that tells me my fate. No way they found me not guilty. Damn she is still as beautiful from the day we met and her hair is longer than what I remembered. She's even a little thicker too, pregnancy always does women bodies good and hers was most definitely done right. I asked for a DNA test to make sure it wasn't my baby boy and he wasn't. I did all that releasing in her for nothing, his weak ass was able to get her pregnant on their honeymoon. I guess that was God's way of letting me know he made no mistakes with their union. It was time for me to accept it and move on. I will always have those moments working together and that one night that was my reality and her dreams. The jury has come in and the judge is asking me to stand. He reads the verdicts and hands the paper to the bailiff so the foreman can read my fate. My head drops as they read guilty to all charges. I hear in muff as people say thank you God and hope you rot in hell. I'm sure it was louder but my body feels as if it is somewhere else besides this body. I hear the judge banging his gravel to bring back order in his courtroom. I feel Mr. Byrd tapped me and as I opened my eyes I saw the judge speaking to me. I have all these tears in my eyes that seem as if they do not want to fall. It has my vision all blurry, I try to speak but my mouth is as dry as the desert. I'm wishing that my mouth and eyes would switch places. Mr. Byrd sees that at this point his client has checked out. I hear him saying something and then helps me sit back down. I don't know what happened to me just now. I knew what that verdict was going to be and I froze up like a little bitch. The judge is talking and his voice is starting to come in and I hear him say that Reign wanted to address me and the court before he hands down my sentencing. We are taking another quick recess.

"Thank God this is finally over and my baby can move on for good," Charlene cried.

"How are you holding up baby girl? Are you sure you want to address him?"

"I'm sure daddy. I need for everyone to know what it's been like for me, my husband, family and friends. I wasn't able to testify and all they have is your all picture of me and video of my nightmare. It's time for the person they brought justice for, to speak."

"Do you need me to stand with you?"

"No baby. You already did that for me, it's time for me to address him all by myself."

"If that's what you need then I'm going to give you that."

"Thank you."

"Reign I know you have this. I want you to also know that if at any moment I see you don't I'm coming to get you off that stand."

"I know you will Jazz."

"Alright just as long as we understand each other."

"The court is ready to reassume."

"Thank  you bailiff we are coming," Lillian reassures him. "Reign do you need me to help you go over what you are going to say? I can get your more time if you need it."

"No, I'm ready to get this over with and get back home to my children."

"Okay let's get you up there and out of here."

"Is the prosecution ready?"

"Yes we are your honor."

"How many people is the state calling for the sentencing?"

"We are only calling one person and she is ready to address the court, your honor."

"Alright call your only witness."

"The state calls Mrs. Reign Alexis Santos to the stand."

"Mrs. Santos, you may address the court. Whenever you are ready."

"I just want to thank the jurors for seeing the truth and not the lies the defense was telling on me. I never once cheated on my husband nor carried on any kind of affair with Andre and I'm thankful that you all were able to determine that without hearing from me. I wanted to be here during the trial and I wanted to testify to clear my name. My health and being close to my delivery date wouldn't let me do so. My dealings with Andre were always professional until that night he crossed the line. I know you all saw the video but what you don't hear is us and what was being said before he raped me. I was going back to the office because I grabbed the wrong laptop. I did this a lot, this wasn't my first time doing it. As I go back in my rings and it's Andre on the phone asking me if I could go back to the building. He told me that he had grabbed the wrong laptop. We joked for a moment because I told him that I had done the same thing and that I was already here. I asked him how far he was and he said he was at the light. I told him to hurry because I had to get home to my family. As I walked back to return the company laptop and grab mine I left my purse and keys on the secretary desk because I wanted to be in and out. As I'm cleaning up my office, Andre comes in and says he has his laptop. I'm thinking cool, let's get up outta here and get home. Then he started asking me weird questions like he always does and I'm thinking not tonight Andre I'm tired and as I have told him many times before. Business is business and my personal life is none of his concerns. That night though I just didn't want to go through those awkward moments with him and the more I tried to leave the more aggressive he was. When he kissed me that pissed me off and before I knew it I had fired him and that's when things got out of control and I found myself fighting for my life and at the time I didn't know I was also fighting for my unborn. I don't remember the rape as it was happening my soul was somewhere else. It took me almost a year to watch that video tape but I found the strength to do so. It took rehab and a lot of therapy but I finally got to see what you did to me that night Andre. I saw the monster in you that they warned me about. You violated me in ways I will never forget therefore I can never forgive you. I won't be here to hear you address the court. I won't be here when they sentence you. I just want you to know no amount of years handed will ever justify what you did to me, my unborn child and my husband. You are a truly sick person and may God have mercy on your soul.

# *Chapter Twenty-Four: Plans Change*

I know I am not supposed to swear but damn it I am. Why do Sunday mornings come so goddamn fast? I swear the weekend needs to be three days instead of two! Give us Friday or Monday but two days is just not enough. Although I'm an entrepreneur I rarely get days off, I guess that's what being a boss means. This shit is still exhausting to me. Maybe things will be better when Sincere comes out. He has really been wearing me out lately and today has been no different. "Baby boy you are truly slowing mommy down and I'm not used to being this damn tired. You have to meet mommy halfway at least move off my left side a little son. No? Okay fine I will adjust. I have so much to do before the wedding in a couple of months and a honeymoon to plan after you come into this world." I had everything under control and moving smoothly then all of a sudden problems started popping up here and there. I had to spend time on that and it took away from me meeting Miss Janice and my mother or Reign had to step in. Now Sean and I have to decide on a good seafood cater and we still haven't picked out a bakery to do our cake. I thought I had the perfect person to do the cake but Sean didn't like she was located in Greenville. Now we are searching for someone in North Carolina closer to our wedding venue. I mean it makes sense now that I said it out loud to myself. I bitched of course when he told me it wouldn't make sense to use her and play extra for them to deliver it out of state. At the time I thought he was being cheap, in reality he was being smart. I'm trying hard not to be a bridezilla but the closer we get our date the more I become one. I need a fire ass cater though. I love me some crab legs and I love for them to be season just right. There's this guy in Greenville that makes them, how I love them and I'm tryin to convince Sean to at least hire him and pay for his expenses. He promised me he would if we couldn't find someone in NC. God please let everyone we test taste suck. We are traveling up there next weekend to do that and my greedy ass can't wait. Our menu for the wedding is fire. You have a choice of steak or lobster. Plus we have a little soul food to go with it. When you are doing a small wedding you can spend crazy everywhere else. And since we both like to eat and drink that's where the majority of our money is going.

"You look comfortable."

"No thanks to your son! He is being a butthole today, literally."

"He still won't move his butt from your left side?"

"Nope."

"Damn he has been there since Friday. Here let me see if I can convince him to give you a break."

"It's okay babe. It took me a minute just to get this position to work."

"What are you doing?"

"I'm online looking for stuff to add to the bridesmaid gift bags."

"Jazz I thought you were about to say you were looking for more carters for Saturday. I was about to snatch your computer from you."

"No lie. I just got off of google searching. I said Sean will kill me if I add one more damn thing to do this weekend."

"I'm glad you know that. Damn I need to step up my game for the groomsmen. You are getting them all of that?"

"Is that too much?"

"Not really. I just got them a watch and a hundred dollar gift card to Footlocker."

"Babe really?"

"What?"

"Sean let me help you make that a little more thoughtful, after I finish ordering my stuff."

"We are men, what else do they need? The watches are sterling silver with everyone's favorite team. I think that's good."

"I am tuning you out."

"Don't be tuning me out woman. Don't you order those knuckleheads anything else."

"How about some alcohol and some fly groomsmen t-shirts to add to your gift bag? Look here's a website where you can design them how you want too."

"Okay that's not a bad idea actually it's pretty dope. You said I can pick out any designs right?"

"Yep, here have at it. Baby, I'm going to the kitchen, do you want me to bring you something back?"

"I'm good."

"Alright, don't you ask for a sip or bite Sean. I mean it."

"I'm good, Jazz. I'm not hungry or dehydrated."

"Remember what you said fathead!" As she entered the kitchen she decided to make herself a baby club sandwich. She places four pieces of bread in the toaster. She walks over to the fridge and takes out a tomato, lettuce, bacon, turkey, ham, cheese mayo and pickles. She places four strips of bacon in the pan and sets the stove on medium. She cuts up the tomatoes, ham, and turkey. She then takes one Swiss and American cheese out of the wrapper  as she was finishing up on that her toast popped up. She grabbed a plate and placed it on the counter. She started layering all of her stuff and waited for the bacon to finish cooking.

"Jasmine. I thought you said you were grabbing a snack? You are in here making a whole meal."

"What I actually said was, "I'm headed to the kitchen." Stop staring down at my sandwich son, you said you were good remember?"

"That's because I thought you were grabbing snacks. It's fine I will fix my own sandwich."

"Sounds good to me since I'm not sharing mine."

"You made that clear in the bedroom."

"Did you finish designing the t-shirts?"

"Yeah and I ordered them too. I put a rush on it so it's supposed to be here Thursday."

"Are you going to get them alcohol too?"

"I will tomorrow or when the shirts get here. Let me have a bite, baby?"

"You are so lucky I love you, here."

"Damn that's good. I wish my bacon hurry the fuck up. What did you put yours on?"

"Medium."

"Oh no wonder. There we go!"

"You are so crazy. Montez is still riding with you later, right?"

"Yeah he said he will be here around three so we can go get the kids. Why?"
"You know why?"
"If he canceled you were going with me. I'm still not cool with that muthafucker like that."
"I'm going to need you to get cordial like I have with Dana."
"I didn't cheat on you with Dana. It's easier for you to be cordial with her."
"Really Sean?"
"I'm just keeping it one hundred with you. I'm not throwing it in your face but that's just facts."
"Okay."
"For real baby I wasn't saying it
"I said okay Sean. Leave it alone!"
"Jazz for real
"I'm going back to lay down. I'm tired. If I'm not up before you leave just wake me up to let me know you are gone."
"Jasmine! Seriously man! Damn!"
        "What time is it?"
"A little bit after ten."
"Aw man I overslept. I need to feed Rome."
"I already took care of him, lay back down and rest."
"He went back to sleep?"
"No, but Abs and Sades have them, you're good. You should take advantage while they are here. You know they leave with me to go pick up the kids."
"You're right let me get some z's in."
"I'm going to get them in with you."
"Now you know if you get behind me, there will be no sleeping."
"We will be on our best behavior, I promise."
'Uh huh."
"While you were giving your best sleeping beauty this morning. Sean called and his ass is in the dog house. You should be hearing from Jazz when we are on the road."
"All he has to do is feed that girl. How did he end up in the dog house? They ran out of food or something?"
"Why you gotta be like that about your sis?"
"Did I lie though?Jazz only bite your head off if she hasn't eaten. We all know this."
"I mean it's facts but he really did put his foot in his mouth and it could have been avoided."
"Don't tell me. Let Jazz do it that way I can react accordingly. I need sleep to show up. I hate trying to force myself to sleep."
"Do you want me to play Anita Baker or Sade?"
"Oh um tell Alexa to play both. I don't know why but those voices knock me every time."
"Excuse me! Are you two decent?!"
"Yes Mersades! Come in!"
"Rome is running low on diapers, can I get someone keys so I can get him some?"
"Take my car. My keys should be in my purse on the bathroom door. Do you need money?"

"Nope I got my nephew. I don't know if you two want to trust Abs by himself with them. Although Rome is on his way out again."

"He will come and get us if he needs one of us."

"Alright. I will be right back."

"I love this song. You should text Sean and tell him to play I Apologize."

"You are wilding."

"I'm trying to help him," she said laughing.

"The lyrics don't even match their situation. They live in the same house."

"All he has to do is keep saying the chorus. He will be fine."

"Close your eyes and go to sleep baby you have run out."

"Okay tell him to play it to her once y'all get on the road. He can call her and then as soon as she picks up let it play.

"We are not in the 90's Reign. Seriously babe go back to sleep."

"This is exactly what's wrong with men today. They have no love songs or creativity.He will remain in the dog house if he doesn't come up with something out of the box and totally left field."

"If I tell you that I will suggest it, will you drop it?"

"Consider it dropped."

"Thank you. Reign?"

"Hmm?"

"If you sing every song that comes on. You will never fall asleep."

"I forgot how many hits she had. Alright, I'm just going to listen. Let me turn this way so you won't be tempted."

"It really doesn't matter which way you lay. I'm always going to be tempted, facing me really not going to help the situation." As he kisses her on the forehead she closes her eyes and lets the music and his soft kisses help her drift off. When she opens her eyes, she finds herself in the parking lot of her old office building. Immediately she knows that she is dreaming and tries to wake herself up but to no avail. She tries to change her thoughts because she feels she controls her own dream, still nothing changes. She realizes she has no other choice; she walks in the vacant building and lets her dream play out. When she opens the door the building she once called her own has been changed into some kind of redemption center. Tamara asks her who she is there to see and she is confused because Tam is acting as if she doesn't know her.

"Ma'am I said, "Who are you here to visit?"

"I don't know how I arrived here, therefore I have no idea who I am here to see."

"Did you receive a phone call or a letter ma'am?"

"Neither."

"Did you just walk in out of curiosity?"

"Yes."

"Okay this is a redemption center for men who did women wrong. They come here to learn from their mistakes in bad relationships and how to better themselves from it. Any time a woman comes in here she is usually a woman from their past. That came to check on her ex or exes. Do you think that your ex is here?"

"I wouldn't care if he was or not. He's an ex for a reason and once we are done I wish him well and move on."

"Oh I see. You are one of those women. Again why did you walk through those doors? Why not just turn around and get back in your car?"

"I tried several times but I can't seem to end this dream."

"Dream?"

"Yeah dream. No way this is real. I was just being kissed and held by my husband and when I woke up. I'm at my old office talking to you and you are carrying on like you don't know me."

"Because I don't know you. Ma'am is there someone I can call for you? You don't look well. How about your husband? What's his name?"

"Tamara you know who my husband is."

"My name is not Tamara, it's Tam."

"I know it's Tam that's what we call you when we don't feel like saying your whole name."

My whole name? Um Miss my whole name is Tam, it's not short for anything.

"Reign is that you?"

"Damien?"

"How did you know I was here?"

"I didn't."

"There is so much I wanted to say to you. I wanted to reach out when I heard about you being raped but I figured you didn't want to hear from me. Then I come around the corner and you are here and for a split second, I thought you did wanna hear from me."

"It would have been nice if you did reach out. I would have accepted the call but you didn't and I'm fine with that too."

"Since you are here can we take a walk and talk a little. There were some things I wanted to say to you that I never got the chance to because of your father's final threats to me."

"I thought this dream was about Andre. I wasn't expecting you."

"Dream? You are not dreaming. Reign this is real." She wakes up with Jazz all in her face. She jumped back so fast she almost fell out of her bed.

"The hell, Reign! Girl are you alright?"

"Just let me catch my breath real quick! Where's Montez?"

"They left about ten minutes ago. He said you were sleeping and I came up here to wake your ass up. Well I raided your fridge first then I came up. You are sweating, were you having a nightmare?"

"Did he seem upset?"

"No. Why did he say some stupid shit to you like his boy did to me?"

"No. My dream was just crazy as fuck that's all. What happened with you and Sean?"

"Montez didn't tell you?"

"He said he would leave it up to you. Now tell me what happened."

"I figured I would forever wear the Scarlet Letter with him. Be honest with my sis. Did you bring up Dame's infidelities every chance you got after accepting his ring?"

"Why are you bringing him up?"

"I know you and I always talked about his cheating. I was just wondering when it was you and him did you throw it in his face out of the blue?"

"Out the blue? No. During an argument? Damn near every time. Did he bring it up out of the blue or were you two arguing?"

"He went totally left field on me. I can honestly say I didn't see it coming because we were not arguing at all."

"Well that's fucked up. What made him bring it up? What were you two talking about?"

"He said if Montez wouldn't have been able to ride with him to pick up the girls. I would have to ride with him. He's still not cool with him for him to be around Marcus by himself. All I said was I needed him to be cordial with him like I am with Dana. This muthafucker is going to say it's easier for me because he didn't cheat with my ex like I did. He didn't stop there. He continued and said I'm not trying to make you feel bad or start an argument. I'm just keeping it one hundred."

"When keeping it real goes totally wrong."

"You know the saying never ask a question that you don't want an answer to?"

"Yeah."

"I really want to know how many more times he's going to bring that up? Do I have to put up with this shit while we are married? If so sis, he needs to let me know now. I have no problem returning this ring and being by myself."

"Whoa Jasmine! That's a little too dramatic don't you think?"

"No I don't Reign. Who really wants to be in a marriage knowing it's constantly going to be thrown in your face?" Not me. I wouldn't want him to be with me if I was doing it to him."

"I understand that I do. I just think this can be fixed without you calling off the relationship and wedding. That's all I'm saying."

"I don't mean to sound insensitive when I say this. It's been two years. He should be over that by now. I haven't cheated on him since and I'm not understanding why he is still bringing it up out of the blue like this. Can we at least be arguing and then hit me below the belt that's all I am saying."

"When is y'all next marriage counsel with the pastor? Don't you two have one more before the wedding next month?"

"Yes a week before the wedding. I don't want to wait that long though. I need to get this over with before we return home."

"I know that. I wasn't about to suggest that you wait till then to resolve it. What I was about to say is make sure you two get the pastor to help you two through this. That way it can be agreed to never be brought up again once you two say I do."

"Remind me that next month. Right now I need us to come up with something tonight."

"Just tell him how you feel Jazz. You should have done that instead of going to bed pissed. Now you have to sit in that piss till they get back. Do me one favor?"

"What's that?"

"Leave the kids here. I don't want my God babies around all that negativity, therefore I am volunteering a sleepover. I haven't had the girls in awhile anyway and I need some girl time. I love my boys but there's not too many things I can do with them."

"Let me see if I have this right. You are going to wake up EARLY in the morning and take them to school. Pick them up after school and hang out with them a little before bringing them home. All that so I can get in Sean's ass tonight?"

"Um so you all can talk and get to the bottom of this without worrying about the kids hearing you."

"That's what I said."

"Yeah. Okay."

"Reign. I haven't forgotten about you."

"What'cha mean?"

"Bitch! Nice try! What were you dreaming about that almost had your ass on the floor, that you didn't want your husband to hear?"

"Nothing."

"Spill it!"

"Alright! I had a dream about Damien."

"Ew! Why"

"I wish I knew."

"You two wasn't having sex were you?"

"It wasn't a sex dream, Jazz. Before you ask, it wasn't a dream about us getting back together either. I was at my old office and standing in the parking lot and I just knew when I walked in it was going to be Andre waiting on me. I tried waking up and I couldn't. I had no other choice but to walk in."

"Dame was waiting on you?"

"No actually Tam was in her usual spot but she didn't know who I was. Instead of being my secretary she was a receptionist for a Redemption center."

"Oh wow. What unfinished business do you two have?"

"I don't know, you woke me up."

"You are not going to reach out to him. Reign? Dear God, you are. Listen to me, leave it alone and move on from this dream. It was just a dream, leave it alone."

"Funny. This is the first time I've heard it's a dream. I kept saying that in my dream and Tam, Damien and even you kept telling me it wasn't. I mean shouldn't I finish the conversation we started?"

"You weren't having a discussion with him. That shit wasn't real, baby girl. Reign listen you are forgetting about someone. Montez is not going to let you reach out or meet up with him. You can't be serious right now. You're actually going to meet up with him without telling your husband, are you crazy?"

"I didn't say that. The fuck?"

"You don't have to say it, its clearly written all over your fucking face. I'm telling you listen to me, leave it alone for the last time."

"Okay! Can we please talk about something else."

"Reign you are so fucking hard headed but okay we can. I'm hungry, let's grab the boys and go to Chili's."

"Whatever. Let's go."

# Chapter Twenty-Five: Juneteenth

Thought about it so many times to postpone the date until after Sincere was born. The bigger I got the closer I came to doing it. Sean had to convince me so many times that I would be beautiful in my dress. That it didn't matter to him all he needed was for me to say I do. Now here I am fat and happy that our wedding day is finally here. We decided to have a beach wedding and once again I am having second thoughts. I have to maintain a balance in sand. One misstep and I'm taking my dad, myself and Sincere out. Lord give me balance and give my father balance and strength. I must have been deep in my thoughts because Reign was in my ears snapping her fingers.

"If I ask you one mo time and don't get a response I know something."

"What was said?"

"Girl, where are you right now?"

"Sis I'm scared. Why didn't you talk me out of this beach wedding?"

"How am I supposed to talk you out of something that you and your man wanted? Girl now is not the time for cold feet."

"I don't have cold feet, I have wobbling feet."

"Huh?!"

"I keep seeing myself having a tumbling wedding."

"You are not going to fall because you have my nephew in you and you know I will kill you if you hurt him."

"Ugh. I can't stand you! Put more pressure on me, why don't you."

"Girl! You will be fine I promise. Now can you please answer my question."

"What did you ask me?"

"Did you want another bottle of water? We need you hydrated in this damn heat."

"I'm good, I just released the last bottle and now that my dress is on I'm good."

"Well your mom said she will have an extra one just in case."

"Okay."

"I wanted to give you something and since it's just you and me. I wanted to give you something old and borrowed. Do you remember this?"

"Reign! You kept that?"

"Well of course I did! It was the first birthday gift you ever made me why wouldn't I? I wanted my daughter to have it but it doesn't seem as if I'm going to have one right now.I want you to keep this till I do have a baby girl."

"I hope this sister bracelet still fits."

"It does, see?"

"Thank you babe you are the best."

"Please do not cry."

"I can't help it, you are so sweet and thoughtful. Plus my hormones are all over the place."

"Oh God! Here Jazzy dap your face. Do you have to do the ugly cry?"

"Yes!"

"Okay, okay! Toya!"

"Are you two okay in here?"

"Mama Lillian can you get her MUA? She's a little emotional from my gift."

"I see. Let me see if I can find her."

"Thanks a lot friend, now you have your mother side eyeing me."

"Sorry."

"Now Reign what did you do."

"Being too good of a sister is all I'm guilty of Toya."

"I made this for her when we were ten years old and she still had it."

"Aw, that's so sweet. Is that something old?"

"And borrowed, she wants me to hold on to it until she has her first daughter."

"Well hell I'm not pregnant and that's making me tear up."

"I can not with you two. Can you please get her back to what she was while I go talk with the other bridesmaids."

"I sure will.

"I don't look that bad do I?"

"Girl no. I just need to touch you up a bit that's all."

"Have you seen the set up out there?"

"Yes. It is so gorgeous out there. The black and red decorations are different but you all did great with it. I have never been to a sunset beach wedding before. I can't wait to see the outcome of it."

"You? I can't wait either. I just need to make it to my groom and I will be fine."

"You will girl, I have known you since our college days. This bump will not get in your way plus Mr. Butler won't let that happen."

"You right I just need to relax and get over these last fifteen minutes."

"It will be over before you know it and you will officially be Mrs. Jasmine Nicole Gray. Look just like that I am done, my beautiful black queen."

"Toya I keep telling you that you need to be doing make up for the stars! I know a few celebrities that need you desperately. Thank you so much for coming through at the last minute for me again. I know you were invited just to attend the wedding so good looking out."

"No problem love. Well if you need me again I will be right out here."

"I'm not crying anymore til I'm walking down the aisle, go be with your husband. I will see you after the ceremony."

"Alright Jazz, the bridesmaids are ready. Miss Janice is setting everyone up."

"I am ready. I am done crying and ready to get the ceremony started."

"They are ready and in place. Yasmine, SJ, and Marcella are waiting with your dad. Only person missing is you. Do you need a moment to yourself?"

"No I'm good and ready to go."

"Alright let me get out here because Mrs. Janice has my ass."

Jasmine looks at herself in the mirror and gives Sincere a rub. She says a quick prayer to God and then opens the door to see her father waiting to escort her. They don't say a word to one another, their eyes say it all. He wipes his tears and holds out his arm for her. As she tries her best not to mess up her makeup she exhales one more time and pulls down her vail. She connects her arms with her dad and slightly squeezes his hand to let him know she is ready. The children are signalled by Mrs. Janice signals for SJ to come first, he looked so handsome with his white suit and red bow tie. He was giving the crowd a show with his little strut he had going. Once he is half way done Mrs. Janice signals the Jazz Orchestra and they switch the music as Luke James walks out. They started playing I Was Made To Love You by Gerald Levert. As Luke serenaded the crowd with his smooth vocals, Yasmine and Marcella came down the aisle throwing down white and red rose petals. As the people stood to watch Jasmine make her entrance all you could hear was the oh's and awe's she was receiving because her maternity bride dress was fit for a black queen. The dress was off white with a long train with red rose petals. She had her eyes on Sean and he had his eyes on her. He smiles harder as they get closer and Montez gives him an elbow nod. She passes her bouquet to Reign. The preacher asks, "who gives this woman to be married to this man."

"I do," Rome says as he places his daughter's hand into Sean's. Sean removes her vail from her face and when he sees her tears escapes his eyes. She takes her hand and wipes them from his face. As the preacher continues with the wedding scripts she places Sean hands on her stomach so he could feel his son's movement. When the pastor says, "If anyone can show just cause why this couple cannot lawfully be joined together in matrimony, let them speak now or forever hold their peace." Everyone turns their attention towards Marcus as he puts his head down. There were a few laughs and the pastor continued with the ceremony. "These two have written their own vows, Jasmine."

"When we first met, I never knew that this would be our outcome. At the time I was just looking for a male companion to spend personal time with while I was in a new city. As time went by you became more than a companion you became my best friend my confidant. You saw things in me that I didn't see in myself you gave me the confidence to strive for my dreams. You loved my daughters from day one and treated them as your own. You have always been a strong black king in our home and you led by example. I am so grateful for your love and support. I'm so thankful for the husband and father our family has gained. There's not enough words for me to tell you how much I love and appreciate you Sean. I only pray that as we become one that everyday you can not only see it but feel until death do us part."

"Sean, your vows for Jasmine."

"I thank God everyday for bringing you into my world on July 19. I remember that day like it was yesterday. You came to the door with your bonnet and PJ's on. You thought you looked a hot mess, all I saw was your true beauty. I remember you were so mad at Montez and Reign for not giving you the heads up that day. You said you were going to get ready but I heard you on the phone giving them two the business."

"Babe you heard me," she said laughing, you never told me that?"

"Too funny," Reign said laughing with her.

"Yeah baby you were pretty loud even with the water running."

"Oh, God."

It's okay though I knew then that I wasn't going to let you. I said to myself that's a woman who will always be straightforward and will always keep it real with me. We had a moment that we were apart, my life felt incomplete. That time apart made me realize I never wanted that again. There is no me without you, I'm just grateful I figured that out before it was too late. I love you and cherish everything about you. Being with you made me a better man, father and now husband. This union is forever only death can do us part on earth. But our soul will forever be a union in the afterlife." As he spoke tears flowed down her face and he kissed them away when he was done. She wasn't the only one crying; his vows to her touched a lot of people that were there. They exchanged rings and the pastor announced them husband and wife. They went back to the venue to eat and celebrate. The jazz band they hired was playing all the hits as they party into the night. They had to put the honeymoon on hold until Sincere was born. Montez and Reign had gifted them a trip to Bora Bora and Tahaiti. They thought they were going to have to choose, their friends made sure they didn't. Once they were done for tonight they headed to their hotel. When he opened the door and carried her through the threshold she saw that the room was covered with white jasmine chinese flowers. He also had red and white roses in vases on the table and throughout the bathroom. In the background he had their favorite love songs playing. He also had her favorite fruits from strawberries to kiwi with a bottle of sparkling white grape juice.

"Oh wow baby this is so beautiful," she said as she walked through the room. "Thank God I am already carrying your child."

"You already know. You really like it? It's not too much?"

"No, not at all. I absolutely love it. You are so thoughtful, I love you for that. I hate that you can't drink tonight."

"Please. Being drunk off on your love is all I need for these next three days. I wished our wedding could have lasted longer. I will never forget how beautiful you were coming down the aisle. I tried to play that shit cool until I pulled up your veil."

"We almost made it."

"Almost. Little man did good today. He got a little excited during the vows but he seems rested now."

Of course, I fed him well at the reception. We have the green light for the rest of the night. Oh this is my song! Dance with me husband." She puts her hands out for him to grab. He pulls her close and they stare into each other's eyes as their bodies find the same rhythm to the music. She takes her nails and softly glides them on the back of his neck. He leans in and they share a passionate kiss as Jazz begins to unbutton his shirt. Once she unbuttoned the last button she rubs his abs and trails her nails up to his chest. In a seductive move she takes her hand and places it on his shoulder to remove his shirt from his body. She places soft kisses on his lower back. The tingle sensation made his manhood rise as he let out a moan. She made herself  back around to face him again so she could unbutton his pants before she could pull them off. Sean grabs her hand and puts two of her fingers in his mouth, then he removes his pants. She takes the slightly wet hand and begins to give him a honeymoon special. He took as much as he could before picking her up and carrying her to the bed. He began to undress her and was pleased to see she already had on her sexy lingerie from Savage X Fenty. He removes her bra and kisses on her lower back. He gently bends her over and places his face in her cinnamon bun and lets his tongue taste all of it. The way he was satisfying her back there made her take her fingers and please herself in her wetness til he made his way there. Now that he had her joining in his honeymoon special to her. He positions himself underneath her thighs and helps guide her to sit on his face.The more her legs trembled the deeper his tongue went in. Jazz finally taps out and lays on her side. He finished removing what little clothing they had and got behind her. He placed all nine inches in and worked her until he released in her. Tears flowed from her eyes and now she understood what Reign was telling her about her and Montez first night. It was different when you became his wife. The passion is on another level, the love seems different and the emotions are definitely on another level. Sean kisses her on the shoulder, before turning her towards him. He kissed her on the lips and finally noticed her tears. Concerned that he hurt her while making love. He wipes her tears, "baby are you okay? Did I do something wrong, was I too rough?"

"No you were perfect. My emotions are just all over the place, I can't wait to bring your son into this world. He really has mommy going through it." He rubs her stomach and tries to help her get comfortable.

"It won't be too much longer, he will be here soon enough."

"I can't wait to see what he looks like and whose personality he will have."

"He will be all me."

"You think so?"

"You want to make an all you? We can plan to do that once he turns one."

"You better get these babies out the way. Because when I hit thirty, it's a wrap. I am not bearing anymore kids."

"Just as long as I get my baby girl, I am fine with that."

"Stop making all these boys then. I know I can give you a daughter so it's not me that is the problem."

"I'm not worried you will have my princess before you are the big three zero."

"I hear the confidence, I hope God will bless you with her. You see Reign is 0-2, maybe you and Montez are supposed to only produce boys."

"Please he isn't my brother by DNA we have nothing in common when it comes to that. Just as long as you agree we can try again, that's all I need."

"You know what I need right now?"

"Food?"

"Yassss!"

"What do you want?"

"The fruit you have in here will be just fine. I just need a little nutrient for round two." Sean damn near broke his ankle trying to get out the bed to get the plate of fruit. She clapped her hands when she saw that he regained his balance and made it to the table without getting her. "My husband has speed and skills," she said laughing. Now come and feed me Seymour.

# *Chapter Twenty-Six: Dragging*

Dr. Leslie put me on bedrest because Sincere decided he wanted to go over my due date. Now he is talking about inducing me by the end of the week if my water doesn't break. I must say being on bedrest after a wonderful pre honeymoon has me hoping these last few days go by slowly. Sean will be home soon and I have our entertainment room setup for movie night. He was out with our munchkins at Frankie's Fun Park, tiring them out so it won't be any interruptions for our date night. I love old classic movies and movies from the 90's. I love to laugh and a sucker for great love movies. Tonight I wanted to do an Eddie Murphy movie-athon. I forgot this man has an unbelievable catalog. That made me settle for his top five in Sean and I opinions .Nutty Professor, Coming To America, Beverly Hills Cops, Boomerang and Life. I know he has some classic ones we left out. We will have plenty of movie nights to watch them all. I couldn't wait for them to get back. My hubby promised me a foot rub. I also brought everything he needed for that. I think my little set up is cute. I have the aroma candles lit and the room dim. I have Billie Holiday playing in the background. We have fresh cut peaches and strawberries, cheese cubes, grapes, and two cucumber water. He wanted to do the popcorn because he knows how to season it just right with butter and hot sauce. I seem to over do it with the hot sauce, what can I say I love my food hot and spicy. I can admit though his popcorn is better than the movie theaters. Although I have hot sauce in my bag it's hard to get it just right at the movie theater. That's why we get the large so we can refill that bad boy when the movie is over. I mean twenty damn dollars for a large bucket and two medium drinks is a lot. You better get your free refill, I don't give a damn what your income status is. It's the principle of the whole thing.

"Hey mommy," Yasmine yells as she runs into the entertainment room.

"Hey Yas! I see you won it big at Frankie's. Did you have fun?"

"Yes and we rode the go carts! Can I get one for Christmas mommy? They are so much fun!"

"Um we will have to see if your dad is comfortable with that. I'm sure it won't be a problem."

"Sean said he would get me and SJ one. Why do you have to ask daddy?"

"Yasmine."

Okay mom, okay. We will ask daddy for permission too."

"Thank you. Where is the rest of the crew?"

"They are coming. Marcella was asleep so Sean is carrying her to bed. SJ is grabbing the other stuff out of the car. I'm going to take a bath and go to bed. Can I get on my ipad for a little a while after I am finished?"

"That's fine sweetie. Did you want me to come and help you run your tub water? "

"No I got it, she yells as she runs upstairs."

"Hey mama Jazz, I won you something."

"Aw you did. Thank you for the bracelet, this is so sweet."

"I got me and my brother this basketball."

"I know he will like it when he gets here."

"I can't wait until he arrives and gets bigger. I like playing with daddy but I want to play with my little brother more."

"I know baby. You are an awesome big brother even to Marcella and Yasmine. Sincere is going to be lucky to have you."

"Can I touch him before I go to bed?"

"You know you don't have to ask."

"Hey Sincere.I got us another ball to play with. I have a basketball this time. Okay lil bruh see you later." He kisses her stomach and then kisses Jasmine on the cheek. Good night mama Jazz."

"Goodnight sweetie."

"Hey baby. I'm going to lay her down and I will be right back for our date night."

"Okay baby."

"SJ hey man! You need to take a bath! Come in here and use our bathroom!"

"Daddy that's not fair! Celly doesn't have too!"

"Hey first of all Celly wasn't doing all what you and Yas were doing. Second of all, as you can see she is asleep. She doesn't have to get one tonight. Now get yourself in here and run your bath water!"

"After I'm done can I play video games?"

"No man, you are going to bed. I'm trying to have date night."

"Daddy why the girls get their way and I don't. Yasmine said she was getting on her IPad. She plays games on that."

Yas is going to bed too."

"No she's not. Mama Jazz said she could."

"Fine SJ. You can play for a little while then go to bed."

"Thanks dad."

"Why did you have me take them to Frankie's to wear them out and then give them permission to stay up?"

"They are in their rooms, they are not coming down here with us. Besides a few minutes on their devices they will be sleeping just like Marcella."

"I hope you are right. I see you have everything set up. Let me get the popcorn started and put on something comfortable. I will be right back."

"What movie do you want to watch first?"

"Life!"

"Baby!"

"Yeah!

"Can you bring my throw on your way back down!"

"Yeah babe, I got you!"

        "Hey daddy. What are you doing?"

Hey princess. What are you doing up this late?"

"We just got back from Frankie's Fun Park and I rode the go carts."

"You did? By yourself?"

"Yes! Sean rode with Marcella while me and SJ rode by ourselves."

"You are becoming a big girl on me."
"I'm growing up and will be in the fourth grade when school starts back. I was wondering for Christmas if my grades stay great. Can I get a go kart for Christmas?"
"What did your mother say?"
She told me to ask you and if you say yes I could. So can I daddy? Please?"
"I don't have a problem with it. You know it depends on your grades, right?"
"No problem daddy."
"Okay well if you do that I will get you one."
"Thank you daddy, you are the best."
"No problem baby girl. Now where's Marcella?"
"She's already asleep."
"Okay well tell her I love her and give her the biggest hug and kiss for me."
" I will daddy."
"Goodnight baby girl."
"I love you daddy, goodnight."
I love you too, Yasmine."

# *Chapter Twenty-Seven: Sincere Nicholas Gray*

   I woke up constipated around three am and I have been sitting on this toilet for at least an hour. Now my foot has fallen asleep and I have to wake up my baby to help me back in bed. I couldn't find the strength to yell so I called him on the house phone instead. I knew he had turned off his cell phone so there was no point in calling that. He answers with an attitude ready to curse out the person on the other line before I let that happen. I hurried up and said, "hey baby it's me and told him that I needed his assistant to get me back in the bed."

"Did you call out to me and I didn't respond?"

"No. I couldn't find the strength to do all of that."

"Oh okay, I'm on my way."

"Thanks babe."

"How long have you been in here?"

"About an hour. I got caught up on this game and next thing I know my foot was heavy and I couldn't feel anything."

"Did you at least finish your business in here?"

"Yeah I'm done. I thought I had to boo boo but nothing came out so I'm ready to get back in bed and knock out."

"Me too. I was sleeping real good until you called the house phone."

"I figured that since you didn't wake up when I got up an hour ago. I said then my baby is tired. Whew! Okay that hurt."

"What hurt?"

"I don't think I was constipated anymore Sean. I think those were actually ouch, damn it! Baby I think I'm going into labor."

"Oh shit! For real? Okay alright I got this! Stay calm while I call my mother.

"Hello?"

"Mom! It's time!"

"Okay! I am on my way! Stay calm, I will be there shortly."

"My mom is on her way to watch our kids. Let me call your parents so they could be on their way. I'm taking your bag to the car while I do that. Are you good right here til I get back?"

"Yes! I'm calling Reign now so she can meet us there."

"Okay baby I will be right back."

"Hey you have reached"

"Damn it Reign why do you have your cell off. Let me try the house."

"Hello, a grumpy voice whispered."

"Ouch, ouch, ouch. Um Tez can you wake up Reign. It's time ouch."

"Huh?"

"Tez! Man, wake your wife up. I am in labor!"

"Jazz?"

"Fool! Who else would be calling saying that?! Ouch!"

"See God don't like ugly! I'm up damn! I'm about to get Reign up so she can meet y'all there."

"Thank you!"

"Alright baby we are set. Let me get you in the car so when mom pulls up we can roll out. I already called Dr. Leslie, he has notified our nurse. Smooth sailing baby smooth sailing."

"Says the man who ain't getting his ass kicked right now! Ain't nothing easy over her, shit!"

"No babe I wasn't saying

"You know what let me just cut you off right there. I don't give a damn what you meant ouch!"

"Remember the class baby. Inhale. One Mississippi two Mississippi and exhale. Feeling a little better."

"Uh huh."

"Okay come on I got you let me help you in. You want the seatbelt on?"

"No. Baby I need your hand."

"Jazz please don't break it. Okay again aw one Mississippi two Mississippi. exhale. Jazz, it's Abs."

"Put him on speaker! "

"Hey man you are on speaker."

"Where's Jazzy."

"I'm here Abs."

"Hang in there we are on our way. You good?"

"Mm hmm the best, baby brother."

"Okay you are lying. You don't have to be strong for me Jazzy."

"Okay okay! I am in some serious ouch, pain! I will see you all when you get here. Love you Abs!"

"Love you too. Hey man step on it and get my nephew there on time."

"Man I'm doing over a hundred with the hazard lights going."

"Fool don't wreck trying to keep them there!"

"Make up your mind Absalom!"

"Get 'em there safe that's clear enough for you?"

"I will! See you all when you get here.

"Alright man, it should be in an hour."

"Cool. Baby I need my hand so I can get around this curve."

"Baby I'm sorry I forgot I had it!"

"We are pulling up to the ER. Besides the labor pains are you okay?"

"I'm good baby. Just let them know what is going on."

"We are going to need a wheelchair, she's in labor."

"I got you right here sir. Okay ma'am lean on me so we can safely get you transported. They will park your car for you sir. Does she have a bag?"

"Back passenger seat."

"Alright got it sir. Are you folks ready?"

"Yes! One Mississippi Two Mississippi."

"Alright follow me sir."

It feels as if time is moving slowly once we arrive. It could be this epidermal they have me on but how I was feeling in the car. I thought Sincere head was already on it's way out with a couple of pushes. I only dilated to four when they checked me out and I couldn't believe it. The last time I ate was last night during date night. Now I'm regretting just eating those damn snacks. I am hungry and these ice chips are not doing anything but pissing me off.  I can't wait to push so I can eat. I am determined to push him out with just two, hmmm maybe one. Yeah one big push and he will be here. I am banking on it.

"Baby can you rub my shoulders. I feel myself tensing up."

"I got you. How does that feel?"

"Mm good baby. I have the best husband in the world. When did Dr. Leslie say he was coming back to check on me? I think I dilated some more."

"You have about thirty more minutes."

"Ugh. I am so bored and ready to get this over with. I'm so hungry!"

"What do you want to eat when this is over with?"

"I honestly don't care. Just have something hot and fresh waiting on me."

"How about some wings with fries?"

"Sean? Really?"

"Dang, my bad. I will just go get you food."

"Bitch you still pregnant?"

"Yes heffa, I am! What took you so long to get here?"

"What do you mean? Hell I am early, you are just at 4. Hey Sean boo. She put you to work I see."

"You know how your friend is. Where's my boy?"

"He said he will be here when his parents relieve him. It's just me for now representing the both of us. Have you talked to our parents?"

"Yeah a few minutes ago. They said they are about twenty minutes away. Why?"

"They cut me short when I talked to them. It sounded like they were out."

"They probably stopped by Gaffney Outlets, they love that place."

"Yeah you are probably right. I know my parents have brought their grandchildren more damn gifts. I feel as if me and the Amazon delivery man know each other a little too damn much."

"Lord! I finally got out that stage with mine, you know they are about to be right back on it. They always buy the most annoying toys too."

"Listen to you two. Sounds like jealousy. Let your parents do their jobs and spoil them."

"Sean, my brother. I want you to remember this conversation when Jazz's parents get started. I'm just going to put it out there that I'm just going to repeat what you said. All I need from you is to remember this discussion, okay?"

"They can't be that bad."

"Oh you poor thing, you don't know what you have married into yet. Baby trust me they are the absolute worst."

"Ask Montez when he gets here. I'm surprised he hasn't told you."

"He has. He just wasn't being dramatic like you two. I mean he did say MJ's birthday was a nightmare but that was about it."

"Hey baby! No Sincere yet?"

"No. He is still refusing to come out."

"Oh no. Tell him to come on his grandparents are here. We have so many gifts for him and the rest of the grandbabies."

"And it begins," Reign said laughing as she elbowed Sean in the side.

"What's up family," Absalom says as he comes in with bags. "Where should I put these?"

" Over there by the window is fine Abs," Jazz responds.

"Damn sis! No nephew yet?"

'Listen I wish he was here like everyone else unfortunately he said no net yet. Hopefully he was waiting on you all."

"Hey baby girl."

"Dad. Really? Where did you get that at?"

"I bought this lion when I found out you were having a boy in July. What is this too much?"

"Not at all father."

"I told you that was too big David. You had to ride the elevator by yourself with that thing. You should have just dropped it off at their house before coming here with that thing. He embarrassed me and Abs when we were waiting on the elevator."

"They were hating. Everyone is jealous because my first grandson has the best gift. You are hating too Lillian, you know nothing in those bags top this."

"David stop it you do not want to get in a competition when it comes to who can buy the better gifts. Everyone in this room knows that is me."

"If you say so, but today it's me."

"You all are a trip. Where are my parents?"

"They said they wanted to see their grandbabies so we dropped them over your house," Lillian answered.

"Wow. They could have called me and told me they were headed there first. Jazz, I'm going to step out so I can call them."

"Okay, sis."

"How is it going Mrs. Gray?"

"You tell me doc. I hope you are here to see if I dilated."

"I am. Whoa! Now that is a huge lion, did it walk in here by itself?"

"See what I mean David?"

"He didn't say he didn't like it."

"No, I like it. Where did you get that from?"

"I bought it off of Amazon, I forgot the company name."

"That's my dad, Dr. Leslie David. My mother Lillian and my brother Absalom."

"It's nice to meet everyone. If I could just have a few minutes with the parents. Alright Jazz let's see where we are at when it comes to Sincere. Well look there, we are about forty five minutes away. You have dilated to seven, let me get the nurse in here to prep the room."

"Thank God, because I'm hungry."

"We will have you eating before you know it. I will be back."

Two hours later Sincere Nichlos Gray was born. He weighed 7lbs 2 oz and 21 in inches. The kids were so excited that their new brother was here, they were fighting over who was going to hold him first. Sean settled it by doing their name in alphabetical order: Marcella, SJ and Yasmine. Sean's mother had brought Jasmine some wings and fries. She wasn't concerned at all at the fuss that was being made about her baby boy. She had held and fed him and it was time to do the same for herself. She let the family have their visit time, she already told Reign to handle getting everyone out after an hour. She just wanted her Sean Montez and Reign afterwards. The family had added one more to the family, bringing the total of five Gray's and Santos'. Sincere and Rome were going to be the next them, they were going to raise that brotherhood like their mother's did for them and their sisterhood. Yes they have other siblings but they also had one another. As they all sat in the room and reminisce on each other's childhood and how they all grew up. They wanted their son's to have the same relationship as their father's. They have been through a lot but they stayed close through it all. It's funny how God blesses people and they feel very blessed for their generation and their kids' generation. They were determined to to raise their family on the same values their parents raised them.

# *Chapter Twenty-Eight: Moving Forward*

I know it wasn't easy for our husbands to plan a trip and convince their wives to take it. Especially since they both are dealing with newborns but somehow they did. I feel as if the last six months went by in six hours. Time flew so fast and I'm just now catching my breath. In just two weeks we will be on a plane headed to the Motherland and I'm excited. Although it took a lot of convincing from our baby daddies, I for one truly needed the break. I just opened Greenville's first black owned grocery store and the business has been crazy. We added a soul food restaurant and sushi bar. Best business move ever if I do say so myself. I'm stopping by today to make sure inventory is stocked and see if they need anything from me before we leave. Then I have to meet up with Sean to check on a house he wants to buy and renovate it. Once he was done he wanted to rent it out to college students. It was in the perfect spot for students attending Furman University. I don't know how much of a deal we can get on it, since it is an old two story house that we can make five bedrooms instead of four. The location of the house will drive up the price. We are looking at from anywhere from one hundred thousand to one hundred seven five thousand. I know how to negotiate and persuade the banks to get great deals but mostly the houses around that area start at two hundred thousands. I think the cheapest house I saw in the neighborhood was eighty five thousand and that was a one bedroom. We meet up with the bank later today and I will be able to work my black girl magic. I'm on my way to Reign's office now and see if she has plans for lunch. I want a good club sandwich right about now. As I pull up to her parking lot, I notice her car not there. I know this heffa did not leave and have lunch without me.

"What's up Jazz?"

"I'm hungry. Where are you?"

"On my way to feed Montez. Why didn't you tell me you wanted to do lunch when I saw you this morning?"

"I wasn't thinking about it at the time. Enjoy your time with hubby, I see if Tam wants to go."

"Alright sis talk to you later."

She gets on my nerves, she always having lunch with him or should I say sex. I like how she tried to word play it like I didn't know what that meant. She will be pregnant again soon, watch. They don't believe in wearing condoms or taking birth controls. I have three kids and I am not ready for number four just yet. I want to at least have Sincere out of diapers before trying to give Sean a daughter. Reign and Montez are the definition of rabbits fucking and creating life. I personally don't think they have ever waited the full six weeks.

It's the beginning of another school week and I am already counting the days until Friday. I have training with my baby planned and we are getting these eight miles in at Paris Mountains. I am so excited because I convinced him to ride bikes out there and he does not do well with height and woods.I promised him if his anxiety made him freak out too bad we would park the bikes and run it. I hope he doesn't pretend to have one and really give it a chance. I love the thrill of it all and want him to experience it with me. Then I just want to spend the rest of the day there to have a picnic and explore the lake and waterfall. Just want to show him other adventures besides the mall, movies and chillin downtown. Plus I think this will also help him for his footwork and training for football. My girls want us to meet up Saturday and head to Atlanta but I am not that confident in bae's driving in their traffic. Those people are crazy on I-85, everytime we go visit Tea I dread it. I wish she would move to the outskirts so we don't have to do their traffic. No matter the time of day there's always traffic. Abs say he can handle it but none of them have convinced me to go. I just really want to spend some alone time with him and do some YouTubes videos.

"Miss Santos are you with me?"

Hell no. Mr. Taylor is going to have to repeat that if he asked me a question. "Yes sir I am."

"Good tell me your thoughts on climate change."

"My thoughts on it?" What the hell did I miss? I want to say it exists but I'm not sure that's what he is talking about.

"Yes. Do you think it's too late to change?"

"It's never too late to change it, but let's be real it's going to continue. It's too many human beings on this Earth who are not taking it seriously. I feel bad for little nephews and nieces, I also feel bad for my future kids. I don't think we are leaving them a great Earth when they take over."

"Anyone disagrees with Miss Santos."

"Derrick, what about you? Do you think we are too late to change it?"

"Yes I agree with Sades. Do you really think these billion dollar corporations are going to stop drilling oil or cutting down trees? Climate change will get worse and I wouldn't be surprised if this was God's plan to destroy earth and rebuild it again. To those who believe in the bible and to those that don't. It will be some kind of ice age."

"Thank you Mr. Garrison. Is there anyone that believes the human race will get it together before it's too late."

"Mr. Taylor I just don't see it. We can't come together in the world for anything. At this point I just feel bad for nature and the animals. We have truly ruined their habitat," Danielle responds.

"You all don't believe in your generation to do it?"

"These adults in the USA alone are going to leave us with so much stuff to fix, I doubt we have time to fix the climate change," Stacie responded.

"Alright class tonight's assignment is to think outside the box and tell me how you plan on slowing down climate change. I need a two page report on what you are going to focus on to help out the environment."

"Sades! Wait up! Are you doing your assignment during your free period or at home?"

"I'm going home today, Rick. I have to babysit my nephews today, so I won't be cutting up with you all today."

"Dang it. I need my study partner. How about I come over to their house and we can knock this out together."

"Let me see what they say about it and I will text you later."

"Cool. Where are you headed now?"

"About to grab some food before my next period. Dallas said he wanted to talk so we are headed to Dairy Queen."

"Alright I will see you when you get back."

**Hey baby! Just letting ya know I'm about to head out with Dallas.**

**Cool let me know when you arrived back at school.**

**I will. I love you!!!!!!!**

**I love you too Mersades.**

"Are you ready?"

"Yeah, just let me text Reign real quick and see if she is still coming to get me today."

"Here let me get the door for you."

"Thank you."

"No problem. How is everything going today?"

"Nothing much. Same old shit just another day. Ready for the weekend like always. How about you?"

"Same. Are you going with the crew this weekend to Atl?"

"I haven't decided yet. How about you?"

"Yeah I'm going. That's why I wanted to talk to you today. I wanted you to hear it from me and no one else."

"Okay."

"I'm going with Ty."

"Ty who?! I know you are not talking about my best friend Tyesha! Are you fucking serious right now?!"

"She wanted to tell you herself

"And you should of fucking let her! The fuck!"

"Mersades please get back in the car!"

"Stay the fuck away from me Dallas!"

**Bitch! Where is your ass at?!!!! Answer your goddamn phone!!!!**

"Sades please! Hear me out! We didn't plan this, it just happened! Sades!"

**I know you are heated right now. I can explain. I can meet up with you after school.**

**Hell no! We are meeting up now! Bring ya ass to the student's parking lot!**

**I'm coming.**

"I told you to get out of my face! Why are you still in it?!"

"I just want you to hear from me what happened. This is on me more than it is on Ty

"Fuck outta here with that! Step the fuck off Dallas!"

"Sades. I swear I didn't mean for this to happen."

"You bitches knew too?"

"Knew what? Listen I'm only out here because Ty asked me to come. I don't know what the fuck is going on therefore I don't know shit," Jada said.

"What about you Selena?"

“ I was just told today. I had no idea until now.”

“Well someone wants to include my ass? What is going on?”

“Dallas and Tyesha are a couple now. I mean it makes sense now that I think about it. Ty fucks anything including my ex boyfriends. Any other of my exes you opened your legs to that you want to tell me about?!” At this time a crowd had gathered at the parking lot and students had their phones out. Mersades didn’t care at this point she was beyond hurt. Ty and her had been friends since second grade. Betrayal wasn’t a strong enough word to describe how she was feeling. This was worse than Harper sleeping with Mia or Maxine taking Kenny from Teri. As they went back and forth some teachers finally arrived and separated the girls. They took them to the principal office to get the situation sorted out. Mrs. Duncan thought it was best to send them home for the rest of the day. Lucas came to pick up his daughter and was upset with her once Mrs. Duncan told him what happened. The car ride home was complete silence and she headed straight to her room. Abs had been texting her all day that but she never responded. He saw what happened on snapchat and wanted to make sure she was okay. Nothing he text made her respond back. Reign told Montez that she would go pick her up to see if she could get her to talk. Since him and Maitea both fell at getting her to respond to them. When she walked in her room she saw that she was doing her homework and tried to have small talk with her.

“Lil mama, you have everyone concerned. What you need right now? Don’t tell me to be alone because that’s no longer an option.”

“Can you and I get outta here?”

“Sure. Where do you want to go?”

“Can you take me to one of your spots?”

“Yeah. Come on.Do you want to play some music?”

“No.”

“I saw the snapchat of you and Tyesha. That was rough, I can’t imagine how you are feeling right now.”

“Did Jazz ever do that to you or vice versa?”

“Hell no! Excuse me I meant no and no we never did that to any of our friends. We believe in the girl code especially when you are best friends.”

“I thought Ty understood. Never thought she would have done this to me. I mean she didn’t even wait. It makes me wonder how long she wanted him.”

“Did she show interest in him before you two got together?”

“Not to me. She seemed to be happy for me when I told her that he was my boyfriend.”

“Do you want to know how they hooked up or are you done”

“I’m done. I’m glad she showed me who she was now. I understand our friendship will never be the same and that I can’t trust her around any of my men. I mean high school love comes and goes. I hate that she chose a boy over us. What pisses me off the most is she let him tell me instead of her. Who fucking does that?!”

“Not a real friend, I’m just going to be honest with you. I think you should let things calm down and talk about it. After you two do that and you still feel the same then yes be done. I just wouldn’t throw away damn near ten years of friendship without talking to one another first.”

“If Jazz did you like this when y’all were in high school?”

"Honestly?"

"Yeah."

"We would have physically fought it out and worked it out later. It's different with her though, we are sisters like you and Maitea. Now if your sister did you that way what would you do?"

"I see what you mean. I will talk to her just won't be any time soon that's for sure."

"She has to respect that too. Don't make her pressure you until you are ready."

"Oh don't worry I won't. Can I ask you something else?"

"Listen I'm here for you. Whatever you need to get off your chest today. By all means get it out."

"How old were you when you lost your virginity?"

Reign cough damn near choked when she asked her that. She cleared her throat and wiped the tears from her eyes and said, "I'm sorry. What did you ask me?"

"How old were you when you lost your virginity?"

"Yeah that's what I thought you said. Yeah I was about fifteen going on sixteen. Why do you want to know that?"

"All the women in my life had sex before marriage, one of the reasons I wanted to wait. Now with this happening and the decade I'm living in. If I'm not having sex it's hard to keep these high school boys interested. I will be in college in two years and the college life will have more pressure."

"Never think that sex keeps a person in a relationship. Sometimes the sex is whack and your mad that you gave it up to the wrong person. If the person you are with can't be with you because you want to wait until marriage. Then he is not ready to be the husband material you are looking for. What you want is just as important: never put another person above you and your morales. Do you hear me Mersades?"

"Yeah I do. What if I don't feel like that anymore though?"

"If that's how you feel that's just how you feel. If you don't want to wait anymore and you found someone that you want to lose it to. Make sure you both are protected and you have him tested especially if he has had sex."

"I will when I find him or he finds me. I didn't break up with Dallas; he broke up with me. He kept telling me it was because of my friendship with Absalom. We both know it was because of sex, he's not fooling me. He is with Ty for that very reason. If that's all he wanted he should have chosen her from the beginning and left me alone. I can't believe I wasted two years on him."

"Thank God it was only two, I wasted a decade and then some with Dame."

"Boys!"

"I know that's right sis! These damn boys!"

## *Chapter Twenty-Nine: Diani Beach*

   This trip to Kenya has been an experience I'm going to remember for a long time. As we lay here getting a tan and watching the people walk the beach. I find myself reminiscing on my life. I remember we always said not us, we are not our mothers. Eleven years later that is exactly who we became….. Our mothers. We ended up pregnant around the same time and we married a year apart from one another and we have sons that are three months apart. Life is crazy and unpredictable. We wanted to be grown so fast. Then when you get your first bill, you are looking at your parents wondering why they didn't tell you. Although they have plenty of times. You still were looking at them to say no you didn't. If you really did explain it like this, I could have lived under your roof a little while longer and not been eager to leave. I love my life, don't get me wrong. I just wished I would've enjoyed my twenties a little more. I wished I had Yasmine and Marcella in my thirties but it's all good. That just means my forties will be lit. I will make it the rebirth of my twenties. My girls would be finishing up college and my son should be entering high school. I know Reign is praying for that girl in the future. As for now Tez has received his sons and is smiling from ear to ear. She won't admit it but her and Kia are having a contest. Every time Kia is pregnant Reign is close behind. I finally joined them but I'm officially done for at least one more year. Then I will try to give Sean his little princess he wants. The things we do for our men are just crazy.  I have to say I am not only grateful for all that we have accomplished individually but also as friends. We have truly been through hell and back together and we haven't even reached the milestone in our life. I can't wait to see what we will do ten years from now together and apart.

"We have to come back and visit the motherland."

"We really do. We also need to look into some property here like we did in Hawaii and Tennessee."

"If we can get more people I told you I'm cool with doing it. This is going to cost us more. We are flying over to the other side of the world on a continent they swear is poor. Until you try to buy property then all of a sudden you need your million dollar friends and associates to make it happen."

"Says the woman who is about to make her first million, hell with Montez's income you two are passed millionaires."

"We are ain't we," she said with a smile. "Just think we did it by being smart business people. No athletes status, no entertainers status, no doctor's, lawyer's, or politicians status. Just two black people starting black wall street silently and making our own mark. Soon you and Sean will be there. If you two keep this commercial lot booming. Which I must say that the parking lot stays packed."

"Give our people what they want in their own community, will do that. Hiring your own will keep it prospering, so many non blacks profit off us. When you walk in their stores you don't see many of us employed there or treated fairly while shopping. Soon a lot more will get tired of it and start taking back our community and making it look like us. I'm just happy I'm already part of that movement."

"I am proud of you Jazz. You saw what the Latinos and Asians were doing and you said why not us? Why our black people can't do the same? You showed us we can and we will. President Obama and first Lady Michelle would be proud."

"I know my parents are," Jazz said laughing. "Right now that's the only two black people approval I am looking for to be honest. Let Sasha and Malia do that for them. I love the Obama's but my dreams were long before they existed in our lives for eight years."

"You right you right," she said with a head nod. "We always wanted our parents' approval, especially our mother's. Dad's were going to be proud regardless. I mean our mom's too but seriously we could have been YouTube famous and our dad's wouldn't have cared."

"Speaking of YouTube have you caught Mersades and my brother's page?"

"Jazz you sent it to me a hundred times you know I have seen them all."

"Do you still think they ain't having sex?"

"Did Abs tell you that they are?"

"No. I'm asking you. On the last upload they did would you say they had? Did you really watch the video or did you just look at it?"

"Oh my God you are so invested in their YouTube page! This is not love and hip hop or College Hill. They kissed a lot and they were doing the chapstick challenge. I mean was it a little too steamy for seventeen year olds, yes. Do I think they are having sex and haven't confided to one of us, no."

"Maybe you are right. I mean if they did they probably wait till we come back to the states and tell us."

"Jazz let's dead this conversation before our husbands get back. Montez hears you talking about his sister possibly losing her virginity. He will end this trip and fly back to South Carolina without us."

"What? I haven't said anything to them in a while about this. I only tell you."

"Great. Let's keep it that way."

"Are you saying you don't want to ask them about this when we get back?"

"I want you to stop stalking their YouTube channel and let them be."

"No can do, that's my little brother."

"Jazz, he is my little brother too and Mersades is my sister in law. If they want to tell us anything let them do it on their own."

"Are you sure that's the best move?"

"Oh my God! Okay I'm done with you and this conversation. Let's talk about something else."

"Okay. I have a question?"

"It better not be about Sades and Abs."

"It's not."

"What is it then?"

"Where are our damn husbands with our drinks?"

Reign burst out laughing and threw her towel at her. She had a legitimate question though. They had been gone an awfully long time to purchase some drinks. They looked around to see if they could spot them. If they moved from their spot they were afraid someone would take them. It was already hard enough holding on to their husbands spot. These people on the beach were like vultures ready to swoop down and snatch your shit.

"Here they come now," Reign says as she finally spots them.

"Damn it took y'all long enough. What happened? Did they make you make our drinks?"

"Ha funny babe. We went the wrong way. We thought you two were somewhere else. The bar line close to us was too long. Tez thought the one on down the beach was moving faster. We went there and then our asses forgot where we left y'all at," Sean said laughing.

"It's amazing how many of these women look like you two from afar. Everyone here has a light skin dark skin friend combo," he said laughing.

"Babe they really do, it had Tez and I shook."

"I'm not even following that up," she says as she rests her head on his shoulder. "Just give me my drink man."

"Here you go. What did we miss? I know you two out here cracking jokes on some of these people."

"Actually we were discussing Sades and Abs. We're off that now, right Jasmine?"

"The discussion has been tabled until we get back home."

"Good because that's not even on my brain. As we were waiting on the drinks we heard people talking about a party tonight. We thought that would be a nice way to end the trip. That's if you are up to it baby."

"I fell asleep one time at the club while we have been here and y'all still on that tired ass joke. Yes Teezy I am up to it. I swear you all can run something into the ground. I was jetlagged damn it."

"We all were but we didn't fall asleep at the club like you did."

"We all were but we didn't fall asleep at the club like you did," she said mocking Jazz.

"Oh, you are mad now? You are acting like Yas and Celly when they get into it."

"Whatever Jasmine. What time does this party start?"

"At eight. We have time to grab dinner and do some more sightseeing before we go."

"That works for me Sean. Right now though that water is calling my name. Are you all ready to lose these spots and get in?"

"Hell yeah come on and let's have some fun in Kenya's water!" They all get up and run towards the water without a care in the world. Once they had enough of the water they decided to head back and change. They wanted to ride the camels before it got dark. Reign and Jazz bought some cute Komono to cover their bathing suits. They couldn't resist getting the bright oversized hats. What supposed to be a quick run in and out. Actually turned their husbands into bag men. They bought so much shit that they had to return back to the room before getting on the camels. This time when they left out Montez and Sean literally picked them up and took them straight to the camels before they got sidetracked again. They were having the time of their life. They got to feed them and take pictures with them. They learned a lot about the Digo tribe when they did the Kaya Kinondo Sacred Forest tour. They only had two days left in Kenya and they knew they had to come back. There was so much more they wanted to do and they knew six days being there wasn't enough time. Like that it was night time and they were back in their own rooms getting ready to enjoy another night life.

"I really think you are trying to stay in tonight wearing that baby. That dress has your husband at attention, all I want to do now is lift it up and give it to you."

"We have time," Jazz says as she looks at him seductively through the mirror. She watches him get up from the bed and walk over to her. He unzips his pants and pulls it out. He grabs her by the waist and pulls her closer. He moves her hair to the side, and licks her neck before leaving a love mark. She lowers her head and grips the corners of the dresser as the sensation of his love bites tingles through her body. Turning her on she grabs his nine inches and puts it in her. The tightness of her panties and the hardness of his manhood made the quickie even better. She threw it back meeting his strokes every time. She was determined to make cum because she didn't want to be caught by their friends getting it in. Sean knew exactly what she was trying to accomplish but it felt so good he didn't want it to end. He instead pulls out and turns her around. He places her on the dresser and pulls down her panties off. He pulls her inner thighs closer to his mouth and puts his tongue to work. Realizing they were going to be here for awhile, she takes off her dress and gets comfortable. She guides his tongue to her spot by placing her finger in her wetness. He sucks her finger and her spot before stopping so he could watch her please herself. "Play with her for me baby," he whispers as he gets back undressed. As Jazz continues pleasuring herself, he puts her breast in his mouth and sucks it slow. He moves to the next one and does the same. He then takes his hand and meets hers. Once his fingers were inside she took her wet fingers and placed them in his mouth. They pleasure each other with foreplay a little longer before taking it to the bed. As they made love, the Santos were blowing up their phones. After the third try with no response they figured they were on their own tonight.

# *Chapter Thirty: Misunderstood*

It was their last night in Kenya. They had decided to spend the night in each other's rooms and tell stories about their lives before meeting one another. Jasmine was telling them about how people from their neighborhood thought that her and Reign were more than friends. They thought they were too close to be just best friends, especially the females. After middle school the two got tired of trying to convince anyone that what they had was real sisterhood.

"I told Montez I thought you two slept together."

"Really? Why did you think that though?"

"When you and Tez started dating, I was nosy as hell on y'all social media pages. The majority of y'all pictures were you two."

"Okay? And? Our pictures do not look like two females in a relationship. Plus I had just broken it off with Dame so all of our pics had been deleted by me. Which left a lot of pics of me and my girls. I never had a lot of male friends unlike your wife."

"Dame wouldn't let her. It's always the cheating and insecure muthafuckers who are mad jealous."

"Hold on now. I chose not to have male friends it wasn't because he didn't allow it. I was focused on my school and his games. Hell I really didn't have time for new friends."

"Yet you and Kia became instant besties. You had time to make friends with the athletes' significant others or wives."

"Let it go Jazz, geez you made friends outside of me as well. You don't see me throwing it in your face."

"This is another reason I thought you two had more than friendship going on. When y'all get into it, y'all sound like a couple."

"What about you baby? Did you think I was fucking Jazz?"

"Nah. You and Jazz sound like me and my sisters when we get into it. See Sean, is the only child like you so he doesn't know how it is between siblings. When you told me how you two were brought up it made sense to me."

"At first Montez man. Not when you all got to know one another."

"I still didn't Sean and you know it. Hell you thought Reign was bougie as fuck just from the car she was in. You had a problem with my wife from day one."

"Thank God you didn't listen to my judgemental ass huh?"

"Exactly! You were so wrong about my baby, I would have missed my blessings if I would have listened to your ass that day and days after that."

"You were pretty hard on my sis babe. You came at her with me a few times."

"Okay damn! Reign I apologize. I was a complete asshole back then. But now you are the sister I wish I had."

"It's all good Sean. I mean I was engaged to a NBA player, that alone gets me a bad rep."

"I still can't believe you thought I scissored with Reign."

"Really Jazz," she said laughing. "Why do you have to be so direct with it."

"No more X videos for you and you need to cancel your Brazzers account."

"Stop fronting Sean, that Brazzers account is yours."

"No you stop fronting, acting like you don't watch it with me."

"I didn't say I didn't watch. I said that is your membership and account."

"Both of y'all are some damn freaks," Montez said laughing.

"I know you ain't talking bruh? You and Reign are the last two that need to sit there. Pretending to be Mother Teresa and the Pope, please stop it."

"I'm done. I have nothing."

"First time ever Reign doesn't have a clap back. Write this day down for the books."

"Fuck you, Jazz. Make sure you add that to your footnotes."

"I know you two went to different colleges. What's the craziest shit you all ever did there?"

"Montez you go first. I know you have some wild stories."

"I mean I was a regular college student. I worked hard during the week and party all weekend."

"Listen. Reign has given you two kids and said I do til death do you part. Name the wildest shit you did in college man! Stop sugar coating shit!"

"What? I just told you."

"It's that bad babe? Come on, what did you do in college. What are you going to tell MJ and Rome when they go?"

"Have fun and don't waste our damn money."

"Alright. I will go first and then maybe my husband will come clean. The wildest shit I did in college was for Dame's twenty one birthday."

"Oh no sis! Montez doesn't know this?"

"Nope."

"Nah. Game over let's not do this. Wait have you ever done it for him?"

"Um, no."

"Yeah game over. Let's go out and get something to eat."

"I want to hear this. What you did to his ass and we haven't done?"

"Tez! Trust me, let's not do this anymore."

"In my defense. He asked for it and I didn't volunteer it."

"Damn now I want to know," Sean said.

"Me too. Let me hear it."

"I tossed his salad."

"No! Not you sis! Wow, and you never did that for my boy?!"

"First of all I never asked Reign to do that. A lot of men don't request that unless they are

"Wait a minute. He can't be freaky, he automatically is considered undercover?"

"I'm good on that. You don't have to worry about me asking for it. Leave my butthole alone for my prostate exam."

"I can respect that, bruh, Sean said, giving him the head nod."

"You never had your salad tossed baby?"

"I didn't say that. I just said I can respect him for not wanting it done."

"Oh okay. Are you next? What is the wildest thing you did?'

"Everyone knows I didn't go to college. You all also know I was selling drugs at the time y'all were furthering your education. The wildest thing I did in the street was have sex three females at the same time."

"I hope your ass wore a condom. What kind of Porn Hub were you involved in?"

"Nah I didn't and that's why it's the wildest thing I've ever done. I kept getting tested after that for a good year."

"Montez?"

"Alright. I swapped and let my roommate fuck my girl and I fucked his. Except me and his girl continued to do it."

"You kept fucking his girl? How do you know he didn't continue doing that to your girl."

"I didn't care if he did or not. The reason I continued with his girl was because she was a freak. She let me do anything to her body that I wanted. My girl at the was boring, we broke up a month after the swap."

"You were a dog baby. Why do you do that to a boy like that?"

"Me? Hell he was cheating on her ass too, at least that's what he was telling me. I figured he didn't care. Alright Jasmine. It's on you, what did you do?"

"I only had a threesome in college."

"Only? You said that like that's normal."

"After hearing you all porn stories mine is minor compared to everyone in this room. Reign ate ass, my husband fucking three bitches with no condoms, and Montez getting freaked by his roommates girl. Yeah mine is normal."

"I remember that threesome. Malik wanted me to join you two."

"He cursed out that day. He was another one who assumed me and Reign ate each other out."

"Hey I have apologized for that numerous times. You had a threesome?" Sean asked.

"I did. I had two in college. One with another girl and the other was with a boy. My boyfriend wanted it for a birthday gift. I agreed to it, only if he would join me with another guy?"

"The guy ended up being Marcus and the rest was history after that."

"Yeah I left Malik to get with Marcus. Reign was so happy she couldn't stand his ass."

"When she told me that shit. I told her to dump his ass. I don't know why he thought it was okay to ask me to join in something like that."

"Yeah he pissed me off when he asked me to bring Reign into it. I told him that's nasty as hell. She is a sister to me without the DNA. We literally were brought up as sisters. I told him that I wasn't putting my mouth nor hands nowhere provocative on her."

"Who did you end up getting?"

"He found some bisexual girl. She ended up wanting to get with me and I nicely told her it was a one time thing. I found out that night that I could never be gay that I was strictly dickie. I barely touched that girl that night."

"Did you eat her out?"

"I think I did. I was molly out babe. I don't remember the taste because I whipped cream the hell out of her."

"Okay change the damn subject", Reign said laughing.

"Sis I swear I used the whole whipped cream bottle."

"Your wife is funny as hell man! Gotta love Jazz."

"I ain't lying though I did."

"I bet she was sticky then a muthafucker." Sean said, shaking his head.

"That threesome was a hot mess. It was nothing like the porn videos I can guarantee you that."

"So you don't know if your mouth touches her pussy?"

"No Sean I don't. It could have I never asked her."

"Did she eat you out?"

"Yeah and without the whip. While she was getting from the back she was all in my lips. No lie, she knew what she was doing. A few times I had to push her back before I became addicted and dick less."

"I can not with you," Reign said, blushing. "She almost turned you out Jazz?"

"She had me questioning some things until it was my turn and then my senses came back," Jazz said laughing.

"She was trying to turn you out. I'm glad she fell."

"Me too," she said while squeezing on his neck. To be honest I haven't met a female yet that could turn me all the way out."

"She had to be a bad bitch times ten, in order to get me to switch teams. I can't see myself eating another woman and pleasing her for the rest of my life. I can see myself suck you though until you are no longer able to get it up."

"Man listen. You and Jazz are on something serious today. What the fuck is in these hotel drinks," he asked while examining her drink.

"All jokes aside. I am feeling a little different, do you think they spiked our shit?"

"How different?"

"Horny different. Montez for real did you do something to my drink?"

"I confess. I gave you the pink pill the Youtube couples use."

"I'm the only one? Sean you didn't use it on Jazz?"

"I used mine last night. That's why we were MIA."

"Damn it! I knew it! I was on another level last night and I knew something had to encourage it.

"Reign I am telling you now. You and Montez need to head back to ya'll room because girl that pill is the real deal. If you wanted to stay in last night Sean that's all you had to say. Now we are going out tonight since I wasn't able to because of your Youtube prank. Those pranks are going to have us divorce quickly."

"You ain't going nowhere. Chill the fuck out now, I made sure you were safe and I didn't do it as a prank."

"Sean, I will Solange your ass, don't play with me like that. Look at Reign, just look at her. I told her she was pink pilled and she is still all over you." Take her back to your room Montez!"

"I'm going damn Jazz. We will see you two in the morning. Come on baby, we are leaving."

"Is it me or is it hot in here."

"Man you got my girl gone. I should smack the shit out of you Montez. How many did you put in there?"

"A half one. She will be fine Jasmine. I make sure she will sleep it off."

"What? Why are you looking at me like that? I didn't give her the pill, Tez did."

"Who gave it to him? Exactly! We are going to get y'all asses back. You wait and it will be epic too."

"Whatever you say. Are you getting ready so we can enjoy our last night here or do you want to take another pill?"

"You think that shit is funny. Okay baby laugh it up. I can't wait to get back home. It is so on!"

My last morning watching the sun rise on this beautiful country. I'm feeling emotional about it. We actually had the opportunity to see animals live in their natural habitat and not be caged up. We see how people live without the internet and truly enjoy life without sharing it with the world. Our people are so talented and it's crazy that you have other people making millions off of them. I see so many clothes here that I buy in stores or off line being sold triple to the price that it is here. No lie, it really pissed me off. Makes you wonder how many travel here and was "inspired" by their culture. You all know that's what the culture vultures like to say when they are caught stealing. It's sad they really don't have a culture of their own that's creative and popping like ours. These people would be lost without us that's for damn sure. We just make this world better and they know it. Look at my baby, he just doesn't know how sexy his chocolate skin is when the sun touches it. I love everything about him, it's sometimes hard to put into words. I fell in love with his pride and determination before I fell for anything else.  I would be lying if I say his looks is what caught my attention. When I opened the door that morning and saw his beautiful dark skin and pretty white teeth looking at me. I wanted to strip him down right and there. If you would have told me that we were going to marry and have this beautiful family, I would have bet against it. We both have questionable parents to our children. I mean they are great with our children but their faith in us wasn't that great. Dana just wanted the money and didn't care how he made it, she encouraged the street life. I would have never done that to him if that was us. Marcus always wanted me to shine, just as long as I didn't out shine him. Sean would never do that to me. He wanted me to be the best me and supported me from the beginning. Now look at us here in Africa and for the first time being on vacation, I don't want to leave. "Sean baby", she whispers. "Baby wake up, you are going to miss the sunrise."

"I'm up. Which way is it?"

"Turn this way." He turns in the direction of her voice and wipes the sleep out his eyes. Once the blur was gone and the window became focus, he could see the sun on a rise. He pulls her close to him so they could experience it for the last time. She places her hands on top of his and puts her head back on his shoulders. They watched in silence with only the sounds from the Indian ocean.

# *Chapter Thirty-One: Sneaking Around*

One of the hottest September ever and I'm sitting in this car waiting for Dana to once again bring my son here on time. I have been rotating the air conditioning from the car, to stepping out the car for God's natural air to keep cool. Plus I'm on a hundred and twenty because this woman stays on her bullshit! I'm going to ask the judge to change the original pick up and drop off because this shit is beyond ridiculous. At this point I don't even think she's trying to be funny. She really is just a last minute type of chick. I can't call her ass and she can't call me because I left my damn phone on the counter. I rushed out to come and get Junior and accidentally left the shit.

"Damn it's about time Dana!"

"What are you doing here? I already dropped Sean at your house, we tried calling you. Why are you not picking up your phone!"

"I don't have it!"

"Well don't be yelling at me then. I was running late because your son begged me to take him to get a haircut. I told him that you were going to take him tomorrow. He wanted me to do it so I did. But of course Shannon was booked, he said he would squeeze him in. Shannon and Jazz tried calling you, after I couldn't get in touch with you. I thought you were mad because I was running late again. That's why I had them do it."

"I was pissed but now at myself. My bad Dana I left my phone by accident. This is all on me this time, I apologize. Well shit let me head home then since you dropped him off already."

"Yeah do that, see you guys on Monday."

"Before I go can I use your bathroom real quick."

"Really? Dude come on and make it quick. Do not shit in my bathroom Sean I'm not playing with you on that."

"Girl chill all I have to do is pee."

"Make sure that's all you damn do."

"Yeah, yeah, yeah."

"I noticed the girls weren't there, is this their weekend with their dad?"

"Yeah it is."

"Do they coparent better than us?

"Hell no dude is still salty that she married me and not him. He will be alright though."

"True."

"True what? You siding with him or me."

"What?"

"You said true. What are you agreeing with?"

"Really? Sean, go home and stop asking me silly questions."

"I'm going and thanks for letting me use your bathroom."

"No problem." As they walk towards the door Sean suddenly stops. Not knowing he was going to stop so sudden, she bumps right into him. "You forget how to open the door?" Sean turns around and kisses Dana. She wasn't even surprised, she felt it coming from the moment he

came in the house. It's been crazy energy between the two of them and it's been happening for awhile now. The tit for tat and silly arguments they had stopped them from this moment. She wondered if this could happen if their son wasn't around. Now she had her answer. He wanted her just as much as she wanted him. The passion was still there and it was nothing for them to explore it. They helped each other take off their clothes, while making their way to her sofa. He lays her down and removes her panties. He gives a few kisses to her hotspot then opens her legs and puts his face in her wetness. She lays back on the sofa and adjusts her whine with the motion of his tongue. The way he was slowly tasting her and how she was flowing with his motions just made her wetter. She continues to feed him with her sweetness until he is hard enough to put it in. He gets up and turns her to the side, "This is still your favorite position?"
"Yes baby it is," as she backs it up on it.
"Damn when you got out of that car and your body was looking like this. You made him bulge real quick."
"I noticed why you think I let you in? Damn you still feel good. Jasmine is one lucky woman."
"Don't bring her up."
"Mm okay baby whatever you want."
I'm getting exactly what I need. Damn she really missed him huh?"
"I did, you just don't know how much and not just the sex but all of you. Why did you marry her?"
"Dana, leave this part of the conversation alone." He tries to switch not only conversations but the sex positions as well. Dana was determined to bring up the fact that he got married but still ended up not only cheating but cheating with her. The more the two went with the back and forth the more he concentrated on doing a quick nut. He doesn't know why he did what he did. He just knows at this moment he realized it's not worth it. He knew Jazz was going to end their marriage if she ever found out. He could try to justify how he gave her a second chance when she slept with Marcus. The thing is that he promised never to bring it up again once they were married. Plus they are married and he broke their vows. How the fuck did he let this happen? He was over Dana at least he thought he was. This just proves that he wasn't. As he laid there holding Dana he was thinking of ways to leave without pissing her off. He had to make sure that she wouldn't call Jazz before he had a chance to tell her himself.  All of a sudden there's a tap on the window and it wakes Sean up.
"Hey. What are you doing here? I dropped SJ at your house."
"What?!"
"Sean! Roll down the damn window!"
"Girl what?"
"I scared you? My bad, but what are you doing here? I already dropped our son at your house. We have been trying to call you then Jasmine discovered your phone on the counter."
"Yeah I rushed out and forgot it. Can I use yours real quick so I can call her."
"Hurry up man! I need to get in here and get ready for my date."
"Calm that down it's only going to take a quick second. Hey baby. Yeah left that shit right on the counter. I'm leaving now see you all in a minute. See that didn't take long and good looking out. See you Monday."
"No problem and see you Monday."

What the fuck was that Sean?! The hell you dreaming about fucking Dana for? Shit it had to be the got damn heat that has me tripping. God I don't know what I did to you but please remove these infidelities from my inner thoughts in your name I pray Amen.

"That was your daddy sweetie and he's on the way. Did you want to help me in the kitchen until he arrives?"

"Yes!"

"Alright let's do it! Now what can you cook again?"

"Biscuits!"

"That's right! Silly me! Alright go grab the stuff we need."

"Okay Jazzy."

"Man you are great with him sis."

"You know I'm a great mother."

"Yeah you are," Abs confirm. "Do you need any help?"

"I'm good bro, you can go join Mersades in the entertainment room. Dinner will be ready in a little bit, right SJ?"

"Yes! Your little chef is ready to help!"

"Aw man you took my title. I used to be my sister's little chef. You are learning from one of the best Junior."

SJ laughs as he puts on his apron and helps Jasmine make the biscuits. Before joining Mersades on the sofa he goes in the refrigerator and grabs them some drinks. He kisses his sister on the cheek and makes his way towards Sades.

"It won't be too much longer before we eat."

"Good! Did you hear my stomach just now? I'm so damn hungry that Burger King we had earlier has left. Is your sister making those cheddar biscuits too or just regular biscuits."

"I think it's the cheddar biscuits from what SJ brought back to the counter."

"I think it's so cool how she treats him as her own but in a respectful way."

"Yeah little man has taken my spot. I seriously feel some type of way seeing them in their cooking together. That used to be me."

"Aw baby. I let you help me cook any time and give you these while you help me."

"Now those I never got from my sister. I'm feeling good about her replacement."

"You are so spoiled. I might have to break you on that."

"I know you are not calling anyone spoiled. You have this whole family wrapped around your finger. If I fuck up in any kind of way that's my ass!"

"Yeah you are so right. I am the spoiled one in this relationship. Lawd that food smells so good, where the hell is Sean at?"

"He was at Dana's house."

"They can never be on the same page."

"He left his phone here, that's how they missed one another. But yeah it's always something with them two when it comes to Junior."

"What y'all doing here," Sean asked as he walked in the house.

"We stopped by to say what's up and grab some of sis famous gumbo. Why are you walking in here looking bothered," Abs asked.

"You do seem off, Sean are you okay," Sades asked.

"I'm fine I just wasn't expecting you two that's all. Plus I was waiting in a hot car for nothing. Where's my wife?"

"In the kitchen with the boys."

"Hey babe welcome home, she says as she greets him with a kiss. "Um Sean baby I love you and everything but you are musty. Please go take a shower before dinner."

"Well damn babe it's like that?"

"Ew yeah it is please go now."

"Hey little man!"

"Hey dad!"

"Alright I'm headed to take a shower. Although you say I stink you still have it smelling good up in here."

"We do what we do! Ain't that right SJ?"

"Yes, his son says. As they do they do their dap routine they came up with.

"Sean! Hurry up and throw some soap and water on you bruh! My stomach is eating my back."

"Damn y'all surely know how to treat a hardworking man. I'm going Mersades calm your greedy ass down." He was going to kiss Sincere but then thought twice about it. He knew his wife would have slapped him if he picked him up smelling like he did. While he was in the shower flashes from his dreams kept entering his mind and he wasn't understanding it.

I keep telling myself that this needs to be done and I will tell my husband all about it. That dream I had about Dame has been bothering me and the only way I'm going to get answers is to talk to him. I have been on his mind a lot lately too because when I reached out he said he wanted to see me as well. He just didn't want another visit from my daddy so he just left it alone. I told him about my dream I had months ago. How I thought that was it  until I had another one last night. We clearly had unfinished business and it was time to see just what that was. When my therapist was telling me this, I didn't believe it. I mean we had met up so many times after we broke it up. I just didn't understand why this was so important to her. Nevertheless he agreed with her that so much wasn't said after he put his hands on me. He wanted to apologize and tell me what it's been like for him. I decided to hear him out and said we could meet at Cheesecake Factory in Greenville. I told Montez I was going shopping at the mall for a little me time. Which wasn't a lie I just left out the part of meeting my ex fiance afterwards. I know that's bad but I know my husband and he wouldn't let this happen if I told him. When I had my therapy sections and Dame was brought up.She told us that I need to get closure from the day he beat me. My husband told her not without him. She tried to explain to him this was something I had to do on my own. When we had the sections without him, she said that one day I had to do this to have complete closure. That my husband just wanted to protect me because he feels responsible for not being there to stop him for beating me. I waited months to do this and there's no turning back now. Even if I wanted to change my mind I couldn't because the waiter is bringing him to me. I took a sip of my water, closed my eyes and said a quick prayer.

"Damn marriage looks great on you. I almost told dude that's not you."

"Aww thanks. You are looking good as well. How is Orlando Magic treating you?"

"It's a little better than Charlotte but not that much better record wise. That contract signing was amazing though."
"I bet it was."
"Too bad I didn't have someone special to share it with."
"I'm sure you found a few women to celebrate with."
"Yeah no one special though."
"Dame are you even looking?"
"Nah I'm not," he said laughing.

"I didn't think so," she said with a smile.
"Replacing what we had seems damn near impossible for me. I just take it as God punishing me by not doing right by you. I wanted to kill that man after reading what he did to you. I know I sound like a hypocrite speaking on how the last time we saw each other. I put my hands on you. There's no excuses for it."
"Are we just going to jump right into it?"
"My bad. I just can't believe you went through that."
"I'm not here to discuss that with you. I call you because of these dreams I've been having about you. Also my therapist said that I needed to get closure for that day you put your hands on me. You are the only one I haven't confronted about a tragic part of my life. We have been through a lot and I never thought you would ever put your hands on me."
"I was hurt and I showed you that hurt the wrong way. Before I realized what I was doing it was too late. I knew I fucked up and had to face whatever came my way. One of my charities is for battered women looking for a new start after escaping their situation. I wanted to open three new shelters for them. One in Chicago, Charlotte and Orlando. That's why I was happy that you reached out. I see you and Jazz doing y'all thing. I wanted to call you to see if you were interested in helping me with the one in Charlotte?"
"I have to speak to Montez about it. I will let you know what he said. That's great that you are doing that for those women."
"Reign. I'm truly sorry for putting my hands on you. I know your life hasn't been the same for you ever since that day. I hate that it was our last moments together."
"I wasn't expecting that to happen. I just wanted you to know the truth. I was still in love with Montez and that hasn't changed. He gave me the life and family I always wanted. What you and I had will always be special to me. You were my first love but we were never meant to be where I am now."
"I could never get it right with you. I tried to be faithful but I was scared of commitment. As you can see I still haven't mastered it. I'm not husband material."
"No argument here."
"Damn! You are still quick with it I see. Are you good though? Is marriage life everything you thought it would be?"
"Yeah it is."
"I'm glad you got the life we always talked about. I didn't think cut grass dude would be able to do it. He not only did it, I can tell just sitting here. He did it better than I could ever have done."

"I will let him know."

"No need for that, let that be between me and you. I promise if anyone asks me if I said that. I will deny it.

"I wish you the best Damien. I have no regrets of our time together or that one incident. There was a time I was in a bad space. There was a time I said I will never forgive or forget. I realize that I just buried it after a while and it didn't resurface until I was raped. I never wanted to believe the man I knew the most could ever do that to me. I didn't know Andre like that so when he did what he did, it didn't shock me. What you did held more weight and that was crazy to me. If I didn't have those sections I wouldn't have never understood it if it wasn't for Dr. Green and Dr. Reed."

"Can you help me understand it? I would think being raped would hold more weight."

"It does. That is something I will never get over, but it won't stop me from living. What you did, it made me stop living and believing that I would ever have what I have now. I wasn't with Montez, I chased him away to another continent. Because of our failed relationship and I put it in my head I didn't deserve his love. You truly had broken me during our time together. Those last two years were hell. The lying and constant cheating, me accepting it. Fucking around with light and white bitches made me think my dark beauty wasn't beauty at all. I was insecure when it came to men loving me for me. That when I did finally walk away from the toxic relationship and Montez appeared. I had nothing to give him but the attitude and insecurities that you gave me. To be honest being pregnant by him was God's way of telling me I deserve better than you. That he sent me Montez he didn't send me you for life.  In order for me to receive that message he had to let that night happen. I just wish he would have sent a different sign."

"Damn. I never knew or maybe I did. This NBA life I said would never be me. I let it change me, I let it kill us and I'm paying for it. I'm happy you walked away, that you found better. He is built to take care of you and his family then I could have ever done. I heard he handle the situation with that bastard the right way. I see a different woman then the one I had. Everything you said you wanted back in high school you finally received. I hear your name a lot in the market world and I'm like damn I had that and I fucked it up. I stalked you for a while hoping and praying Montez fucked up. He never did and I realize he never will. It took me today to finally see our chapter close. Maybe now I will be blessed with someone."

"I really hope you find her or she finds you Dame. This is my husband now, it was good seeing you again."

"I feel the same. Take care Reign."

As the night falls and I lay here in the bed with Sean watching The Chi. I could tell he had something heavy on the brain. I wanted him to tell me on his own and I'm trying not to push. If I did something wrong or if he did I wish he would just tell me already. I felt the sleepiness begin to take over as my eyelids were fighting to stay up. Even they know something is off with him tonight. We tried our best to stay awake but ended up losing the battle. Whatever was bothering him would have to wait until tomorrow.

"Jasmine. Are you sleeping?"

Really Sean? "Almost."

"I need to tell you something that happened today."

Hell I am wide awake now but I'm not going to let him know that. "What's going on, baby?"

"I'm only telling you this because it's on my conscience and I want to make sense of it. I just don't know what your reaction is going to be once I tell you."

Jasmine sits up in the bed and turns on the lamp. She didn't like how that sounded and she wanted to see his face when he told her. "You now have my attention. What's going on?"

"Today when I was waiting for Dana to bring me Junior. I had a dream that I slept with her."

"Past or present?"

"Huh?"

"When you were fucking her in your dreams was it when y'alll were together or now."

"Now."

She exhaled and closed her eyes. She was trying to find the right words but none came to mind. All her thoughts were to curse his ass out. "What the fuck do you two do when you meet up to ge SJ?"

"Nothing. I pick him up and bring him home."

"Nah. No way. Tell me the whole fucking dream!'

"Baby I don't remember the details

"Bullshit Sean! You have come this far. I'm going to need you to finish. How did you end up fucking her in your dreams."

"I had to use the bathroom and when I came out it just happened."

"Who made the first move?"

Why are you interrogating me like the shit happened for real? It was just a fucked up dream that has been messing with me. I would never do that to you and you know that. I didn't have to tell you about it."

"Next time don't!"

"Don't worry I won't!"

Good! All I know is Sean, you better not cheat on me with her, I will kill both of you if you do."

Okay Jazz, go to sleep you are taking this shit too far about a goddamn dream."

"You heard what I said. Goodnight Sean and try not to dream about her while laying here with me!"

# Chapter Thirty-Two: Extended Family

Marriage is hard work. I don't care how much love you have for your spouse. Keeping a happy home is a lot of work. Lord knows my marriage has been tested a lot this year. Co-parenting became a problem for us but it didn't last long. I have to trust Sean and he has to trust me. It takes time and we are committed to keep it by always being honest with one another. No matter how bad it is.As we get ready to say farewell to another year I have to admit there have been more great times than bad. As we prepare for our New Year's festivities and welcome in new beginnings, I have to admit that I'm excited. Last year the kids brought it in with their other parents, this year it's our turn. The men were over my house waiting on the babies to arrive. While the women were out grocery shopping for tonight's party. Mersades was responsible for the fireworks show so she was out at one of the TNT booths making purchases. Of course Reign and I were responsible for the alcohol and finger foods. While our mothers were out getting the main course meal. This year's celebration is going to be the biggest one we ever had. My family will be there, Sean's family, Montez's family, and Reign's family. We called, DM, text message and facebook everybody and their mama. We wanted to get as many family members together as we could to ring in the New Year. We weren't expecting a lot of yes and were shocked that we did. There's no turning around now this was about to one big family reunion and I just hope we have enough food, drinks, and entertainment to please everyone. Making these last minute runs with my nephews is a challenge. They love their father but they are clearly mama boys. Rome and MJ move when she moves and it's the cutest thing. Montez is raising them to be his eyes when he's not around. They are top notch Reign security guards, and they are not even over three yet. I told her to wait until they are teenagers, she really is going to have it bad. She didn't take kindly to my prediction. She's thinking about the girls she has to put in check. Already have that mentally that no one will ever get her approval. No lie I'm the same way with mine. Yasmine and Marcella already make me side eye these elementary boys. I volunteer for all the school activities and when I can't make them Sean is there and he is worse than me. They most definitely don't like when he shows up, I hear about it every time. They say that daddy Sean and Uncle Abs are embarrassing. Poor babies haven't seen anything when it's time for middle school. I'm going to go ahead and apologize now because I know it's going to be bad. As we wrap up everything and head back to my house. We get caught up with Mersades and her plans for her last semester in high school. She has the Senior Prom and graduation coming soon. She decided to stay close and turned down Louisiana State University and instead she will be attending University of Georgia. She also wanted to be close to her sister and nephews. Although LSU has the top track team, her closeness to her family made it easier for her to decide. Absalom will be attending Clemson, I screamed so loud when he announced it. I mean Clemson is that football team, Alabama who? That was his other choice and I'm so happy he turned them down, I know he really did it because Mersades decision. If she would have signed with LSU he most def would have chosen Alabama to be as close to her as possible. They are still going strong and it's a beautiful thing to see. I wouldn't mind having her as a sister in law because she is just awesome and very grounded just like her siblings. The

Santos did a great job with them and I'm glad that Reign has them. She would've never had this with Dame, his family does not have that strong family foundation. Hell they helped my hubby get his life back on track after his time in jail. I'm not the only one thankful for them doing that, his mother says it all the time. How grateful she was for Mr. Lucas stepping in and being that positive man figure. He has been building a better relationship with his father since we have been married. Just at the time of his manhood he didn't have him a lot and had to lean on his uncles and Mr. Lucas. Sean has said if he would have continued following his father's footsteps when he was a teenager that he would have ended up in prison longer. Steele is street life and street life is Steele, even till this day. He is still an OG and we have to be careful when it comes to him being a part of his grandchildren's life. We have been doing baby steps, starting with holidays and birthday parties. They recently did a fishing trip, for father's day and that meant a lot to Sean. He talked a lot about it this year, and to see that different kind of happiness from him makes me smile every time. I noticed before he let his father back in how much he admired Abs and our dad relationship. Now he has a chance to build that with his father and sons. One thing about my baby he believes in giving people that is important to him second chances. I am the prime example of second chances. You don't find too many men who give women that cheated those chances. The percentage is not as high as it is for women that forgive the men for their infidelities. Especially in the black community, do not question that. The numbers don't lie; it's rare like UFO sightings. We damn near have to give a kidney to make you stay if we cheat. I mean he did leave my ass when I fucked up, but quickly realized living without me was impossible. I mean he tried, but come on I'm Jasmine I put it on his heart. Once a woman has a man's heart it is hard for him to walk away. Remember anyone woman can get his head between his legs but not many can touch and love his heart body soul and mind. We have to sometimes learn that the hard way, just ask our exes Dana, Marcus, and Damien. We all made choices and had to learn the hard way. That's life though the whole reason why Jesus sacrificed his life for our sins and gave us for will. We make these decisions and blame everyone for it instead of facing that person in the mirror. It's just easier to point then it is to look at oneself. Anyway I'm not going to take you all through a sermon that is not my calling and I'm not trying to send some of you to hell. Don't need you pointing and blaming it all on me. As I look around at my beautiful family that showed up to ring in a new year. I am truly thanking God for all he has done for me. I could never pay him back for having Lillilan and David as my parents, the best brother in the world Absalom. My beautiful legacy Yasmine, Marcella, SJ, and Sincere. The only female I would die for my sister, my rollie, my ace Reign. Last and I do mean last. The last love of my life, last father of my children, my last heartbeat and breath. Till death truly does us part, Sean Gray. As we count it down and say goodbye to another year, I look around and there's no one else I want to do it with then my extended family. HAPPY NEW YEAR!

# *All That Jazz*

You may be wondering what's next with you and the family? Well as for me I will continue building my empire in different cities. Therefore I am finally taking my talents to Utah. I mean it's only right. That I end up in a place where the NBA team has my name, Utah Jazz. I will be there to rebuild the black communities in that state. The plan is to build me a realtor team in six months and move on to another state.  We will head out next month and look for office space. I already have a head start by accepting resumes early. All I have to do is knock out the interviews and train my team. I'm excited about building my own Black Wall Street and encouraging others to do the same. It has to start with us; this generation has to push and kick down doors and make it happen. Other generations run so we could walk and I for one do not want to let them down. I'm only twenty six years old and I have accomplished a lot. My determination took me there. My parents guidance and love had me believing I could conquer the world. I have a brother that rides with me no matter what and a sister who believed in me from day one. Reign and I have done a lot after graduating from college. The world has thrown it's worse at us and we still stand beating out the naysayers. We are strong driven black women going for ours. E made all the doubters say well damn they actually did what they said they were going to do. Speaking of Reign, she is finally going to have a baby girl. It wasn't looking good at first but in 3 weeks I will have a niece Raina Nicole Santos. She has my middle name, all I can say is God bless that child.Our family just keeps getting bigger and we are thankful for that. I want my children to be proud of their mother and father just as I was of mine. Everything I have done and will do was for them.  As I bring this to a close, my preacher would always say keep your eyes towards the sky and keep your faith close to your soul. Remember if God brought you to it he will be there to get you through it. Trust in him for he will see you through it all, failure and triumphant. He gave us all a gift of some kind of talent. It's up to us to open it and use it. Until next you all take care and never stop living.
Love and Blessings,
Jasmine Nicole Gray

## Dedications

*I want to dedicate this book to the women who believed in my talent from day one and weren't here to see me accomplish having my work published. My cheerleading angels, my mother Alberta, and my cousins Linda and Brittany. Thank you for encouragement here on earth and after life in spirit.*

# Also By E.M. McDaniel

Reign's Love
When It Reigns


Coming Soon
D.O.T.S
Livin'
Street Love